A RUNAWAY BRIDE FOR THE HIGHLANDER

Elisabeth Hobbes

MILLS & BOON

First Published in Great Britain 2019
by Mills & Boon, an imprint of HarperCollins*Publishers*
1 London Bridge Street, London, SE1 9GF

© 2019 Harlequin Books S.A.

Special thanks and acknowledgement are given to Elisabeth Hobbes
for her contribution to The Lochmore Legacy series.

ISBN: 978-0-263-26911-6

MIX
Paper from
responsible sources
FSC® C007454

For J, A & A,
who braved midges and camping
so I could climb hills and look at lochs.

Chapter One

September 20th, 1513

They came from all over Scotland, converging on Stirling. The young with fire and anger in their bellies, the old with steel in their sinews. They came from the Highlands and the Lowlands, the borders and the isles. They came bearing weapons and grudges and wounds. Crushed by defeat in battle, yet unbroken in spirit, the Chiefs and the Lairds gathered together.

Stirling Castle loomed on rocks that fell away steeply on three sides. It was an imposing sight by any measure, visible from miles around, far over the winding Forth River. At dusk with the sun blood red behind it, the effect was doubly striking. Flaming beacons at either side of the Forework cast eerie shadows over the six soaring towers and seemed to breathe life into the stones themselves. The Forework became a skull, the windows black eyes and the great central doorway a gaping maw ready to swallow all comers.

Sitting astride his horse in the slow procession that wound from the city huddled beneath the rock towards the great gateway, Ewan Lochmore shivered at the disconcerting image that had entered his head.

He considered himself a rational man, not given to believing tales of eldritch creatures that his grandmother had told him and his brother every Samhain Eve many years ago. Even so, as he drew nearer and nearer he was filled with foreboding that once he passed beneath the stone arch his life would be changed for ever.

He winced and clutched Randall's reins tighter as a stab of grief sharper than the blade of any dagger knocked him sideways. He gritted his teeth, determined to betray no outward signs of his pain. His life had already changed beyond all imagining and what he would do over the coming days would only make it official.

He looked again at the castle, thinking it no wonder that he saw the face of death when Death had claimed so many Scottish lives recently.

'You're quiet. What are ye thinking of?'

Ewan looked at the man driving the small cart alongside him. Angus, his father's cousin and right-hand man, was watching with shrewd eyes.

'My father,' Ewan answered, his voice thick with emotion. 'And death.'

'Aye, we're all thinking of Hamish,' Angus wheezed, filling the words with a depth of sorrow that matched what Ewan was feeling. Cousins who were more like brothers, Angus and Hamish had grown up the closest of allies, with Angus acting as Hamish's retainer and answering only to him. If any man had a claim to share the grief that consumed Ewan, it was this man.

'I found him and held him as he died, a pike still in his back,' Angus continued. 'Even then spitting a curse on the cur who struck him down. A great Laird to the last.'

Ewan bowed his head. 'I should have been there,' he muttered.

Angus shrugged, but did not contradict him, which twisted the dagger in Ewan's conscience even deeper. The loss of his father was a blow so great he feared he might never recover from the grief. What weighed him down even more was the knowledge that the eyes of all Lochmores, young and old, rich and poor, landowner or simple yeoman, would be on Ewan as the new Earl of Glenarris. Leadership had been thrust on his shoulders in the most tragic way possible. So far he had failed to impress Angus, one of the few men now living whose good opinion he craved. Jamie, Angus's sixteen-year-old son, who was sitting alongside him on the seat of the cart, rested a hand on the older man's shoulder.

'We'll drink to his memory tonight,' Ewan said. His tongue felt parched as he spoke. He needed a drink. Lots of them, in truth. He'd been riding long enough today and his throat was dry.

The line was moving forward and before long Ewan and his companions were through the curtain wall and into the Outer Close where visitors with their horses and transport were being admitted. Six sentinels lined the path from the gateway to the doorway of the residence known as the King's House. A neatly dressed man in black robes stood before the door, flanked by two more guards in the royal colours. Beside him, a scribe sat at a table covered with rolls of parchment and an inkwell.

Ewan dismounted and passed the reins to Jamie. He moved to offer his arm to Angus and received a contemptuous eye roll.

'I don't know what sort of weaklings they have in Glasgow, but I'm no' in ma grave yet, laddie. I can use ma legs.'

Ewan took a measured breath, reminding himself that though white haired, Angus was a man of fifty-eight who had fought and survived the massacre at Flodden, not in his dotage. His offer had been an attempt at courtesy, not to insult. He ignored the jibe against the city where he had been living for the past five years. They might walk streets rather than glens and hill paths, but there were men mad-eyed and bottle-brave enough in Glasgow to meet Angus on the battlefield.

Angus clambered down unaided. He adjusted the folds of his *brat* across his shoulders, and pushed back the sleeves of the yellow linen *leine* he wore beneath the heavy length of cloth. Ewan rearranged his own cumbersome length of plaid and straightened the more formal doublet he wore beneath. Satisfied that he was presentable enough for any royal court, he walked to the doorway and made a deep bow to the standing figure. The man inclined his head slightly in return.

'State your name.' The man at the table dipped his quill tip into ink. He waited, hand poised over the parchment for Ewan's answer.

'Ewan Lochmore of Clan Lochmore.'

The secretary wrote his name on what Ewan could see was a growing list.

'Your business?' asked the robed figure.

He sounded uninterested in the reason Ewan was there. His face was unfamiliar, but he was a man of some importance given the rich nap on his black robes and the jewels that bedecked his hat. He might be anyone, from a minor secretary, or an advisor to the Chamberlain of Scotland himself. He knew already why most of the grim-faced men were attending the hastily convened Special Council. The question was simply a formality.

Once Ewan said the words out loud it would be admitting to the nightmare he wished he could wake from, but with the light fading and many behind him waiting to be admitted, he could not permit himself the indulgence of delaying any longer. Ewan lifted his chin and gave the man a firm look.

'My father Hamish Lochmore is dead and I am here to claim my title. I am the new Earl of Glenarris.'

The secretary scribbled this information, too, without raising his eyes.

'And your servants?'

Ewan named them, managing to avoid Angus's eye as he was described as such, and their names, too, were added to the document.

'Stable your horse and stow your cart in the yard to the rear of the Great Hall,' said the black-robed man. 'You will be escorted to your accommodation. The castle is extremely full. Many of the Parliament arrived yesterday and have been meeting continuously.'

'I have matters I wish to put before the Parliament,' Ewan said. 'Many men from my clan fought at Flodden alongside my father. There are tenants who lost their husbands and fathers fighting. I seek alms for them as King James promised.'

The man's expression softened slightly. 'That matter will be dealt and compensation will be given. The council has not yet decided the amount it can afford to spare, but rest assured, your people will be provided for.'

Ewan tried not to bristle at talk of 'sparing' money to support the families of those who now had no other means to support themselves. He followed the directions he had been given, promising himself he would not leave without an assurance, if not the money itself.

The rear courtyard was bustling and finding a convenient space for the cart took some time. Most of their property would have to remain on the cart. The small chest containing Ewan's books of law, papers and other valuables was padlocked and chained to rings set into to the floor of the cart and Ewan had no fear it would be stolen or broken into. There were grander and more tempting vehicles surrounding their modest cart. He ran his hand over the top of the studded chest and another pang of misery welled up inside him. His days of studying law at the University of Glasgow were finished. When Angus had arrived bearing the news, he had left his rooms the same day, knowing he would not return.

Ewan's eye settled on his father's *targe* that

was propped up at the back. The great shield had been no protection against a pike through his back. A feeling of grief overpowered Ewan. Regretting the loss of his future career seemed petty compared to the loss of his father and brother.

The three men rearranged a few rolls of cloth, boxes of dry goods and two barrels of wine, then pulled heavy sackcloth over the most vulnerable pieces of Hamish's armour and sword. The whole cart was covered with a large piece of heavy sackcloth secured at the edges with rope. Satisfied with their work, the three men returned to the entrance and were escorted to a chamber on the second floor of the King's House. The room was small and cramped, with two truckle beds squeezed side by side at the end of the larger bed meant for Ewan. There was barely room for the roll of clothes that Jamie carried.

'It's an insult to you, to be placed so high and distant from the Great Hall,' Angus muttered, prodding his pallet with a foot while Jamie set to laying out their fresh linens.

Ewan grinned at his companion's outrage. When they had been younger men Angus and Hamish would spend days away from Lochmore Castle sleeping in bracken under the skies. Ewan and his older brother had gone with them on many occasion, learning to hunt and snare. He sighed, remembering the good times. Not wanting Angus to see the emotion he was sure his face gave away he straightened the coverlet on his bed and realised how tired he felt deep in his bones. The mattresses were filled with sweet-smelling barley straw and looked comfier than anything he had slept on while travelling and the sheets were clean and tempting. He could gladly tumble back and pull the curtains around himself, blotting out the world.

'I don't mind this room,' he said. 'If we were the only guests I might see it as a slight, but you saw for yourself how many others are here.'

'You should mind, laddie. It's an earl you are now and you should remember you're accorded respect. You should demand it!'

Ewan hid the unexpected grin that he felt forming. He was truly fond of the older man, even if Angus lived in a past where ready fists and a forehead could settle a score easier than negotiations. Fortunately Hamish had been more longsighted in his vision for his second son and, when he saw Ewan's inclination was not for patrolling the borders between Lochmore and McCrieff lands, he had encouraged Ewan to take a place at the University in Glasgow.

'The first Lochmore to be educated beyond reading and numbers!' he would roar proudly, daring anyone to pour scorn on Ewan's accomplishments.

'Do you not think that respect is gained quicker if you *don't* bluster and demand and shout?' Ewan asked.

Angus looked at him as though the concept of not shouting was beyond him. 'Aye, possibly here. But you'll need to command the clan and the men will be wanting more than fancy words and polite bowing.' He cracked his knuckles. 'You'll need to be able to fight. Can you do that?'

This was the fear that had kept Ewan awake as much as his grief. Hamish might have valued his learning, but that mattered little to men who prized swords over quills. 'I might spend most of my life surrounded by documents, but I can hold my own in a skirmish if I'm needed to.'

Angus nodded slowly. 'Then make sure you show it to the court. Now, we're wasting time while there is wine paid for by the Crown. I'm heading down to find a drink. Are you coming?'

Ewan's mouth began to water, craving the sting of hot liquor down his throat. It would go some way to obliterating his grief if only for the night. As soon as he had stowed his belongings, he planned to make his way down and join them.

'I will shortly,' he said.

Angus left. Jamie stood by the window, uncertainly.

'What would you like me to do?' he asked.

Jamie seemed content to act as manservant.

Ewan wondered if his brother, John, had intended to use Jamie as his advisor and confidant in the same manner their fathers had lived and worked together. He would never know, because John had fought and died at Flodden like their father.

'No, you can go find something to eat. Enjoy yourself before we have to return home.'

'I'll do that. I saw a bonny lass with a fine arse on her and a pair of titties as big as twin babbies' heads.' Jamie grinned and headed out eagerly.

Ewan sat on the bed and dropped his head into his hands. If his cares could be worn away between a pair of plump thighs as easily as Jamie's could, he'd have an easier mind. Now he was alone he could indulge himself in a moment of weakness as doubt crept into his mind. He was no leader. No great chief like Hamish had been, or John had been raised to be. Ewan could pray for the strength to be a leader, but his prayers that reports of his father's death were false had gone unanswered. He had no faith this one would be heard. He felt more alone than ever before. He and he alone would have to find the strength to be a worthy leader.

Ewan lifted his head and took a deep breath. No more time to linger here while Angus appeared alone and tongues wagged. There would be a feast that night and the drinking had already started. Had been underway for some time, from the slurring of the old ballads and the volume and variety of the curses that had flitted to Ewan's ears as they passed by the Great Hall. He thought briefly of his father, who had commanded the eyes and attention of everyone in the room with his loud laughter and booming tones, missing him more than he thought possible. John had been the same, vibrant and charismatic, while Ewan had been content to let him. They would have been the first to table, the first to empty a cup and call for more. There was something in what Angus had said. A chief must command and be seen. Ewan would not bring shame on their memories by appearing cowed or withdrawn.

He ran a comb through his jaw-length light-brown hair and shook it out free. He shaped his plaid over his shoulder and beneath his right arm until the long, woven russet-coloured cloth hung neatly. The *brat* was an outdoor garment but the colour proclaimed a man's clan allegiance and at this time the usual rules of clothing would be relaxed. He added a swagger to his step as he left the room, holding his shoulders back and head high. He would make his first appearance as Earl of Glenarris one to remember.

He descended to the ground floor and made his way outside to the Inner Close of the castle. The sun had sunk beneath the height of the curtain wall and the limewashed stone of the Forework was a warm orange. The impression was much more benign than the image of the skull that he had first thought of. The air was warm and sweet with the scent of grass mingling with tempting smells coming from the kitchens beside the Great Hall. Ewan inhaled deeply, his appetite surging back for the first time in days. Since his father's and brother's deaths all food had tasted like ash, but the scent of rich juices from the roasting meat were more than any man could resist. He would eat well tonight and fill his belly, knowing that he had three days' journey to take him home to Lochmore Castle.

A few other late guests were making their way across the courtyard, taking a direct route. The cool breeze on his face and neck made his stiff velvet doublet a little more bearable and Ewan decided to take a longer route. He made his way round the path, past the Chapel Royal, and came face to face with a ghost.

Chapter Two

The apparition appeared before him no more than half-a-dozen paces away. It was small, slight and female, and appeared to have passed through the solid stone of the inner curtain wall itself. The figure was facing away from Ewan. She was clothed from head to foot in grey, with a veil of long, white silk that covered her head and fell to her waist. Late evening sunlight seemed to stream through the wall itself, lighting upon her veil and causing it to glow and shimmer like a sunrise over the loch where the water took the colours of early lavender and slate.

Ewan stepped back in surprise, mouth falling open. His mind refused to believe what his eyes were seeing, but no living woman at court would be dressed in such a strange manner or such a colour.

He must have gasped out loud because the spectre spun on the spot to face him in a flurry of skirts. The veil she wore framed a face that was pale and angular. With the light shining behind her, Ewan could only vaguely make out the woman's features. Black eyes and red lips that became a startled circle.

Ewan got an impression of fragile beauty and of apprehensiveness. The spectre looked more fearful of him than the reverse. His heart began to pound in his throat and his palms grew moist. Was this creature here to herald his death, or seduce him into giving up his soul? If he was going to be faced with proof that the unearthly creatures he had scorned as old wives' tales truly existed, he could not imagine a more alluring example.

The creature raised an arm swathed in a wide, billowing sleeve and swiftly drew the edge of the veil around to cover her face, leaving only the tantalisingly dark eyes visible. Ewan raised his hand to shield his eyes from the sunlight and try to catch a better glimpse of her. He could not have moved from the spot if his life depended on it. He had no idea how long he might have stood there, not daring to move in case the creature vanished, but waiting for her to melt away, because at that moment he heard himself being hailed loudly from across the courtyard.

The bewitchment that had transfixed him was broken. The ghost shuddered and stood motionless, then stepped quickly back through the wall, disappearing instantly. Ewan stepped towards her, hand outstretched. A sense of yearning filled him that such delicate loveliness was beyond his reach. He might as well try to catch mist.

'Ewan Lochmore! It is you I see!' came the voice that had intruded.

He tore his eyes away from the now-empty spot and gave his attention to the speaker. A familiar figure was striding across from the King's House towards him, his reddish-gold hair streaming behind him.

'Struan MacNeill!'

Ewan opened his arms wide, roaring his greeting and genuinely pleased to see someone he had not seen for over a year. MacNeill's sept was a branch of Clan Campbell, neighbours of Clan Lochmore, and the men were on friendly terms. The two men embraced, clapping each other on the back amid loud exclamations.

'My commiserations, Ewan,' Struan said, once they had released each other. 'Hamish was a great man. They both were.'

Ewan passed a hand over his eyes.

'Are you ill?' Struan asked. 'You look as though you're half-asleep.'

'I was looking for a woman,' Ewan murmured.

'Aren't we all?' Struan laughed, grabbing his crotch in an exaggerated manner. 'Don't fear, there are plenty of bonny lasses in the castle who are more than happy to oblige. I cannae think of a better way to heal a wounded heart.'

Ewan forced a crude laugh. Dallying with serving girls didn't appeal, especially when his thoughts were consumed with the unearthly encounter. He looked back over his shoulder. She was, of course, nowhere to be seen. He wondered if the whole incident had been the product of his mind and she had never been there at all.

He took a few steps closer to the place where the ghost had been, stopped and roared with laughter. What he had believed was a solid wall in fact held a small archway that had not been apparent from the angle he had been standing at. An iron gate had been pulled to. Ewan shook his head at his foolishness. The woman had not been a spectre passing through solid stone. She was a flesh-and-blood woman who had simply walked through a gate, albeit one dressed very oddly.

A prickle of excitement ran down his spine. If she was real, she would be among the guests and he might find her. Might even talk with her. He would like to see if she was as pretty as the brief glance had suggested she was. The path led only to the battlements and outer wall, which was no place for a lone woman to be walking. He peered through the gate, hoping to see where the woman had gone, but, seeing no sign of her, joined Struan making his way to the Great Hall with higher spirits and alert eyes. For the first time since his loss, his grief had to compete with another emotion.

The five great fireplaces in the hall were ablaze and filling the Great Hall with the heady smell of woodsmoke and herbs. The building was large, but men and women stood crushed together in tightly knit groups while serving maids and boys wove their way from group to group, replenishing wine cups. Ewan seized a cup from a passing tray and drank deeply, finishing it quickly and taking another almost instantly. He strode from group to group, greeting old friends and paying deference to the men who outranked him, remembering that he, too, was now owed respect as the Earl of Glenarris. All the while, he was conscious that his eye was searching for the woman in white, but she was nowhere to be seen.

Ordinarily a gathering of this many men from so many clans would lead to old grievances and rivalries being raised and fought over but tonight, at least, all within the walls were united in the grief that the devastating loss at Flodden had caused in all hearts. Scotland had lost her sons and fathers.

Lively music came from the minstrels' gallery high in the rafters of the building and Ewan could tell from the way bodies were starting to move in time with the rhythm that it would not be long before the whole company began dancing. Ewan's fingers began to click in time with the music. He decided that he would dance tonight and lose himself in the music in the hope it might diminish the sorrow in his heart.

Ewan was caught by the arm and found Angus by his side. They walked side by side through the milling people. They were almost at the furthest end of the Great Hall when Ewan saw a flash of McCrieff plaid. His cheeks flushed and he knew his previous reflection on peace and truces was about to be tested. If he had thought about it he would have remembered members of that clan would be present too. Donald McCrieff, son of old Earl Malcolm, laird of the McCrieff clan, was with his cousin Duncan.

They were thickset of body and florid of complexion and stood staring at the gathered men belligerently, occasionally whispering with their red heads together. Ewan recognised Duncan by sight, but they had never spoken. Duncan was reputed to have a quick mind that his cousin was entirely lacking. Ewan realised from the sharp intake of breath from beside him that Angus had also seen them. Angus began muttering threats under his breath.

'Now's not the time,' Ewan said, placing his hand on Angus's arm, even as his fingers itched surprisingly to curl into a fist. 'We're all here for peace and to decide the future of Scotland.'

'Aye, though the future would be brighter without a McCrieff in it.'

The gap between cousins widened to admit a third person to the party. The figure that appeared between the two men was small, female and dressed in grey. She was none other than Ewan's ghost.

His heart clenched.

She's real.

Perhaps he had spoken aloud because Angus was staring him with an expression of amusement.

'Pretty little piece, isn't she?'

'Do you know who she is?' Ewan asked. Still pale, still looking wary, but more beautiful in the warm glow of firelight than she had been in the low dusk sunlight. He watched as she dipped a graceful curtsy to the McCrieff men. Duncan loomed over the woman, his thick frame and height serving to make her look small and fragile beside him.

'The Frenchwoman?' Angus leered at Ewan. 'Don't get any ideas about her. She's the poor young lassie who is to become Duncan McCrieff's second wife next week.'

A pit opened beneath Ewan's feet. His stomach lurched with revulsion and, he was startled to notice, jealousy as Duncan took her hand and bowed deeply over it, lifting it to his lips. Ewan bit his in response, fighting the intense urge to be in Duncan's place.

So she was French. That explained her slightly unusual manner of dress and told Ewan something else. Following the custom of her country, wearing white indicated she was in mourning. Well, she was not alone in that, with barely a single person not grieving for someone lost at Flodden.

'A Frenchwoman,' he muttered. 'McCrieff's last wife was English. Why he can't marry a good Scottish woman is beyond me.'

'Mayhap no good family wants to let their daughters breed with him,' Angus sneered.

Ewan grimaced. The girl looked barely past childhood. The image of Duncan's stocky frame heaving itself on top of the slender girl in white soured the wine in Ewan's belly. A woman as beautiful as she should be cherished. He would treasure her, if she were his. He could not guess for whom she grieved, but any woman about to marry a McCrieff would have plenty to mourn in the future.

Marguerite Vallon slipped into the Great Hall. Keeping her head bowed, she walked rapidly through the groups that filled the whole space and made her way towards her future husband. No one had noticed her late arrival. These Scottish men were too busy drinking or shouting—and in many cases doing both simultaneously—to pay attention to one small woman.

She was out of breath from running back to the gateway. Her heart pounded from the exercise, coupled with the agitation from having been seen passing through the gate. Tonight it had been too close for comfort. Duncan did not ask how she spent her days, presumably believing she sat in attendance on Queen Margaret, sewing and reading with the other ladies of the court. If he knew what she really did with her time he would doubtless be furious with her.

On her second day in Stirling Marguerite had discovered the small gate that was unaccountably unguarded. Ever since she had been using it as a way in and out of the grounds without being seen. She had become complacent, however. Now the castle was busier she would have to be careful. She did not want to have to explain to anyone what she was doing.

She caught a glimpse of red hair and made her way towards it. Duncan was standing with his cousin Donald, a man as pleasant in manner as Marguerite's fiancé. He was less handsome, but younger, and whenever Marguerite saw them together it made her want to weep that she was to marry a man who was almost twice her age.

'Good evening, *messieurs*.'

Duncan gave her a charming smile, lifting her hand to his lips. Donald bowed, made an excuse and left them alone.

'I was beginning to wonder where you were. We have all been gathered here for some time now.'

'I was in the chapel,' she replied.

It was not a lie. She had stood frozen in fear while the tall stranger had stared at her openmouthed, as if she was more alarming to him than he was to her. Thank goodness his attention had been called away by his bellowing friend. As soon as he had looked away Marguerite had slipped into the Chapel Royal through the open door while he was distracted.

She shivered in memory of the way the man in the courtyard had looked at her. The expression of open interest when he had looked at her had caused hot prickles around her neck and between her breasts. The flush threatened to renew itself now. It was as though he had never seen a woman before.

He might be one of those men from the distant wilds that women of the French court had spoken of in horrified whispers whenever they discussed the uncivilised country where Marguerite was condemned to make her home. According to them, Scottish Highlanders who lived alone where there were no women took sheep as wives. It was dreadful enough to think a man had such base urges at all, but to consider he might satisfy them in such a disgusting manner made Marguerite flush scarlet and feel physically sick. She hoped she would not encounter the man from the courtyard again.

Although she had wept when her father told her she was to marry a man of thirty-five, she was thankful that Duncan, with his deep blue velvet doublet and close cut hose, seemed to possess an air of sophistication that would not be out of place in the French court.

She realised Duncan was speaking and she had not been paying attention.

'I'm sorry, I was thinking of the peace of the chapel and my mind wandered.'

This was closer to a lie and she felt her cheeks grow warm. Duncan smiled again, though with a touch less warmth, Marguerite noticed. He bent over her, tall enough that she had to tilt her head back to see into his face.

'I said that to prefer prayer over a feast seems overly devout in one so young. You should stay close to me now we are here. We will be eating before long.'

She nodded meekly and looked down demurely. She had no appetite to speak of.

She looked away and as she did her eye fell on a figure that was standing at the other side of the room. Her breath caught, her ears began to buzz and she felt as though she might faint. It was the man from the courtyard and he was staring right at her.

Their eyes met briefly. His flickered in recognition and the muscles at the side of his mouth twitched. She thought he was going to smile, but his expression remained solemn. His brows knitted. He crossed his arms across his chest and tilted his head to one side slightly, regarding her with only a little less curiosity than he had in the courtyard. Her cheeks grew hot again and a faint fluttering in her belly spread out through her torso. It felt as though he was slowly drawing his fingers across the inside of her ribs in a caress that reached to her heart itself. She looked away, dropping her eyes down demurely and hoping that would be the end of it.

Duncan spent the greater part of the meal talking to Donald, who sat at her other side, and Marguerite was left in peace. She tried to muster enthusiasm for the dripping trenchers of roast venison and beef and platters of goose and pigeon that passed before her. She sighed, craving the freshness of delicate white asparagus with lemon sauce, or the *gigot* of lamb with red and black peppercorns that had been her favourite dish at home rather than yet another night of greasy meat lacking in sauce or spice.

When she had eaten as much as she could stomach, she spent her time looking around to see if she could recognise any of the faces about her. The man from the courtyard was sitting at the furthest end of the table at the other side. Marguerite watched him as he ate. He was solemn faced, bordering on surly, and kept his head down and his wine cup close as he devoured a great plate of beef. He spoke only occasionally to the men on either side of him and Marguerite only noticed him smiling twice. The men all wore the same pattern of plaid so she decided they must belong to the same clan.

The meal was drawing to a close when the grave-faced man sitting at the centre of the high table stood and began to speak. These men were the General Council of Scotland, the noblemen who had survived the recent battle against the English. A hush fell on the hall.

'The Prince and Great Steward of Scotland, His Grace the Duke of Rothesay will be crowned King James V tomorrow. The matter of the Regency will be decided forthwith. Tonight we gather and remember those we have lost.'

He paused as a great noise that began as a groan and transformed into a cheer surged around the hall. The man smiled, acknowledging the mix of emotions that all men must be feeling.

'The Parliament has been in session for the past two days. We have decreed that honours will be announced tonight so that tomorrow's coronation may proceed with each man in his rightful place.'

He explained that new titles would be created to compensate for the loss of life in the recent battle, that some lands would be granted to them and others were to be presented to existing noblemen. A black-robed man sitting at the nearest table began to read from a long list detailing which land would pass to which surviving man. Most of the names meant nothing to Marguerite, but she listened in case McCrieff was mentioned.

'The estate between Loch Carran and Gailsyth that was in the possession of William McNab, Fourth Earl GlenCarran, is to be granted to Ewan Lochmore, Third Earl of Glenarris.'

Donald swore beneath his breath and his usually mild expression was thunderous. Duncan leaned past Marguerite to grasp him by the wrist.

'Is that bad?' Marguerite asked.

Duncan whipped his head round and Marguerite recoiled at the anger she saw directed at her. She fumbled with a piece of bread. Duncan seemed to gather his thoughts. He patted her hand, then reached for his wine and drank deeply.

'It is…unexpected. That land was promised to my cousin in the event of McNab's death at Flodden. Now it is to pass to that young pup.'

Duncan nodded contemptuously towards the man from the courtyard. He was sitting at a table among a group who were congratulating him on his good fortune with hearty thumps to the shoulder. He looked remarkably solemn for a man who had been granted lands unexpectedly.

Marguerite eyed him with interest now the attention of the room was on him and it was acceptable to do so openly. He was beardless, with angular cheekbones, and his light brown hair was shorter than the men surrounding him, curling slightly below a narrow chin with a small dimple in it. He was still young and if Duncan had been the same age as this man, Marguerite had no doubt her fiancé would be the better looking of the two. Lord Glenarris was handsome in a lean-faced way, but what really distinguished him from the other men in the room was his eyes. Oh, they were the reason Marguerite's heart raced and a previously unknown sensation woke within her. They were so very bright blue. They were currently grave, but Marguerite could imagine how appealing they would look when he was amused and the fine lines at the edge crinkled.

So he was an earl. She didn't know where the places mentioned were and his name meant nothing to her. She should feel the injustice dealt to Duncan, but the glee on Earl of Glenarris's face was delightful to behold and even though she did not know him, Marguerite was happy for him. Further names were announced. Donald McCrieff scowled when his name was called.

'A spit of barren rocks!' he said petulantly. 'Why did I not receive the McNab land? You told me you could arrange…'

'Be silent, you fool!'

The fury in Duncan's voice made Marguerite quake. His hand tightened on Donald's forearm. They glanced towards Marguerite, who gave a simpering smile and twirled her fingers around her sleeve. She had learned early that men spoke more freely when they believed a woman did not have the wit to listen. She tried to ignore Duncan's whitening knuckles as he gripped. The hand that would lift hers so gently had become a claw.

'I will not let this insult pass,' Donald muttered. 'There will be a reckoning.'

He glared across the room at the Earl, who looked deep in thought, his blue eyes unfocused.

A chill ran down Marguerite's spine. She felt the urge to warn Lord Glenarris. Of what, she was not certain, but she knew that Donald and Duncan McCrieff meant him nothing but ill.

Chapter Three

Servants swept in and bore away the remains of the meal. The minstrels in the gallery, who had been playing a muted, gentle air during the meal, began to increase the pace. The music of the pipes and drums that floated from the gallery above grew louder and faster. Men were beginning to circle and stamp their feet, calling and whooping along with the drumbeat. It was hard to tell whether the unruly leaps and steps towards each other was dancing or fighting.

Many of the ladies had retired to the far end of the hall, but joining them while they spoke of the men they hoped to marry held no appeal for Marguerite. She followed Duncan to his previous place by the great fire, trying to avoid being jostled aside or seized around the waist and pulled into the circles along with the merry serving girls, who protested that they had no intention of dancing while their eyes and lips said otherwise.

Apart from the fact that the steps were unfamiliar and too wild, grief had transformed Marguerite's feet to lead. She hoped Duncan would not ask. He was so much older than she and dancing must be tiring.

'Shall we dance?' Duncan asked, as if he had read her thoughts.

Marguerite declined with the best smile she could muster, which Duncan accepted with a shrug.

'Ah well. We'll have chance to dance aplenty once we're wed.'

Marguerite nodded dumbly, her stomach flipping over. From the inflection in his voice she did not think Duncan meant the sort of dancing they were witnessing here.

'You seem at odds with yourself tonight,' Duncan remarked. 'Are you ill?'

'My head aches.' Marguerite clutched at the excuse Duncan had suggested. 'I would like some air.'

'You're better staying close to me so I can tend you if you become faint,' Duncan replied. He summoned a serving girl and took a cup of wine from her tray. He dismissed the girl with a pat of his hand on her lower back, then leaned close to Marguerite, passing the wine into her hand from behind. His breath was hot on her neck and he let his arm brush against the length of hers in the process as he withdrew it. She tried not to wrinkle her nose too obviously. Usually she tolerated his presence, but tonight it was an endurance. The image of his hand gripping Donald's wrist was too vivid for her to bear being held by him. Those hands on her body…

She looked again at the centre of the Great Hall where more and more men were joining the dance. Some of them were dressed in clothes that would not look out of place in France, but others were bare legged and wore layers of cloth wrapped over jerkins of leather and padded doublets.

Lord Glenarris was among them. She caught a glimpse of the deep russet-coloured cloth he wore across his shoulder as he leapt high into the air with an energy and exuberance that took her breath away, landing sure-footed on the floor, arms outstretched. His head was thrown back and he was laughing with glee, flashing wide smiles at anyone who caught his eye. Marguerite was determined she would not catch his eye again.

She looked back at Duncan, feeling further explanation of her reservation was needed. She gestured with a hand across the room. Greater numbers of men were joining in the dancing, adding ear-splitting yells whenever the music reached a certain point Marguerite could not discern.

'It seems so strange. I miss the statelier ways of France.'

'We are a more expressive people,' Duncan said. 'You will most likely prefer the court of England. You'll discover it is more sedate when we visit.'

He spoke with a hint of disapproval. Marguerite looked back at the dancers, trying to find some beauty in the wildness, some sense of pattern in the steps.

'I am unfamiliar with these ways,' she explained. 'I was not expecting to be brought to Scotland so soon after my mother's death.'

Her voice caught in her throat. Duncan took her hand and patted it as if he was comforting a child. He lifted it to his lips, but must have noticed the reluctance that made her instinctively stiffen because he released it after only the briefest of touches. He rubbed a long finger across his jaw, stroking his neatly trimmed red beard as he regarded her thoughtfully.

'The timing of your arrival when my attention is on matters of politics, not love, has not been the best, I must admit. You will grow to learn our ways soon enough.'

'Should I return to France until matters are more settled before we wed?' Marguerite suggested.

'No, we'll marry as planned,' Duncan said.

'It will give Queen Margaret's ladies something to keep them occupied after the coronation of the new King. They'll enjoy fussing around with chemises and stockings and suchlike.'

Duncan gave her a smile that bordered on lascivious. Had he deliberately chosen to name items of clothing that were so intimate? It was impossible not to imagine their wedding night where he would expect access beneath the delicate layers she wore beside her skin. Cold shivers stroked down her spine at the thought of submitting to his attentions. She looked again into the centre of the room. Lord Glenarris had danced closer to them as the surging mass moved around the hall and Duncan was staring at him, arms tightly folded across his burly chest.

'I will go take some air after all, I think,' she murmured. 'Excuse me.'

She made her way round the edge of the room. As the dancers came closer Lord Glenarris leapt high into a twist, arms outstretched. He landed just as Marguerite stepped out. They collided and his arm caught her a blow across the shoulder, pushing her forward. It didn't hurt much, but she squealed in alarm, her foot slipping on the stone floor, and she bumped into a table. Lord Glenarris staggered, but found his feet quickly and righted himself. He clasped Marguerite's hand and put his other hand on her waist and gently pulled her upright. She tensed instinctively, anticipating the revulsion that followed when Duncan did that, but none came. Instead, her fingers tingled and grew warm. She closed her fingers around his and felt the tension flood from her limbs and core.

Lord Glenarris held her firmly, yet his grip was gentler than she would have assumed from the ferocious way he had thrown himself around as he danced. He spoke rapidly in the language Marguerite was only just starting to speak with any fluency. Every Scot seemed to have a different intonation. His was soft with a melodic roll to the 'r's. Marguerite could only catch half the words, but it appeared he was apologising.

The clamour of other voices dimmed and the room seemed to empty, leaving only them together. Marguerite looked up into intense blue eyes and he returned her gaze, unblinking. She began to set her face into the polite smile she had been trained since childhood to show. To her surprise it came naturally and his lips curled in response. It struck Marguerite that he found her attractive. His fingers spread along her inner wrist, resting over the soft spot where her blood thrummed through her veins. Warmth rose to her breast and neck as she discovered this was far from unwelcome. When Duncan showed interest, her body never reacted in such a way. She hoped the fascination she unaccountably felt for him was not equally clear on her face.

Before she could assure him she was unharmed, Duncan had pushed through the crowd that had gathered around them and the peace was shattered.

'Take your hands off my woman!'

He stepped between them, his elbow coming up to jab Lord Glenarris in the ribs, and he pulled Marguerite away by the arm with considerably more roughness than the Earl had inflicted on her. Both men staggered and came up with fists swinging and angry roars as they threw themselves at each other. They collided roughly. Onlookers reacted quickly and the two men were seized by others and dragged apart.

'Watch where you're hurling yourself, Lochmore!' Duncan growled, shaking himself free of Donald's hold. His cheeks were a red almost as deep as his hair. 'I'll gladly break your arms if you can't keep them under control. If you've hurt my bride, I might do it anyway.'

Lord Glenarris's jaw tightened and his eyes flashed with anger. 'Now's not the time or place, but I'll gladly meet you at any other.'

'I'm not hurt,' Marguerite said hastily. The idea that they might inflict violence on each other because of her was intolerable. 'I was not paying attention where I was walking.'

The Earl tore his eyes from Duncan to look at Marguerite. The fury that had filled his face disappeared, replaced with concern. He held his hands up and stepped back from Duncan and was released from the three men holding him back.

'I harmed you and I am sorry,' he said to Marguerite. In French.

Marguerite blinked in surprise. His accent was appalling, but he spoke her language. It did not occur to her until much later to wonder how he knew which tongue to address her in. She managed a small smile and replied in rapid French, reiterating that she was unharmed.

Duncan slipped his arm about her shoulder, drawing her close. It was a gross indiscretion to touch her so intimately before they were wed. He glowered at the Earl before guiding Marguerite back to the fireplace. He pressed her gently on to a stool.

'I told you that staying beside me was the safest course of action.'

'I'm not hurt,' she protested. 'I fell from a tree once and landed much harder than that, without injury. I am quite hardy.'

'Nevertheless, you had best sit here where I can guard you.'

He called for more wine and bustled round, gathering ladies of the court to sit with her. His anger had subsided and the charming, solicitous man had returned. Despite his vows of guarding her, to Marguerite's relief he only lingered at her side until she was supplied with wine and a dish of sugared fruits before he excused himself and left the hall in the company of his cousin.

Marguerite allowed herself to be cosseted, and listened to the praise heaped upon him. She nodded as she was told how lucky she was to be betrothed to such a gallant and well-looking man, but said nothing. She had never seen Duncan so incensed as when he had faced the Earl. His anger at seeing her predicament and his protectiveness over another man touching her should be reassuring, but instead made her stomach curdle. She would have to try very hard once they were married not to invoke that anger.

She sat meekly as she had been bidden and stared towards the seething mass of men, flailing and leaping around in the centre of the room, but could not see Lord Glenarris. The dancing showed no sign of coming to an end when Marguerite eventually excused herself and made her way—with more care than previously to avoid the dancers—out of the hall.

The night was very cold. She breathed deeply, relishing the freshness after the stifling atmosphere in the Great Hall. She had intended to return to her bedchamber, but instead strolled the short walk to the gate in the wall. It was locked now, but even if it had swung open, to venture through at that time of night would be foolhardy. Instead she leaned her forehead against it, took hold of the iron bars and looked up into the night. The sky was black as pitch, but clear, and the sky was awash with stars. Marguerite sighed in contentment at the sight of the unending vastness of the sky. For the first time in the night her heart was at peace.

It did not last long. The serenity was spoiled by a needle-sharp pain in her neck. One of the never-ending swarm of midges had slipped beneath her veil and bitten her. She slapped at it angrily and hissed, tossing her head to try rid herself of the plague of buzzing, biting monstrosities.

'Ugh! Will you horrid creatures never cease to torment me?'

'They'll die when the frost comes,' said a voice in French.

Marguerite jumped, her heart leaping to her throat. Lord Glenarris was standing almost where he had been when he had seen her earlier in the evening. He leaned against the wall, legs crossed at the ankles and arms folded. He had been obscured by the shadows that fell between the circles of light from the flickering brands set in sconces at intervals along the wall. He had obviously chosen his position with care not to be seen.

'Twice in one day we meet here,' he remarked.

'Were you following me?' Marguerite asked suspiciously.

'No.'

He replied in his own language this time. Perhaps the limits of his French had been reached. Marguerite was vaguely impressed that he knew enough of her language to understand what she had said at all.

'I was too hot inside and growing weary of dancing. I've been out here for a while now. You walked straight past me.'

He pushed himself from the wall in one fluid movement and walked towards Marguerite with the same vigour that he had displayed on the dance floor, arms swinging as he took long strides towards her. Conversing unchaperoned with a man to whom she had not been introduced, never mind one who had assaulted her—albeit unintentionally—would be breaking all the rules of etiquette Marguerite had been taught. She should have walked away, but something compelled her to remain exactly where she was: the way he moved, the way he held her eye and grinned, a slight swagger to his walk. She wasn't sure exactly.

Marguerite stood, hands clasped together inside her wide sleeves, face upturned until Lord Glenarris was by her side, both unable and unwilling to break eye contact with him. He had spread his coloured cloth wider across his shoulders so it acted as a cloak and partly obscured the brocade doublet. His hair fell about his eyes and he appeared a confusing blend of untamed wildness and civilised manners. It was intriguing, to say the least.

He stood beside her and looked out through the iron bars. 'Were you intending to slip out of the grounds again? I wouldn't recommend it at this time of night. The curfew in the city is long past and anyone out now will not be your friend.'

She almost told him of nights when she and her brother had sneaked out of their father's chateau and watched revellers in the roadside inn, of afternoons creeping through the woodlands or walking for hours along the riverbank. She resisted. She had not even shared that private side of herself with Duncan so this coarse stranger had no right to learn it.

'Did you understand what I said to the *moucheron*?' she asked, changing the subject. 'How well do you speak French?'

'Not very well.' His face broke into a wide grin. He laughed, showing even teeth. 'I think accompanied by the flapping hands and tone, the meaning was clear enough.'

'They are horrible,' Marguerite said as another swarm of the small, black creatures surrounded them. 'I hate them.'

He folded his arms across his chest and stared down at her with a grave look on his face. 'You seem to hate a lot of things. I watched you from across the hall when you arrived and during the meal. You did not look as though you were enjoying yourself at all. Was it the company you were keeping or something else?'

A shiver caused by some sensation she could not quite identify ran down the length of Marguerite's back. Uneasiness at the thought of being watched unawares, but also a budding excitement that she had caught his attention. She was halfway to answering before it occurred that he was deliberately goading her to speak indiscreetly. There was some animosity between the Earl and the McCrieffs beyond the granting of land. Marguerite did not particularly care to learn the reason, but she bridled at the idea a stranger to her might try to entice her into disloyalty to the man she was betrothed to.

'This sort of evening is not what I was expecting when I came to Scotland,' she said.

He raised his eyebrows. 'How were your expectations of my country different?'

Marguerite frowned, biting her lip as she thought of the most tactful way to respond. His eyes flickered from her eyes down to her mouth and a keen expression crossed his face. Her pulse speeded up and she stopped biting her lips, not wanting to draw his attention to them any further in case he decided to steal a kiss.

'I had been led to believe that although Scottish men are rough and plain spoken, the court of King James was a centre of culture and learning, of science and arts. That he filled it with poets and musicians from all parts of Europe. I was told I would find it not very different to home.'

The Earl's expression darkened. 'Aye, it was until recently. It will be again, no doubt, given time, but James has been dead only ten days. The country is in mourning for our King. You can't expect life to continue as if nothing has happened.'

'I did not mean to criticise. But this, this…' She waved her hand in the direction of the Great Hall where the dancing was still taking place. 'That roughness appeared more like a battle than a dance.'

'You can't have spent much time in the company of men, I expect. You need to understand that most of these men have been in battle all too recently. Many have lost fathers or sons, brothers or kinsmen, some have lost all.' The Earl looked away, jaw jutting out and lips downward.

'I think you could find it in your heart to excuse their wildness.'

When he looked back at her again, misery was etched on his face. Marguerite's heart pitched in her breast. Didn't she long to scream until her voice was hoarse and the grief that consumed her burned away? Her beloved mother was only two months dead and Marguerite woke every morning with wet eyes.

'Forgive me, my lord. I did not think.'

She wondered for whom the Earl was mourning to speak with such raw pain and who would comfort him. She reached a hand to his forearm. His head jerked down to look and she pulled it away hastily, acutely aware she had transgressed.

'Goodnight, *mademoiselle*.'

Lord Glenarris swept into a low bow. He strode away, head down and arms rigid by his side until the shadows swallowed him once more.

Chapter Four

With a throbbing head and churning stomach, Ewan watched a babe of seventeen months crowned King of Scotland. James V seemed unaware of the significance of the ceremony he was the centre of, biting his fingers and wriggling about in clothes that looked far too formal and uncomfortable for a small child to endure. Ewan wondered if he even understood that his father was dead. He envied the boy if he did not. He felt as equally uncomfortable in the close-fitting doublet as the boy looked. He pulled on his high collar to loosen it and shifted on his seat, feeling queasy. The Chapel Royal was far too hot and crowded and the ceremony was unendurably unending.

Perhaps that was the intention. The nobility of Scotland would remain seated here long enough for the King to grow to adulthood and for the question of who would act as Regent to no longer be an issue.

As the bishop intoned his sermon, Ewan let his attention wander around the faces of the assembled multitude. Most of them displayed eyes that were dark ringed and complexions that were slightly waxen. The heavy drinking had gone on well into the night and Ewan had not been the only man who had indulged far too copiously the night before. Everyone had fasted before attending the coronation and he craved a cup of milk to soothe his stomach and something plain to stop it churning.

Queen Margaret knelt beside her son, stiff backed and iron faced. Now there was a woman who would not easily relinquish control over her son or the throne. The next few months would be interesting indeed. Ewan let his eyes rove further back into the congregation. Margaret's ladies-in-waiting sat to one side of the aisle behind their mistress. They were dressed sombrely in blacks and deep, wintery colours, but among them on the final row of seats was one white headdress and veil that stood out in contrast to the darkness that surrounded it.

Ewan's stomach tightened as he saw the French girl, head bent over in devotion. She was in profile to him. Her stiff hood and veil drew her hair back and obscured it completely, while emphasising her high cheekbones and giving Ewan a perfect view of a delicately formed jaw and slender neck. He felt an alarming lurch below his ribcage and feared his heart had suddenly forgotten how to beat. A heart as burdened with grief as his was could surely be forgiven for succumbing to the load it had been forced to bear. He pressed his fist into the spot as his eyes began to blur.

Had they not, he might have been more aware that he was being watched and looked away quicker. As it was, it took him a moment to realise that the girl no longer had her head bowed reverently, but was looking straight at him. He blinked to clear his vision and stared back, slightly unnerved by her boldness. She had called into question the manners and behaviour of the Scottish court and yet here she was, openly staring at him. He'd thought French women were modest and demure. Some devilry inside Ewan made him wink at her. Her eyes widened and she smiled nervously in a manner that Ewan thought rather sweet. He recalled how she had gently touched his arm when he spoke of his grief the night before, breaking all social codes. He'd drawn away, unable to cope with her kind attempt at consolation, and now wished he hadn't wasted that opportunity to touch her.

Her eyelashes fluttered before she gave her attention to the ceremony and kept her eyes firmly fixed on the bishop with an expression of raptness Ewan envied. Ewan wondered whether his sermon would falter if he noticed her looking so intently, and after those blasphemous thoughts he was unable to concentrate at all. He forced himself to listen, but more than once his eye was drawn back to the girl, hoping to see that she was as distracted as he was. She never looked toward him again and Ewan had to content himself with the pleasant view of her profile.

When the ceremony ended, the nobles moved once more into the Great Hall. It appeared the dancing and drinking was to recommence early in the day. Before Ewan could make his way to the table laden with pitchers of wine a soft hand touched his sleeve and a quiet voice spoke.

'I crave a word with you, son of Hamish Lochmore.'

A small man had appeared at his side so silently Ewan had barely noticed him. He recognised the speaker, however, and the hairs on the back of his neck rose. Robert Morayshill had worked for James IV and now presumably served the new monarch, liaising with operatives tasked with gathering information and relaying it to the government. The two men strolled towards the furthest of the great fireplaces, seemingly engaged in no more than idle talk.

'Your father might have spoken to you before he died about certain ways in which he assisted his country.'

Morayshill let his words tail off. The word that had not been mentioned hung in the air between the two men.

Spy.

Ewan glanced at the fireplace and moved slightly into the centre of the room. A grille might be used for ventilation, or might be a *Laird's lug*, a shaft leading to a chamber where unseen ears might be listening. He noted Morayshill's eyes tighten with approval.

'My father was very discreet,' Ewan said cautiously. 'He kept his own counsel.'

'Hamish Lochmore, discreet! Your loyalty to your father is admirable, but we both know that isn't the case.' Morayshill laughed.

'*Wasn't*. Not isn't. And I would thank you not to defame his memory.'

'As you say. And I say to you that your father was brash and sometimes lacking in subtlety, which worked to everyone's advantage at times.'

Ewan dipped his head in acknowledgement. Spying was too sophisticated a word for what Hamish had done. There had been no covert meetings between velvet-clad and silk-tongued ambassadors, no ciphers slipped from sleeve to sleeve. Instead, Hamish would receive word that a particular group of merchants or travellers who had spent time recently in courts in England or on the continent would be arriving in one of Scotland's ports. They would be greeted by Hamish, playing the role of loud, crass, overly friendly Highland laird—a part which he performed with ease—who would take them drinking and whoring as the mood took him. The visitors would wake the following morning with a headache fit to blind them, unsure of how loose their tongues had grown.

Though Hamish never revealed the details of what he learned or how it was used, his descriptions and impersonations of befuddled Flemish wool merchants or vomiting Italian minstrels had kept Ewan and John entertained long into the night. Ewan's throat tightened with grief at the loss of the warm-hearted figure with the bellowing laugh. There would be no more drinking and laughing. No more days hunting or riding.

'One of the men here today has been communicating with the English court for years,' Morayshill said. 'This is expected. We have agents in England and abroad, naturally. However, recent matters have had far-reaching consequences.'

Ewan listened, anger rising. Someone had passed crucial information regarding the Scottish troops to the English, to be sent to Queen Catherine in King Henry's absence. Instead of hampering trade negotiations or causing dissent in the borderlands, the spy had directly contributed to the massacre of the men at Flodden.

'Hamish believed he knew the identity of at least one agent. Did he tell you anything?'

Hamish had hinted to John and Ewan—if drunken growls of 'I'll skin that redheaded traitor alive, nae mind the consequences' could be counted as a hint—but had never shared the identity of the man.

'I'm sorry, no.'

'Would you be prepared to assist in discovering the culprit?'

'I don't think…that is… I don't have my father's manner.' Ewan's jaw tightened at the thought of another role he doubted he could fill.

To his surprise Morayshill shook his head. 'There might be matters that a young man with more discretion and an understanding of the complexities of politics could undertake. If you can point me down the right path to follow, there are others who can verify the truth.'

'Aye, perhaps,' Ewan answered uncertainly, feeling a little better. His education would be a benefit there, not a hindrance, and being described as discreet warmed him. By the time they parted, he had promised he would do everything in his power to discover the identity of the spy who had done so much damage at Flodden.

Ewan made his way to the table once again, but before he could reach it the crowds parted to either side of the hall. Margaret Tudor, widow of the deceased King, was making her way into the Great Hall. Her eyes were heavy and her face drawn. Her marriage had been political—designed to create a greater bond between the English and Scots—but it was said she and James had been happy. Her grief must have been greater because James's body had not been returned to her from the battlefield, but had instead been taken to Berwick by the English.

Ewan had been denied the chance to lay Hamish and John to rest in the crypt at Castle Lochmore and felt a sudden stab of pity for the Englishwoman. He bowed as she passed and as he raised his head he found himself face to face with the French girl who had been walking in attendance with the other women of court. She paused and looked directly at him, tilting her head to one side and regarding him with wide brown eyes as curiously as if she was examining the apes or civets in the menagerie at Holyroodhouse.

Blasted woman! Those fine brown eyes reached everywhere. The sooner Duncan McCrieff took her away to be his bride, the better. Ewan drew a sharp breath, realising that was the last thing he wanted.

She took her place in the ranks of women at either side of Margaret where the other women started fussing over her as if she were a pet mouse. Ewan paid no attention to what Margaret was saying, but instead stared at the French girl, wondering how he could be so intrigued by her when they had barely spoken and everything she did irritated him.

It must be the strange manner of her clothes that commanded his attention. He examined her now. Her dress was cut from one length of cloth and laced tightly beneath each arm; not a separate skirt and bodice tied at the waist in the Scottish fashion. The design caused the stiffened bodice to draw in closely at her slender waist and fall into a full skirt, hitched up at the front to reveal a waterfall of white underskirts. It was high necked and loose-sleeved. Nothing about it was indecent, but it gave Ewan a definite sense of her figure. The cloth was finely woven and, though without ornament or pattern, was of excellent quality. The cost of the gown would have fed the poorest of Ewan's tenants for a year. She was not alone in that, however. Ewan glanced round in distaste at the wealth on display, himself included. He might inwardly chastise her for her bold behaviour and superior attitude, but could not condemn her for that.

Among the more extravagantly and brightly

dressed members of court adorned with braid and brocade she shone. A dove among peacocks. He wondered how much of this seemingly modest dress had been carefully calculated to draw the eye rather than deflect it. It was no wonder Ewan could not help but look at her.

Satisfied he had solved the mystery of his inexplicable attention to her, he decided to finally find something to drink, but Queen Margaret had finished speaking and the girl was walking towards Ewan. Once again he found himself unable to move.

'Why were you staring at me, my lord?'

She had addressed him directly and spoke without introduction or hesitation, and with a touch of indignation. Ewan shivered. He had noticed last night that her voice was low and deeper than her compact figure and youth would suggest. It should be high and girlish, not the creamy purr that stroked down his belly and made him want to roll over like his deerhound before the fire and submit to whatever attentions she bestowed upon him. Caught out, he blinked and answered more honestly than he intended.

'I was looking at your clothes.'

'Oh!'

She drew in on herself. Her hands disappeared inside the capacious sleeves as she crossed them over her chest and her breasts were pushed flat and upwards. The high-necked chemise that filled the gap between the top of her bodice and her neck concealed them, but the silk was fine and translucent enough that it bunched and dipped. Ewan suspected they would be full and firm when liberated from their bonds. He was consumed by a sudden and highly unacceptable urge to ease the gown from her shoulders and find out if he was right.

'The style is very strange,' he explained. Imagining that he was about to undress her did nothing to dispel the guilt that crept up on him, but she did not seem to have noticed his unease.

'Is that how you knew I was French?' She tilted her head to the right and gave him another of the sweet smiles that made his stomach rise and fall. Her mouth was wide and slightly uneven. It rose a little more to the right as she smiled. Perhaps she had developed the habit of tilting her head to the side so the smile appeared straight. Ewan found himself wanting alternately to smile back or run his fingers over the slight indentation that appeared in her cheek.

'Aye, it was,' he lied, not wanting to admit he had asked Angus about her. 'I'm no expert, but I could tell you aren't Scottish. You wouldn't be English, not here at this time. You're not fair enough to be Dutch or dark enough to be Spanish.'

She looked at him seriously, then gave a rippling laugh. It was high and girlish and was more akin to the voice he expected her to have.

'How ingenious of you!'

He might have taken it as a compliment if she had not sounded so surprised. She had made it clear the previous night that she thought the Scottish were savages. His irritation flooded back and he intended to end the conversation then.

'Did you wish to speak to me for a reason?' he asked brusquely. If she thought him uncouth, why be anything other?

'I know I should not speak to you when we have not been introduced, but I wanted to apologise.' She reached out her hand as she had the previous night, but held it steady between them, regarding him with entreaty in her eyes. 'I did not intend to cause any offence last night when I spoke of the wildness I saw. I am sorry.'

'You didn't cause any offence, at least not to me.' It was a lie, but now she was beside him he had no wish to spoil it.

She looked relieved, but managed to ruin the thawing tension by continuing with a sigh, 'I find it strange. That is all. I do not think the men of my country would behave so if they were nursing wounds after a defeat in battle.'

Ewan rolled his eyes and folded his arms. 'A little more tact might be advisable.'

Her lips twisted down and she pressed them

together to stop them from trembling. Ewan felt as though he had slapped a kitten.

'Tell me where you had been yesterday evening,' he asked impulsively.

She did touch him now, clutching at his wrist with urgency while her eyes darted from side to side. Once again Ewan stiffened. The chill of her fingers on his skin was enough to make him quicken, his blood sparking to life like a flint catching in straw.

'Don't speak so loudly!'

He hadn't been and her consternation told him he had touched on something secret. He clasped her hand briefly before removing it from his wrist with fingers close to trembling, not daring to risk touching any longer. He glanced around. Duncan McCrieff was deep in conversation with Queen Margaret and was unaware his bride was elsewhere. Ewan privately thought that if this delicate little lass with large, innocent eyes were his woman he would not leave her alone in a room full of lecherous Scots to fend for herself.

'No one will hear over the music, but I shan't if you tell me,' he said, grinning to cover the bewildering surge of emotions that her fleeting touch had awoken in him.

She cast him a look of pure indignation.

'I shall not, for it is no business of yours!'

Her hands moved to her breast and she began

to fiddle with a heavy pendant that hung from a long gold chain, her thumb rubbing in small circles over the etched patterns. The gesture looked like a long-formed habit and Ewan wondered if she was even aware she was doing it. He watched her fingers moving over the polished gold. They were long and slender with nails shaped like almonds and he could not tear his eyes from them as they moved deftly.

He narrowed his eyes. 'I would have said you were meeting your lover, but I know McCrieff was in the hall before you.'

'He is not my lover!' She blinked rapidly, which made her thick, dark eyelashes flutter in a manner that caused Ewan's heart to do similar. 'I have no lover. If you slander me in such a way, I shall have to tell Duncan.'

'You'll inform him that I saw you slipping in furtively from somewhere you should not have been?'

She pouted, dropping her head.

'I simply wanted to be alone.' Her voice was filled with melancholy that spoke to the misery in Ewan's chest in a language that needed no words. Had her necklace been a gift from whomever she was mourning? It was all Ewan could do to stop himself from drawing her into his arms in an attempt to comfort them both, but from the corner of his eye he saw Duncan McCrieff was now winding his way through the groups, heading in their direction. He wore his customary surly expression. Ewan thought about leaving the girl alone, but McCrieff had already seen them standing together and had increased the speed at which he jostled his way towards them. To depart now would be more suspicious than to stay. The girl had noticed his approach, too, and Ewan didn't like the way her pale cheeks grew even paler.

Ewan lowered his voice and inclined his head a little. 'It is probably not my place to say, but in a strange country with an unfamiliar husband I would try to win as many friends as I could.'

'Yes. I do need friends,' she whispered.

Her eyes grew wide and gleamed. She looked as if she was about to cry and Ewan felt a stab of remorse that he had contributed to her unease. He wondered if she was aware that she had edged closer to him as her bridegroom approached so that her skirt was brushing his leg. He could say nothing because Duncan was upon them.

Chapter Five

~~~~~~~~~~

Duncan's smile exuded warmth that Ewan believed was entirely false. He lifted his bride's hand to his lips, then nodded curtly at Ewan, all warmth frozen over.

'Lochmore.'

'McCrieff.'

The girl was looking at them, surprised by the openly hostile tones they spoke in.

'I hope you are not assaulting my bride again.' McCrieff held up his hands in a parody of submissiveness. 'Wait. I jest! I jest!'

Ewan eyed him coldly, wishing he had a sword to hand. 'I merely stopped to speak with her to confirm she had not been injured last night,' he said.

Duncan looked suspiciously between Ewan and his bride. She spoke rapidly in French, too quickly for Ewan to follow every word, but he understood she was confirming what he had said.

It gave him a curious pleasure that she was joining him in the lie.

If Ewan had to gamble on anyone betraying Scotland, he'd bet every piece of silver plate in Castle Lochmore it would be a McCrieff. He tried to curb his prejudice, reminding himself that he had no evidence and the only reason for this was the longstanding enmity between the clans.

Duncan was the middle son of the Chief's brother. He spent his time travelling around Malcolm's lands, assisting when his cousin Donald was not capable, or venturing abroad or across the border into England. By any measure Duncan was nobody, yet he had risen high and risen fast. He'd had the knack of being in the right place at the right time. Some men were born with a kiss from Fortune herself. Duncan McCrieff was one such man, it seemed, and now he had won that delicate little blossom of a woman who looked up at him with nervous eyes and lips that were quivering.

'My congratulations on your betrothal,' Ewan said. 'It must be five years since Elizabeth died.'

'Almost six,' McCrieff said, referring to the death of his first wife. 'My congratulations to you also. You've acquired yet more land, I see. You'll be hard pushed to keep it all under control.'

If Ewan hadn't genuinely feared the same

thing he'd have had his dagger at McCrieff's throat for the slur without hesitation.

'Fortunately there are men I can trust to ensure the tenants are well cared for and safe from attack by raiders.' He let that hang there. They both knew it was from McCrieff men the Lochmore farmers were most at risk where their lands shared boundaries. 'It's a shame you weren't equally fortunate yesterday.'

Duncan smirked. 'I don't crave land. It's my wealth I'm trying to increase. It's less bothersome to keep control of and doesn't require me to throw a costly feast at it every autumn and spring.'

Ewan laughed. The twice-yearly gatherings of as many of the clan as could make it was one of his favourite traditions. 'Some of us enjoy the feast and dancing. Perhaps your new wife would enjoy it, too.'

'I think Mademoiselle Vallon has experienced enough of your dancing.' Duncan gazed down at her and patted her cheek affectionately. Ewan tried not to show his disgust openly at the sight of a man of thirty-five leering at a girl young enough to be his daughter. Mademoiselle Vallon simpered. Disdain crept into Ewan's heart that she could appreciate such behaviour. To think he had been on the verge of feeling sorry for her when, with her fine clothes and jewellery and silly opinions of his country, she was nothing more than a pampered pet.

'Where is your cousin?' he asked Duncan.

'Donald left at first light for Castle McCrieff to take news of the land he was granted. I'm sure he will pass on your good fortune to Malcolm.'

Ewan was sure of it, too, and that the reaction would not be favourable. The land he had been granted was at the meeting point of both the Mc-Crieff and Lochmore borders. It was fertile land further inland from Kilmachrie Glen and would provide a good income.

'I'll be leaving myself in the morning,' he said, preparing to bow farewell. 'I need to distribute the alms to my tenants.'

'We'll be staying a few days longer,' Duncan said. 'I'm interested to see who becomes Regent for our new King.'

'It will be Albany, surely,' Ewan said, his intended departure delayed by the opportunity to discuss the impending regency. There had been such great losses at Flodden that there seemed to be barely anyone left who was able to stand to the role. 'He is closest to the throne.'

'Possibly the widowed Queen will wish to rule in her son's name,' Duncan suggested.

'An English Regent?'

'Aye, it will be unpopular at first, but she has

friends here and the backing of her brother in England.'

'But a woman!' Ewan scoffed.

'Why should she not be Regent? Are women incapable?' Mademoiselle Vallon had spoken. Her cheeks flushed and her eyes were bright. She looked at him sternly, her straight, dark eyebrows coming together, and Ewan was astonished to see fierce intelligence in the dark brown eyes that flashed in his direction. It gave her an earnest air that he found surprisingly endearing. He didn't want to argue as much as coax her into agreeing with him.

'Do you think the English Widow Queen should be Regent for Scotland?' Ewan asked, giving her his full attention. 'Isn't your allegiance towards a French faction?'

She looked delighted that he had answered. She raised herself to her tallest, straight backed and chin tilted up. 'Why should I feel more allegiance towards my country than to my sex? Besides, your country is my country now, or will be before long.'

She tailed off, her fierce expression replaced by a furrowed brow and look that Ewan could only interpret as disgust. His hackles rose to hear her casting yet another slur on Scotland. She seemed to gather her thoughts and dropped her eyes.

'I merely question your belief that a woman is not capable of ruling.'

'You are best suited to ruling our hearts, Marguerite, my sweet. Best keep to your sewing and playing. To give you our kingdoms would be unwise.' Duncan gave an indulgent laugh and patted her hand again. Ewan wondered that she did not ball her fist and give him a blow to the ear for his cloying pawing at her. She merely gave him another simpering smile, but her eyes were dull and placid. Ewan wondered how often her intelligence was allowed out to play and once more felt a stab of frustration that she was to be married to Duncan, who would not appreciate such forthrightness in a wife.

'As for the Queen,' Duncan continued, 'while her husband lived he guided her. I am sure she will be able to make her case well. She has friends as well as enemies at court who will doubtless support her claim.'

'Do you count yourself as one of her friends?' Ewan asked. 'Your first wife came from England with Queen Margaret. You must have some inclination to believe she has a claim.'

'Ah, but as you can see, my new bride is French.' Duncan smiled, but his eyes were steel. 'No one could doubt my support of the Auld Alliance with such a treasure at my side.'

Ewan smiled back, equally frostily. 'An admirable cause for a wedding celebration.'

'It would be, if I had not fallen deeply in love the first time I saw her and begged her father to give her to me.'

The future bride gave them both a brittle smile that did not reach her eyes.

'Then I wish you good fortune on your wedding,' Ewan said. He had never wished anything less.

'That reminds me, my sweet,' Duncan said. 'I was telling Her Grace how well you play the clavichord and she is eager to hear you. She plays herself, as you know.'

Mademoiselle Vallon shrunk back. 'I don't think…that is… I have not played for a month at least. I am sure to disappoint.'

The expression of modest denial of her skills could be an affectation, but Ewan thought not.

'That won't matter in the slightest.'

Duncan took her arm under his. She glanced at Ewan in appeal, but as much as his heart lurched in pity, it was not his place to intervene in their dispute. Duncan did not appear to notice how distraught Mademoiselle Vallon was as he swept her away, but her expression of panic played on Ewan's mind.

What had compelled him to warn her in such an alarming manner to make friends? She had given him no reason to become her defender, but he wondered if he had been wrong about the cause of her distaste. Perhaps it was the thought of her future husband that caused her dislike for Scotland. And, Ewan thought as he followed behind, who could blame her for that.

'I did not know you had been married before,' Marguerite said as Duncan escorted her down the side of the Great Hall.

'Did your father not tell you?' Duncan laughed. He looked down at her with an expression of surprise. 'I'm five and thirty, my sweet. Did you expect your husband to be a virgin like yourself?'

'Of course not.' Men had wants and needs. No man would be content to wait until marriage, or would be censured for not doing so. Sometimes she could almost understand them, when impulses raced through her and her body cried out for fulfilment of something she could not explain. 'You have never spoken of her and I wondered why not. She was English?'

'Aye, she was from close to the borders near Berwick. And why not, when our King married an Englishwoman himself. Elizabeth died from a childbed fever.'

'Did you love her dearly?' Marguerite asked softly.

'Yes. Yes, I truly did.'

Duncan looked down at his hands and for the first time since they had met she felt she was seeing his true thoughts. She knew then that his heart belonged to a dead woman and he would never love her. When he raised his head again, his face was hard, all emotion under control.

'Her death was tragic, doubly so as she died before she was able to give me an heir. Our child is a daughter.'

'You have a daughter?' Marguerite couldn't hide her surprise at the revelation she was to be a stepmother. 'When will I meet her?'

'Soon. When we travel to England. Liza lives with her aunt and uncle. Better placed for stability and good alliances for a girl than living with a father who travels between lands.'

He gave Marguerite a look gleaming with desire. 'I hope you shall be more successful in providing me with a son than Elizabeth was.'

Nausea flowed over Marguerite. How easily a man spoke of such matters as childbirth!

'I hope so, too,' she said faintly. 'I do not wish to die.'

Duncan smiled warmly and chucked her under the chin, but his eyes were iron. 'Of course. That is what I meant. A flower as delicate as you should be cherished and kept safe from harm. Don't fear. We'll get you with child as soon as we are able.'

Her mother, Dominique, had warned Marguerite and her sisters that a wife's path was perilous and, sure enough, she had been proved right. Visions filled Marguerite's mind of her sister Marie lying limp, her pallor grey, pleading weakly for some relief from the agony of childbirth. Marie had been granted her release and now lay cold in her grave. Marguerite could not bear the thought this would almost certainly be her fate, too.

Duncan gestured for Marguerite to approach the dais where Queen Margaret sat and it took all her strength to walk there.

'I hope my fiancée might favour us with a song from France our court might not have heard. She plays excellently.'

Marguerite could gladly have screamed at Duncan for bringing her to the notice of the court. Nevertheless she gave her prettiest smile and, amid murmurs of assent, took her stool before the instrument that had been brought into the room and placed at the foot of the raised dais beside the last of the great stone fireplaces. The heat was stifling and she had an urge to feign illness and run to the safety of the courtyard, but such a thing was impossible.

She bent her head over the clavichord, taking longer than necessary to feel her way around the keys, giving herself an opportunity to compose herself. She picked a merry tune that the peasants in the nearby village used to sing at midsummer. She knew it well enough to play without thinking and let her fingers find their positions. She played the first refrain, then began to sing as she repeated the melody.

A murmur rippled through the audience and Marguerite drew courage from their astonishment. She played well enough to pass in company, but her strength was the voice that dipped to lower notes and greater heights than her size would indicate. She was proud of it. Now she dared to look at the audience and see what effect her performance was having. Duncan was nodding his approval. Other faces she recognised smiled at her or stood rapt.

Her eye fell on Lord Glenarris. He alone looked unmoved. He stood with his arms folded across his chest. His face could have been carved from the same granite that the castle stood on. His eyes flashed cold as they met hers. The hostility that emanated from him was strong. He didn't like her. He found her attractive, though, she could tell from the way his eyes caressed her almost as freely as Duncan's did. Oddly, knowing this did not make her shrink from him as she did from Duncan, but she needed privacy and time to untangle why not.

His words had made her shiver with a sense of foreboding. Why would she need to win friends?

Possibly he only meant as a stranger in an unfamiliar country, but, remembering his heated exchange with Duncan, Marguerite could not help but imagine a more sinister reason. It had sounded more like a threat than friendly advice.

She finished the song and dipped her head at the applause. Duncan wore a smile of approval and gestured to continue. She shot him a look of entreaty, but he did not appear to understand and called for another song.

Marguerite began to play a gentle air that her mother had loved, but realised instantly it was a mistake to have chosen a song with so many memories attached to it. The words spoke of the coming of dark nights and winter snows, something her mother would never experience again. Her back and neck grew damp and she knew from the heat rising in them that her cheeks and throat would be starting to flush. The song required more subtlety than Marguerite felt capable of, but she continued into the refrain with a voice that was growing breathy and frail. Her eyes blurred as each note seemed to echo into the high rafters, with no end in sight. She had only sung one line of the second verse, in a voice she could tell would not last out the song, when she heard someone starting a gentle clapping. Others joined in.

Marguerite's fingers faltered and she looked up. Lord Glenarris was striding towards her, hands raised before him and leading the applause. She could no longer be heard over the increasing volume and dropped her hands to her lap. Had her performance been so poor that he could not bear to listen any longer? She was torn between a sense of humiliation that he had interrupted and relief that she would not reveal her weakness to the entire court. She would no longer *have to* continue playing.

'Beautifully played and sung, Mademoiselle Vallon,' he said. 'You remind us that the Auld Alliance benefits our country in matters of culture as much as in politics and trade.'

His eyes glinted and his lips were twisted into a smile that looked sincere enough, but which Marguerite suspected was as false as his praise. 'Forgive me for bringing an end to your performance, but this is a time for celebration, not slumber. Who will give us a song from Scotland and lift our hearts?'

Voices cried out as quarrels between men promoting the songs of their clans broke out. Marguerite slipped from her stool with relief that she was now forgotten. She adjusted her hood and slipped away, coming face to face with the Earl, who was leaning against the carved fireplace. He had assumed the same position he had in the courtyard, arms folded, legs crossed at the ankle and head resting back. The top point of his doublet was unlaced and it displayed his throat and a small V-shape of skin between the nubs of his collarbone. Still uncomfortably hot from the fire and her ordeal, Marguerite felt her back and chest grow warmer still and a slight trickle of perspiration began to make its way down her lower back. He had been watching her and she had been unaware.

'You are not offering to sing, my lord, since you have interrupted my performance?'

The Earl ran a hand over his hair, causing it to flop across one blue eye. He tossed his head to send it back into place and looked at her keenly. 'I only sing when I want to keep the wildcats away from the hen house. They flee screaming, thinking a monstrous one of their type is upon them.'

Marguerite stifled a smile at the image and noticed the way his eyes flickered to her lips, then back to her face, his pupils growing wide. She had not intended to show amusement. She was angry with him, after all. Annoyed that he noticed how his words had affected her, she lifted her chin and gave him a cold stare.

'You doubly insult me if your singing is so

terrible yet you still cannot bear to hear mine to the conclusion of a song.'

He frowned. 'You're still looking red in the face and a little sick. You should find your fiancé and ask him to take you somewhere cooler now you're at liberty from the obligation to perform.'

He made a clipped bow and strode away towards the throng of men who were still debating which clan had the best songs. He raised his hands above his head, beating his hands together and beginning to sing a loud, stirring march in a voice that was as tuneless as he had threatened it would be. Other men took up his song or began to sing their own with different degrees of discord. Some of the rhymes she caught made her blush to hear.

Marguerite leaned against the fireplace in the spot the Earl had vacated, feeling the cold stone pressing into her back and gradually cooling her down. She did not understand him. He made no effort to hide his dislike, but he alone had noticed she was becoming distraught and had succeeded in freeing her from the obligation of performing. Whether or not that had been his intent, she was unsure, but the fact he had made a point of showing he was aware she was uncomfortable, and his wounded air, suggested his interruption had been a rescue after all. Perhaps he had been trying to be kind earlier, too. She wondered if Ewan Lochmore might be a good friend to have and what she would have to do to make amends.

Chapter Six

Duncan found her shortly afterwards and consented to take Marguerite outside. They strolled around the courtyard in the fine rain that Marguerite welcomed as it washed the heat from her cheeks.

'That upstart whelp needs a whipping for insulting me in such a manner,' Duncan said.

'How did he insult you?' Marguerite asked.

Duncan placed his hand on her shoulders. 'Why, by interrupting your performance, of course. You played and sang beautifully. He just could not bear to see you bring credit to me.'

Marguerite said nothing. That interpretation had not occurred to her. She resolved to keep her own to herself.

Duncan's fingers travelled beneath her veil and pushed it behind her shoulders. He ran his thumbs over the wide braid at the neck of her gown.

'I wish you would wear colours that might reflect your beauty. White draws attention to you. No wonder Lochmore couldn't tear his eyes away.'

Marguerite buried her hands in her skirts, wishing Duncan would remove his, but he spread his fingers wider and began slowly running them down her arms, smoothing her voluminous sleeves down. She knew her refusal to put away her mourning clothes angered Duncan. On her wedding day she would have to lay them aside and appear as a joyful bride in brighter colours. Until then it was one small act of rebellion she was determined to maintain.

'He has not been looking at me in any particular way. Beyond growing bored of my playing.'

Duncan's hand tensed, fingers growing firm.

'Your face is unusually flushed,' he said. He finally took his hands from Marguerite's arms, instead tilting her head and stroking his finger across her cheek. 'I hope you are not growing ill.'

'You may be right. I think I should lie down on my bed for a short while until I feel better.'

'Then I will escort you to your chamber.'

Duncan's eyes lit up with an expression of open craving that made Marguerite shudder, a hunger that she knew he was eager to satisfy. As they travelled towards her chamber, she reflected that he had not touched her beyond what propriety allowed, but he made no secret of the fact he desired her. The thought terrified her. It kept her awake at night. It made her want to scream whenever he touched her.

'Rest well, my sweet,' he said. 'I shall be counting the hours until our wedding day. In the meantime I shall have your maids sent to assist you.'

His eyes followed Marguerite as she slipped into the room and she did not turn her back from the door until she heard the catch shut. She did not wait for the maids to arrive, but tore the hood from her head and let her black hair tumble the length of her back. She reached beneath each arm to unlace her gown and tore it off, removing her chemise until she stood clothed only in her sleeveless shift. She filled the ewer of water and began to scrub her neck and arms until they smarted, but at least she had rid herself of the sensation of Duncan's hands.

By the time maids and two Ladies of the Queen's Bedchamber arrived Marguerite was sitting composed on a low stool before the narrow window with her chemise on and her embroidery in her lap. The maids twittered around her like a flock of birds, brushing and scenting her hair. As Duncan had predicted, the women were more interested in the forthcoming wedding than the coronation of King James. Now the babe was their monarch they were unable to coo over him as they had done previously. They talked of the wedding feast, Marguerite's dress and her fortune in marrying such a husband. The little French they spoke was halting and worse than her grasp of English so Marguerite was able to shut out most of their conversation and retreat into her head until she could bear it no longer and dismissed them, claiming a headache.

The room was stifling and she felt restless. It was the time of afternoon when Marguerite's mother would have escaped her pain in a drugged slumber. Marguerite had relished the hour or more of freedom to roam outside and it was as if an internal hourglass had tipped, drawing her outside. She dressed and made her way out of the King's House and along her customary route to the small gate in the wall that led to the path out of the castle. She paused as she drew near, half-expecting to see Ewan Lochmore waiting for her as he had done the night before, but he was nowhere to be seen. Presumably he was still inside the Great Hall, singing songs about doxies and tanners.

After passing through the gate, the path wound down and around the front of the castle, away from the vertical cliffs and towards the flatter, rougher ground below. From here she was able to walk through the knee-length tangle of bushes and weeds towards what had once been a formal garden. She had discovered it on the second day in Stirling. This place alone reminded her of her home and her mother's gardens full of lilies and irises stretching down to the lake. As she walked she began to hum the song she had been unable to complete. Now she was alone she could allow her grief to emerge. A small knoll of thick grass faced over the town below and it was here Marguerite spent her days. When she arrived now, she discovered it was already occupied.

The Earl of Lochmore was sitting on the bracken. He had his back to Marguerite and sat with his elbows on his knees and his hands cupping his chin as he stared out over Stirling. She would have fled, but he looked round as she approached.

They stared at each other.

'Why are you sitting in my spot?' Marguerite demanded. It was unbearable to think that her refuge had been discovered and invaded by this man of all people. 'Are you spying on me?'

Lord Glenarris unfurled himself from his huddle like a long-limbed marionette being taken from a case. He faced her and ran his hand through his hair. 'I wondered when I came here whether this was where you had been creeping away to. No, I'm not spying on you, or waiting for you.'

'Then why are you here? Have you come to criticise my singing further?' Her eyes fell on the bottle that was lying at his feet. It had crushed a posy she had left the previous day and she was filled with unreasonable anger that he had violated her sanctuary.

'Or to pass judgement on my choice of flowers!'

He followed her gaze and unearthed the bruised bouquet from beneath his bottle. Marguerite was about to demand it from him, but paused. His lean face looked gaunt and he was lacking the vitality he had displayed so far. His blue eyes were startling in their brightness and rimmed with red.

'Surprising though it may seem, you aren't the only person in the castle who craves solitude on occasion. Even more surprising, you were not even in my thoughts when I set out.'

He held the posy to his nose and inhaled, then straightened one or two stems and held it out to her. She took the flowers from him, noticing how careful he was not to touch her. After Duncan's constant fondling she appreciated the unexpected sensitivity. She tweaked another flower into place and he grinned.

'I'll admit to choosing the gate you used deliberately, but only because I was curious to see what drew you to it.'

He sat down again and looked out over the city towards the distant mountains. Marguerite stood, uncertain what to do now her plans had been thrown into disarray. He cocked his head back to her and patted the grass at his side. After hesitating for a moment she joined him, taking care to keep her skirts away from his legs.

'I can see why you like it here,' he said presently. 'It's very peaceful.'

'I can think of home and don't have to remember I'm in Scotland,' she explained.

His expression darkened. 'Aye, and you wouldna' want to do a thing like that now, would ye!'

Marguerite had had enough of politeness with this man. 'No. I wouldn't. I did not ask to come here. I do not wish to be here. I would go home tomorrow if it was within my power to do so.' She stood and gestured up to the castle walls. They loomed above the garden like a faceless ogre from a folk tale, dark and foreboding in the drizzle. 'This grey drabness is stifling. It is not what I am used to. Do not condemn me for how I feel!'

'You aren't seeing the best of the country,' he said. 'Come with me and I'll show you.'

Unexpectedly, he jumped to his feet and held his hand out. She should leave. To be caught alone with any man would be scandalous, but to be found with someone Duncan disliked would be disastrous. She eyed him fearfully, disinclined to obey. He stared back at her with such intense blue eyes and she recalled what he had suggested about making friends.

'We won't be walking far, if you're worried about becoming tired,' he said.

He had misinterpreted her hesitation and that decided her. 'My lord, I can walk for hours without tiring.'

She reached out. His hand closed over hers and she tried to ignore the way her flesh seemed to grow warmer. He dropped her hand as soon as she was beside him and strode ahead. He seemed as unwilling to touch her as she was to be touched.

She followed Lord Glenarris further round the side of the hill, as he pointed out mountains in the distance with names that sounded harsh to her ears. They walked all around the castle and arrived at the gate. Marguerite glanced around, not wishing to be seen in his company but Lord Glenarris continued walking and climbed the steps to stand on the walls themselves.

'You see nothing of beauty here?' he demanded. 'Have you ever seen mountains so imposing?'

The mist was thickening into fine rain, but Marguerite could see the hills beyond the flat plain in the distance. They seemed nothing compared to the jagged, snow-capped peaks that were visible from her home in Grenoble, but she admitted their beauty, which drew a smile from the Earl.

'We have mountains, too, where I live,' she told him. 'I mean, where I used to live. Bigger than these. They tower to the sky and are white with snow until at least April. I wish I could return there.'

She sighed with longing and noticed from the corner of her eye his face was grave.

'You said you are returning to your home tomorrow,' she said.

'Aye.'

'Tell me about where you live.'

He chewed his thumb before placing his hands on the wall, staring out along the river. When he spoke it was grudgingly.

'It is a high tower, built centuries ago when times were more dangerous. It has been changed over the years. It is not as large as this, of course. It's on the coast, high on a small spit of land, surrounded on two sides by sand and rocks. The sea is rough at times and the sands are treacherous, but where the sea becomes a loch it is calmer. It's beautiful when the sun sinks over the turrets and the water becomes gold and amethyst.'

Marguerite smiled. 'That's almost poetry.'

He grew serious again. 'We're not all the savages you seem to think us.'

She ignored his taunt. 'Imagine if you could never see your home again, but were taken somewhere else against your will. You can go home tomorrow. I never can.'

He stepped towards her, but drew back. 'Can't you? Why not persuade your husband to take you after you are married?'

Marguerite bit her lip. 'I don't think so. He says the first place we will visit will be Berwick.'

'Berwick, you say?' His head snapped up and he tugged her sleeve, staring keenly at her.

'My lord! Please, release me.'

'Forgive me,' he said. His grip loosened and he stroked her sleeve back into place, smoothing it out before withdrawing his hand. It was a gentle gesture she could not imagine Duncan performing. She forgave the indiscretion immediately, wondering why Berwick was of such interest to him.

They stood side by side and watched the clouds growing dense and heavy over the distant mountains. The rain would become heavier and already there was dampness in the air.

'At what hour do you leave tomorrow?' Marguerite asked.

'Soon after first light. My cart is already packed and ready.' He pointed to the Outer Courtyard where coaches and carts were parked in rows. He singled out a sturdy looking four-wheeled cart with high sides and rough, home-spun sacking covering the contents. 'All I need is to collect the alms I am to take to my tenants.'

'Then I shall say farewell now for I am a late riser,' Marguerite said. 'I do not expect we shall meet again.'

Impulsively she held her hand out to him. Lord Glenarris bent his head and brushed his lips across the back, keeping his eyes fixed on Marguerite's. She curled her fingers around his hand and her nails grazed his palm. His head snapped up. His blue eyes looked grey in the dim light and were gazing at her with a look of longing almost as intense as Duncan's. A delicious shiver raced over Marguerite's skin. Her body wanted to answer the silent question his eyes asked. She would never willingly touch Duncan, whereas she almost craved the opportunity to do so with Lord Glenarris. She could enjoy the thrill of that unsettling reaction, but she would never have to act on it and submit to what she dreaded with Lord Glenarris. Perhaps this was why she did not mind knowing that he found her attractive.

'Thank you for showing me your country,' she whispered.

His eyes crinkled at the corners. 'I hope one day you will grow to love it. Farewell, my lady.'

Marguerite waited until he was out of sight before she descended and returned to her room.

She had spent a whole afternoon in the Earl's company and it was growing dark. Even so, she was surprised to see lamplight flickering beneath her bedchamber door. She pushed it open cautiously and found Duncan sitting in the high-backed chair by the window.

'Ah, you return! I thought I would see if you were faring any better and to offer you some succour. Imagine my distress when I discovered you were not here.'

He gave her a broad smile. She did not return it.

'I went for a walk to clear my head. Have you been waiting long?'

'Long enough to grow a little tired myself. We could rest together.'

He looked pointedly at the bed and a chill ran down Marguerite's spine. Sleep was not his intention. She would have to admit him to her bed and allow him to do what he desired with her body once they were married, but for now she did not belong to him.

'Please, don't ask that of me when you know I must refuse.'

She walked to the table close by to wash her hands in the ewer of cold water. Duncan joined her and dipped his fingers in the water.

'We shall be married within a week,' he said. He smiled and Marguerite was reminded of a fox, red haired and deadly as it prepared to devour its quarry. 'Would anyone blame us for getting to know each other a little better than we already have?'

He took hold of her hand, sliding his wet thumb around until it rested on her pulse. She became aware that her blood was racing. She hoped Duncan did not feel it rushing beneath his thumb and interpret her fear for excitement at the prospect. Her room was on the highest floor at the end of the passage. No one would pass by at this time of day. If he decided to take her now, she knew she would not be able to prevent it.

'One week is not too long to wait when we will have our lives together,' she said, aware how shaky her voice was. She gave him a coy look and wriggled free. She moved towards the open door, hoping he would follow and leave, but he stayed where he was.

'A kiss, then!' he said. 'To give me something to anticipate if you will not permit me any other token of your affection. Then I shall leave you to prepare for the evening.'

If she obliged he might leave. She nodded and he strode to her. He leaned an arm against the top of the doorframe, blocking her exit, and inclined his head. Marguerite stood on tiptoe and brushed her lips across his. Immediately, Duncan's hand came up, gripping the back of her head. He held her steady and pried her lips open with his tongue, forcing it deep into her mouth until she almost gagged in shock and disgust. He moved it slowly and firmly around before withdrawing it. He trapped her bottom lip between his teeth, scraping as he released it and bringing tears to her eyes. He pressed his nose against her neck and inhaled deeply and loudly. Bitter bile rose in Marguerite's throat.

'That's my sweet, obedient child,' Duncan murmured. 'I look forward to availing myself of the rest of your treasures before too long.'

Something ugly flashed behind his eyes and Marguerite realised she really, *really* did not want to marry this man. He lowered his hand and stepped into the passageway, bowing too deeply to be respectful. Tears of humiliation made his face swim before Marguerite's eyes. She slammed the door and collapsed face first on to her bed, clutching the heavy woollen coverlet between her fists. Burying her face in it, she muffled her rising scream and gave free rein to her tears of shock and hopelessness.

The Duncan who had violated her so crudely was not the polite, courteous man she had believed him to be since arriving in Scotland. Oh, he spoke of love and tokens of affection to her, but it was lust that drove him. Her mind tumbled down a dark well of horror at the prospect of those lips touching her elsewhere or the hands roving beneath her clothing.

She could not—*would not*—marry Duncan McCrieff.

She would return to France to plead with her father to release her from the engagement. If she could make her way to the port at Leith, she could board a ship heading to France. With the jewels she had inherited from her mother she had more than enough money to pay for passage. Whatever remained she would donate as admission to a convent and take holy orders. Marguerite sat up and wiped her eyes, never subdued by tears for too long. A plan started to form. She did not even have to get to Leith in one journey, only far enough away that Duncan would not be able to trace her. Thanks to her conversation with Lord Glenarris she knew exactly how to put distance between herself and Stirling. He had told her he lived on the coast. She would conceal herself on his cart and get as close as possible to the port.

Removing her mourning gown and veil caused a pang of sadness for her mother. She pulled the long gold chain out from between her breasts and held the locket tightly, running her thumb over the D and V that were etched into the gold. It was a legacy to Marguerite before Dominique's death.

'I'm sorry, ma fille, *I could not prevent your marriage...'* Her mother had wept.

Dominique would have forgiven her. Marguerite would only have worn the clothes for another week before Duncan insisted she stopped wearing them anyway. She slipped coins into the bottom of her stockings and put on her sturdy boots, reassured by the feel of the cold silver beneath her feet. A band of linen around her torso held more coins close to her body. She put her rings and necklaces into her jewel casket, wrapped them in her spare linen chemise and shoved them into a leather bag. She dressed in a russet petticoat and a gown of olive-green wool.

When a knock at the door brought a servant calling her to the evening's meal Marguerite answered weakly that she was indisposed and could not attend the coronation banquet. She would most likely stay in bed the next day, too. She listened to the retreating footsteps, then forced herself to eat a whole dish of sweetmeats and drain the water from the jug, uncertain when she would next eat.

Marguerite had waited until curfew was imminent and other guests would start to go to bed. She put on a heavy wool cloak with a large hood that concealed her face and she was ready. With heart drumming a march, she kept to quiet stairs, pausing only to snatch up a small loaf of bread and a round of cheese from a tray as she passed the kitchens. She reached the Outer Courtyard unseen, found a dark corner to curl up in and waited for morning.

The fine rain had grown heavier in the night. In spite of her heavy cloak, it penetrated every layer she wore. Somehow she had slept, with Lord Glenarris's gentle burr winding itself into her dreams, and woke to a pale sun trying to break through heavy clouds. Her first thought was that she was too late and Lord Glenarris would have departed, but his cart was still there. She hesitated. It was unfair to involve Lord Glenarris in her escape, but with luck she would be able to slip away when they reached a town and he would not even know she had travelled with him. He would be able to tell Duncan truthfully that he had nothing to do with her disappearance.

She wriggled under the covering. The carriage was crammed with boxes and barrels and there was barely space to hide, but Marguerite squirmed to the front and discovered a shield that had space for her to curl into a ball behind. Her belly churned as if wild snakes filled it, but beneath her trepidation a small knot of victory began to grow. True, her damp shift stuck to her legs unpleasantly and she was shivering with cold, but she was safe for now and the longer she remained undiscovered, the greater her chance of success.

She could not tell how long she waited for the cart to start moving, but soon after the lurching of wheels began, she allowed them to lull her as a babe rocked in a cradle and Marguerite could no longer fight the tiredness she had been denying. The cart bore her away from Stirling, away from Duncan McCrieff and back towards France, and with this comforting thought, Marguerite fell asleep.

Chapter Seven

Despite his intention, Ewan was unable to leave at first light. There were courtesies to be observed and proper farewells to be made. The matter of alms needed to be settled. It might take half the day, but Ewan was determined not to leave without the compensation owed to his people. He woke Angus and Jamie and ordered them to leave with the cart as soon as they had broken their fast. He would ride and catch them up as soon as he was at liberty to leave.

He instructed them to make sure the contents were secure, but as Ewan watched Jamie tuck a basket of provisions on to the seat beside Angus, he knew they had done a half-job at best. Ewan threw an eye over the bulk of boxes, barrels and sacks that made lumpen shapes beneath the covering and was satisfied none of them seemed to be missing. He tugged the back corner back into place where it had come loose and sent Angus and Jamie off. The cart trundled down the path, becoming part of the slow procession of other men returning to their homes.

It had been a remarkably trouble-free gathering, Ewan mused as he returned to the King's Hall. Naturally some eyes had been blacked and noses broken, and plenty of stomachs would be raw and empty this morning, but in the wake of Flodden even the most hardened feuds had been put aside for two days.

Morayshill caught him as soon as he stepped over the threshold.

'You have not managed to identify the traitor?'

'Since yesterday morning? It would take skills beyond mine to work that quickly.' He scratched his beard and thought about what he had learned at the coronation banquet the night before.

'I know he has red hair, but that does not narrow the field much among Scots. There are some possibilities.' He named three men who had been loudly critical about the previous King's decision to strike at England once they had drunk more than advisable.

'We can ignore dissent, especially at this time,' Morayshill said.

Ewan nodded in agreement. A spy would not be foolish enough to openly draw attention to himself. The spy must be someone Hamish encountered frequently enough to have cause to suspect. That meant someone close to the Lochmore lands.

In his bones he felt sure he knew the most likely suspect but paused. He sucked at his teeth, uncertain even now how much of his suspicion against Duncan McCrieff was down to the long-standing feud between clans and his instinctive dislike of any McCrieff.

'It is the future stability we are concerned with,' Morayshill continued. 'Our Queen has been a faithful wife to her husband and to Scotland. There is no reason why she should not continue to serve her son as Regent in such a way. It would be a shame if the influence of her English brother were to divide her loyalties.'

'Duncan McCrieff has strong relationships with the northern families in England through his previous wife,' Ewan said, now that particular door was open. 'He has ample opportunity to pass information to interested parties as he communicates with his daughter's guardians. I have also learned McCrieff is intending to travel to Berwick after his marriage.'

Ewan felt the corner of his mouth twitch at the mention of the marriage. How much of his dislike of Duncan McCrieff was fuelled by jealousy that Duncan had negotiated marriage to a woman Ewan was finding increasingly hard to push from his mind? She'd disrupted what he had intended to be an afternoon of solitude and contemplation by appearing in the old knot garden and her small, white hands playing with the jewelled locket around her neck had slipped into his dreams. He felt a little guilty that he had wasted an afternoon with her rather than investigating, but it had been worth it to see the appreciation in her eyes as she had admitted Scotland was beautiful and the way they lit up further when he had kissed her hand.

'The reivers are notoriously changeable in loyalties,' Morayshill said, referring to the families that lived on the ever-changing border between Scotland and England.

'Did McCrieff persuade his kin to throw their lot in with the English in promise of reward following the battle, I wonder?' Ewan suggested.

Morayshill raised his bushy eyebrows. 'But he is making a marriage with a French family and has been speaking much of his commitment to the Auld Alliance.'

'A cunning man would profess loyalty and what better way of demonstrating it,' Ewan answered. 'I do not believe McCrieff is in need of money so any dowry would not be a consideration. He could be wildly in love with the maid, of course. She has a certain charm.'

'Though a singing voice that offends you, I understand.' Morayshill's expression gave nothing away. 'I believe the marriage was delayed because the bride refused to leave her mother, who was ill for over a year with a tumour.'

Which explained Marguerite Vallon's mourning garb. Ewan had not even thought to ask whom she grieved for. Their losses—her mother, those of Hamish and John—were doubly tragic, forcing unwished-for responsibilities on to both of them. It was no wonder she had seemed alternately spiky as the prickles of a hurcheon and as nervous as a starling. Ewan was aware of a growing cauldron of emotions regarding the girl and currently sympathy was bubbling to the surface. He wished he had been a little kinder to her rather than teasing and rebuking her and perhaps they could have offered each other a little comfort.

'Thank you for your intelligence,' Morayshill said. 'It shall be noted and investigated further. Farewell, my lord. I wish you safe journey back to Lochmore. I have been asked to pass this to you. Alms to compensate for the loss of your clansmen.'

He held out a drawstring leather purse that seemed rather small in Ewan's opinion. Divided between the many Lochmore kin it would not go far to ease the trouble of a wife who had lost her husband and who might struggle to replace him from a greatly diminished stock. Ewan took the bag, wondering if it would have been given so readily if he had not provided names. These games angered him. The court strangled him even after two days. It was time to leave.

He had hoped to glimpse Marguerite Vallon before he departed. A kind word or smile to let her know he understood her pain would go a long way to settling his churning conscience, but she was not in the Great Hall. Duncan appeared to be angry about something because he was striding around with a thunderous expression. He gave Ewan a long, hard stare, which Ewan returned. Provoking Duncan by asking the whereabouts of his bride was tempting but would most likely mean trouble for her, so he left. The girl could be in Queen Margaret's apartments, but Ewan had no intention of invading that female domain in search of a woman he had no right to be seeking out.

It was with regret that he made his way to the stables and ordered Randall to be readied. He had the memory of her sweet smile, a stolen hour in her company and the scratch of her nails on his palm as he had kissed her hand. Stealing those from under the nose of a McCrieff was a victory enough to satisfy him and would be something to brag about on dark winter nights. He could even get the bard to write a song to celebrate it so he went down in clan legend along with figures such as the great Chiefs Rory, Camron and Fergus, whose names he knew from the chapel in the grounds of Lochmore Castle. 'The Ballad of Ewan and the Glaistig Who Wasn't' would pale in comparison to their exploits, but the thought made him smile nevertheless.

A sudden, violent shower brought him back to the present and Ewan decided he did not wish to linger to get a soaking. He pulled his *brat* over his head to ward off the worst of the rain, lowered his head and spurred Randall into a gallop out of Stirling Castle in pursuit of Angus and Jamie. The cart had been Hamish's finest and his pride. It was four wheeled where many used two, was fast and the horses pulling it were a good pair bred from a sturdy mare. Once out of the town and on to the road it would make good speed and Ewan knew he would be likely to catch it before midday in this flatter part of the country. He had lost more time than he planned trying to squeeze money out of the treasury, but after the conversation with Morayshill, he was glad of the chance to ride in solitude to gather his thoughts.

Leaving the formality of the court was welcome, but a weight settled on his shoulders nevertheless. He had been accepted as Earl of Lochmore by the court, but would the clan accept him? Hamish had been a popular chief and John was well liked. Ewan with his milder temperament would have to work hard to prove himself. The matter consumed his thoughts as the road passed beneath his horse's hooves. Peace looked to be settling on the country for the time being so he would have no opportunity to show his abilities with a sword or bow. Only a foolish man would wish for further conflict, especially in the aftermath of the recent battle, but a gathering with tests of skill and strength might be a way to prove himself. The yearly autumn feast for the Lochmore tenants was due. That would serve as an arena where he could demonstrate he was capable of fighting.

The cart was approaching a small cluster of houses nestled together in the shadow of the hills before Ewan caught up with it. They had made good progress, but the journey was close on a hundred miles and it would still be a week before they arrived home.

Keen to make miles, they passed through a village and travelled until after sunset, stopping at a croft by the road to beg a bed for the night. Hospitality deemed that no one would deny a traveller a bed, even in this modest home. Ewan saw to Randall and the mares, rubbing them down vigorously. He whistled as he stroked the velvet withers and it took him a full minute to realise it was the lively folk tune Marguerite Vallon had sung before she started the slow, sad air that had made her look so grief-worn it had torn a hole in Ewan's chest. He glanced at the sky in the direction of Stirling and saw it was black with clouds that promised a thunderstorm over the city.

'You won't have been walking out today, lass,' he murmured. A burst of jealousy made his belly curdle at the thought that instead she would have been in Duncan McCrieff's company.

He walked to the house and found Angus and Jamie in the process of drinking ale with a flame-haired, handsome woman who stood by her doorway, exchanging jokes. This must be the crofter's daughter. Ewan greeted them all cheerily, his spirits lifting at the sight of the dark brew. He asked for a pot and was taken aback to see how the woman's laughter ceased. She bobbed up and down deferentially and vanished inside, returning with a pewter tankard that she filled and handed to him with another bob and averted eyes. He drained it quickly, aware of the uncomfortable silence that had descended on them. All through the meal of stewed lamb and barley the crofter and his family sat in silence, mumbling short answers to anything Ewan said.

'Did I say something wrong?' Ewan asked as he walked behind Jamie up the narrow staircase into the hayloft where they were to spend the night. Jamie looked almost as worried as the family had. Angus came up behind Ewan, slapping him on the shoulder.

'You're dressed like something they've never seen before, or if they have it's on someone squeezing them for rent. They ken you're of noble birth, Lord Glenarris, and was treating you with the respect you're owed.'

Ewan tugged at his collar. Angus was right. With the stiff velvet and slashed sleeves he was dressed for court, not travel through the Highlands. He untied the braided points and shrugged his cream-leather jerkin off. His doublet and hose followed. He wrapped himself in his *brat* and a blanket and tried to ignore Angus's snoring. He dreamed he heard Marguerite Vallon's deep tones shushing him back to sleep, but it was only the whinnying of the horse. Her dark eyes haunted his dreams as her white-clothed figure passed through the wall, coming to Ewan's waiting arms, but passing through him, too, leaving him restless and unendurably aroused. He tried to ignore his erection and refused to relieve himself, feeling that to use Marguerite's image in such a way would somehow defile her, and spent an uncomfortable night until the stiffness subsided.

The following morning Ewan replaced his formal attire with a longer, looser *leine* with gores beneath the arms and sewn into the back. With a padded woollen jerkin instead of the leather one, and his great *brat* gathered over his shoulder and belted, he now wore clothing that would allow him to pass unnoticed through the countryside. He fixed his father's favourite blade at his waist, smiling a little at the design of the handle that would have made genteel eyebrows rise if he had produced it at court.

He was still greeted with solemn faces when he came downstairs and anxious looks at the door.

'There was someone outside in the night,' the crofter explained. 'I heard moving.'

'It must have been the horses.'

'Nay, unless a horse can lift a latch and help itself to cheese that my wife had drying in the dairy.'

The mystery went unsolved. The cart and contents looked the same as the night before. Any vagrant who had been in search of something valuable must have been satisfied with the stolen cheese. The rain that had continued solidly throughout the night must have put him off and Ewan felt a stab of pity for anyone unlucky enough to have been caught outside in it. He helped Angus hitch the mare, wondering if he should check the contents more thoroughly, but decided against it. Even though he was more exposed to the rain that was threatening to resume at any moment he felt freer and more comfortable than he had in a long time. He wrapped his *brat* around his shoulders and strode round to the front of the cart with a swagger he did not have to force.

'Let's be leaving!' he said, swinging himself into the saddle. 'I want to get to Druinunn and sleep in a proper bed tonight.'

In years to come he wondered how different his life would have been if he had inspected the cart at the croft. If he had discovered the additional contents of the cart when he was close enough to Stirling to turn back.

The rain did come down again. Hard gobbets of water that exploded in the road, turning it to a quagmire and making for slow going. On top of their *brats* the three men wore cloaks of felted wool pulled close over their heads and backs that staved off the worst of it. The cart was not as fortunate and before long the sackcloth clung to each item, moulding itself into the shape of each casket and chest and creating an odd undulating mass of forms that even Ewan, who had placed most of them there himself, would be hard pushed to identify.

Almost a full day had passed and the settlements were growing further apart when Angus beckoned Ewan over and pointed behind him into the cart.

Someone there, he mouthed. *Heard movement*.

Ewan peered behind Angus. Now he bothered to look closely he noticed a rounded bulk between his father's *targe* and the driver's board that he could not identify. A stowaway. Ewan narrowed his eyes. He pulled the edge of his cloak back to reveal the hilt of his sword. Angus nodded in approval and made a slitting moment across his throat. The chance to prove himself a fighter might have come sooner than Ewan anticipated.

They had been climbing steadily up the first of many hills and the small town of Druinunn where they intended to spend the night lay nestled in the glen before them, curving round the bank of Loch Lomond where the road split. The rain had eased, turning to thick drizzle that hung in the air, chilling Ewan to the core. As much as he wished to reach the inn he did not want to deal with his unwanted stowaway there. A track led away to the left towards the forest and as they came upon it Ewan took it.

When he was satisfied they were far enough away from the main road, he called loudly, 'I need to piss. Stop the cart a moment, Jamie.'

Jamie grinned and tugged the reins with an

exaggerated cry. Ewan dismounted, saw to the need he'd mentioned and walked around the cart.

Nothing moved. If there was someone hiding there, they were very good at remaining motionless. At a nod from Ewan all three men drew their daggers. Ewan pulled back the corner of wet sackcloth with a flourish. A small figure lay huddled in a ball. This was undoubtedly the vagrant who had stolen the crofter's cheese. He was dressed in a dark cloak with a large hood and Ewan's first impression was that a monk had hidden himself in the cart. His second, more accurate realisation, was that this was a youth not a fully-grown man. His third was that the cloak was finer quality than a common thief could have afforded. The stowaway burrowed deep down between the *targe* and the seat.

'Come out of there, thief,' Ewan barked.

The stowaway did not move. Ewan leaned over and grabbed him roughly by the back of the hood and one arm. He heaved on both none too gently and dragged the boy over the side of the cart backwards. The vagrant cried out in pain and twisted against Ewan, kicking wildly at his shins.

The voice was angry and scared. And, Ewan realised in astonishment, female. Ewan let go abruptly. The stowaway fell forward to the ground with a loud exhalation that ended in a weak groan. She rolled over to sit up and pushed her hood down. Long, wet tendrils of black hair clung to her face like an oil-soaked rope. She raked her fingers through it with long, slender fingers and raised her head. Ewan looked down into the face of Marguerite Vallon.

She was dressed in dusky green rather than her white and grey mourning clothes, which somehow was more unnerving than finding her there at all.

'What are ye doing here?' he demanded.

She made a move as if to stand, but her eyes fell on Ewan's knife. She recoiled and looked at Ewan with an expression of helpless entreaty.

'Don't hurt me!' she gasped.

She sprawled supine on the ground, resting her weight on her elbows, with her legs splayed out in front of her. Ewan's limbs grew hot with desire. If a woman had presented herself in that position to him from the comfort of his bed he would have considered himself a fortunate man. He was not feeling particularly fortunate under the circumstances. Her dress had ridden up to her knees and Ewan had an unobstructed view of a pair of sturdy boots that looked out of place on slender calves that were sheathed in fine silk stockings.

'Did McCrieff send you to spy on me?'

'I'm no spy!' she cried, tossing her head back and glared up at him from the ground.

'Then why did he send you?'

'He...' She bit her lip and looked guilty. 'He does not know I am here,' Mademoiselle Vallon said at last.

'Are you trying to trick me?' Ewan brandished the dagger once more, glaring at her over the top of his outstretched hand.

'No! He does not know, truly.' She looked very close to tears. Her mouth was set in a firm line, her crimson lips pale with the pressure of keeping them rigid, and she blinked too frequently. 'I have left him.'

Ewan shook his head in disbelief.

'And you chose my cart to do it in!' Ewan bunched his fists because otherwise he would have wrenched half the hair from his head in frustration. 'Are you trying to bring the entire McCrieff clan down on my head, you foolish woman?'

'No!'

Angus and Jamie were waiting for orders, the younger man with an expression of pure worship on his face as he looked at Mademoiselle Vallon. Ewan became uncomfortably aware that he was allowing—no, forcing—an unarmed young woman to cower in the mud. He sheathed the knife and put both hands to his temples, burying his fingers deep into his hair, hoping the pressure on his brain could help him make sense of what was happening. He looked down at Mademoiselle Vallon again.

'Get up.'

She didn't move so he held out a hand and eventually she took it. Her fingers were icicles and her grip was weak as he helped her to her feet. She swayed a little as she stood and Ewan instinctively put a hand to her arm to steady her, running his fingers from wrist to elbow. Her eyes widened, but she tensed and he drew his hand away, but not before feeling how unpleasantly damp her sleeve was. Every layer she wore must be wringing wet and heavy, right down to the intimate layers that sheathed her body. Ewan did his best not to imagine them and failed.

'What exactly is your intention?' he asked her.

'I planned to hide until we arrived close to your home. I am going to try to find a ship to take me back to France and return to my father.'

'From my home?' Ewan blinked. 'Why on earth did you think that would be a good plan?'

'You told me your castle is on the coast.'

A great guffaw burst from Ewan before he could stop himself. 'Scotland has more than one coast, woman, and I live on the west.'

Chapter Eight

Ewan folded his arms and watched with amusement as the information sank in. She looked stricken and his stomach clenched with guilt for having mocked her. If she cried Ewan knew he wouldn't be able to prevent himself from offering comfort.

'Where were you hoping to get to?' he asked, a little more gently.

'I wanted to go to Leith. That is where my ship docked.'

'You've got a long walk back ahead of you.'

Her whole body slumped. She looked defeated and exhausted. Deep purple ringed her eyes. He wondered how well she had slept.

'Did you steal the cheese last night?'

'Only the smallest. I left three pennies beneath another for them to find when they look.'

Much more than the meagre round was worth.

'Get her an oatcake, Angus,' Ewan instructed.

She snatched it from his hand and devoured it, then began to look around her with a slightly desperate expression that was easy to interpret.

'The bracken is thickest over there,' Ewan said. She rushed off with more urgency than gracefulness.

Ewan swore loudly. 'Two days and both wasted! Angus, turn the cart around.'

'Now?'

'The town is so close,' Jamie said.

Ewan ground his teeth. They were right. They wouldn't find anywhere else before nightfall.

'Three men and a woman together. How will that look at the inn?' Ewan asked.

Angus shrugged. 'I want a bed and beer. That silly woman shouldna' stop me getting them, if that's all the same to you.'

'No, it isn't. I want rid of her as soon as I can,' Ewan snapped.

Mademoiselle Vallon was returning. She held her skirts high to keep them free of the mud as she picked her way through the thickest of the bracken. She had combed the worst tangles from her hair and it hung loose over her shoulders, almost to her waist. It was blacker than anything Ewan had seen before; slick and wet, it gleamed like the wing of a raven. She dropped to her knees before Ewan, eyes raised in supplication.

'Lord Glenarris, forgive me for using you so

badly. I knew you were leaving and saw no other means within my power to slip away without being caught. If I had realised you were not going where I wanted, I would not have involved you.'

That went without saying. Deliberately travelling in the wrong direction wouldn't be anyone's plan.

'It's all well and good to say that now.'

It would be easier to remain angry if she wasn't shivering from cold and those thick-lashed lids weren't doing their best to keep tears at bay. 'Just make sure you make it clear to your fiancé that I played no part in the matter. Peace between Lochmore and McCrieff is fragile at the best of times.'

'There will be nothing to make clear,' she exclaimed, clambering to her feet. 'I'm not going back to him.'

Ewan could not look at her because the expression of misplaced bravery that sparked in her eye threatened to skewer his heart.

'And if I decide to take you back anyway, what exactly are you going to do about it?'

'When we reach the first town I shall say you are forcing me to go with you.'

Desperation gleamed in her eyes and Ewan had no doubt she would do it. Stuffing her back under the sackcloth until Stirling seemed awfully appealing. He rubbed his eyes wearily. Angus wasn't the only one who wanted to get his head down for the night.

'If you want to go to Leith, you'll have to pass by Stirling,' he pointed out. 'Whatever caused you to quarrel can be mended.'

She gave a great sob and the tears she had been holding back began to fall. She bowed her head, her slight frame juddering as she wept. Ewan swore under his breath. He patted her on the shoulder and she looked up at him.

'I have no one to turn to. Please aid me.'

He gave Mademoiselle Vallon another stern look.

'I'll make no decision tonight. Angus and Jamie, go to the inn as planned. Buy provisions in the morning. If anyone should ask where I am say my horse became lame and I slept rough.'

He gathered some essentials.

'You're coming with me. We're sleeping in the woods tonight until I can decide what to do with you.'

Mademoiselle Vallon drew her cloak around herself and began backing away. 'No! I won't. You won't…'

Her meaning was clear enough to Ewan. 'I won't touch you,' he growled, casting an obvious eye over her. 'I like my women tall and buxom and fair, not scrawny and looking like drowned kittens.'

That was a lie. Some women drew eyes when they were dressed in velvet and jewels, others when they were clad in nothing more than a chemise. Bedraggled and wet, Marguerite stole Ewan's breath away. Her dress clung to her breasts, belly and thighs. She might have been draped in a bolt of finest silk. Ewan wondered how he had ever thought she was a boy.

She still looked uncertain. She had made it clear on the first night they met that she thought the Scottish were wild brutes after all. He wondered what McCrieff had done to provoke her to flee and spoke a little more gently, spreading his palms wide.

'You're very pretty, I'll own that, but I'm not going to touch you because I like my women consenting, not forced. You have my word your virginity is safe with me.'

She nodded. 'I want my luggage.' She retrieved a bulky leather bag from the cart. Ewan held out a hand to help her mount the horse and was taken aback when she ignored it and swung herself into the saddle, sitting astride.

After watching Angus and Jamie leave with the cart, he climbed on to his horse behind her. She stiffened as he passed his arms around her but before long he felt her relax as they both rose and fell to the rhythm of the horse's stride. He followed the track deep into the forest until the undergrowth grew thick before stopping. As he helped her dismount she gazed up at him from beneath her long lashes. She placed her hand on his shoulder with her fingers skimming the place where skin met *brat* and Ewan's throat tightened. He noticed the moment it occurred to her that she was touching him because her creamy complexion deepened to a soft pink and she drew a sharp breath. For a woman who was fearful of being alone with a man, she was making herself far too charming.

'Go sit over there,' he said, gesturing to a tree that offered some shelter. He began to make a fire, keeping his back to her. He heard her move and was surprised when she knelt beside him to help, dropping good kindling on to the ground. He was more surprised that she knew how to lay the kindling and tree bark well.

When the fire took hold he sat cross-legged beside it and took a long swig from the bottle of wine he'd packed in his pannier. Mademoiselle Vallon knelt at the other side, leaning close to the heat with her hands stretched out. Shadows stroked her cheeks and caught the lights in her black hair. She looked unearthly, pale face surrounded by darkness. The ghost he had thought she was. Faced with a night under the sky when he should have been in a bed, Ewan had no desire to make conversation, so for a while they simply stared at each other through the flames until he noticed she was beginning to shiver more violently.

'You're soaking wet,' he said as he realised. 'Take your cloak and dress off and spread them over the bracken to dry before the fire dies. It's a terrible dreich night and it will just get colder.'

She began to fumble with the laces at her side, though seemed to be struggling. Her fingers had been cold when Ewan had touched them.

'I expect you're used to a maid. Do you need help?' he offered.

She glared at him. 'I am perfectly capable of managing by myself and I most certainly do not want you to undress me. Please turn your back.'

Ewan obeyed. Before long he heard the rustle of foliage and she told him to turn back. She was clothed only in her shift, which a cursory glance told Ewan was mainly dry. A cursory glance was all he was prepared to risk, given the way his senses tingled at the sight of the close-fitting white linen that followed the outline of her full breasts and hips. She'd freeze dressed like that. Already her lips were tinged with white. He beckoned her over.

'Come here and lie down.'

She grew paler, if that were even possible.

'I'm not going to hurt you, or violate you,' Ewan said irritably. 'I'm only going to help you get warmed through before you shiver yourself to pieces and I'm left with a corpse. I'd have a hard time explaining that to Duncan McCrieff.'

She didn't move so Ewan unwrapped his *brat* and held it out to her. 'You can wrap yourself in my *brat* to save your modesty.'

She came round the fire in small steps and held the heavy cloth as if she had no idea what to do with it. Ewan took it back and began wrapping it around her from shoulder to feet, swaddling her like a babe. She gazed at him with eyes that were far too trusting, given the thoughts that ran through his head as he wound the cloth tightly around her frame. He helped her to lie down, doing his best to ignore the prickling of lust that raced from his scalp down his spine. He lay beside her and dragged the sheepskin over the pair of them. Before long Mademoiselle Vallon's shivers reached him, each convulsion causing her to body to brush up against Ewan's side, softly at first but with increasing strength that caused all manner of thoughts to assault him. He clenched his teeth, forcing his imagination to behave. He had no business becoming aroused by her suffering. He rolled on to his side and wrapped his arm cautiously around her, drawing her close to him.

'Take your hands off me!' Her voice was a horrified gasp.

'Hush, lass,' Ewan whispered. 'I'm not going

to harm you. I'm trying to stop you freezing to death.'

She turned her face to his. For a moment her breath was teasingly warm on his cheek and the scent of rose oil in her hair sent him dizzy. The curves of her breasts and thighs were so tantalisingly obvious even through the layers of plaid.

Kiss her!

Don't kiss her!

Sense and lust fought for dominance. Ewan swallowed.

'You'll stay warmer this way,' he muttered. 'And you're less likely to keep me awake wriggling. Or you could go sleep on the other side of the fire.'

She did not protest, but her body remained stiff and she twisted her head away from him. She was still lying rigid when Ewan fell asleep, his mind whirling with what on earth he was going to do with the troublesome woman in the morning and what he was resisting the urge to do now she lay so close.

It was just as well he was a man of his word.

Marguerite woke feeling warmer and more rested than she had gone to sleep with any expectation of. The dappled sunlight on her face had woken her and with that sensation came a lingering feeling of disorientation. The air smelled sweet and earthy, with an undertone of musk that she identified as belonging to the cloth she was wound in.

'I'm on the floor of the forest,' she murmured. Saying it out loud helped to make it feel more real. At least it was not raining and after two days of being soaked to the skin it was an improvement on her circumstances beyond expectation.

I'm lying in the arms of a man I barely know.

She was in no danger of forgetting that! She had stayed awake long into the night, trying to keep her body rigid in Ewan Lochmore's embrace. She had been determined to stay awake longer than him and had not been aware of exactly when she passed from exhausted drowsing to true sleep, but it had been only after the arms around her began to slacken that she dared close her eyes and lower her guard enough to fall asleep herself.

She tried to move away from him, but the cloth she was wrapped in was pinned beneath him and she was unable to pull free. She had no choice but to wait for him to wake up and free her. In truth, she did not object now he was asleep. It was barely light and she was still very tired. True, her feet and nose were icy and painful with cold, but the rest of her was warm and comfortable inside the cocoon the Earl had made for them from his cloak and the sheepskin, and the length of cloth he had called his *brat*.

She lay with her eyes closed, trying to keep perfectly still so that she would not wake the slumbering man in whose arms she lay pinioned. The Earl had been so irate the evening before and Marguerite was uncertain how he would respond. Her sister Françoise's husband hated to be roused from sleep. His wife received most of his ire, as wives so often did, but the entire house suffered his wrath if he was woken before he was ready. If all men were like Pierre as Marguerite feared, she could expect Lord Glenarris's tolerance to be stretched even further.

With her eyes still closed she concentrated on each part of her body in turn and received a shock. She had gone to bed lying straight, but in sleep she had drawn her knees up, presumably as her body tried to keep as much warmth as possible, and slept half-curled up. Her legs were pinned between Lord Glenarris's and his body was pressed against hers with his arm wrapped tightly around her. Her skin prickled from head to icy toes at the realisation that she was lying with him as if they were husband and wife. She was wound tightly in the thick *brat* with no part of her flesh meeting any part of his, but it was impossible to ignore the way his body had moulded to fit the shape of hers in the night. She tried to reassure herself that there was nothing improper in the way they had slept together and straightened her body until the insipid sunlight fell on her face and Lord Glenarris began to stir.

He unwound his arms from her waist and rolled on to his back, taking the cloak and warmth with him. She shivered and squealed in protest. With a groan he opened his eyes and looked at her in confusion. It was the first time she had been close enough to notice that his blue eyes were flecked with hints of cornflower. They reminded her of the sky in spring when the sun rose over the distant mountains.

'Of course. You.'

It was not the most civil reception she could imagine and she had to remind herself that it was her doing. He rubbed his eyes and sat up.

'Have you been awake long?'

'A little while.'

'And you didn't wake me?'

'I did not want to disturb you and cause you further irritation,' she admitted.

'More than you already have by being here at all?' His words confirmed her fears, but his eyes smiled. 'Did you sleep well?'

Marguerite ached more than she had first realised, but had no intention of telling him that.

'Much better than the night before. It was nice to stretch out rather than curl up.' She raised her arms high and rolled her head from side to side, but stopped when she noticed how his eyes followed the movement keenly. He had said she was safe with him and he had been true to his word, but she knew he was attracted to her. His restraint would only last so long. Remembering how their bodies had become entwined, she lowered her arms slowly and crossed them.

'I'm hungry,' she said.

'We'll get some food when we get to the inn at Druinunn. The quicker you dress, the sooner you'll eat.'

Marguerite pulled her petticoat from the bush and slipped it over her head. Her precious bag of clothing and the jewel casket were where she had left them beside her. She considered changing her linens, but that would mean unwrapping them and possibly revealing what she had with her. She was startled to see her companion watching her with an intent look on her face. Perhaps she was not as safe as she had thought. She pulled the bodice into position and laced the neck, aware of his eyes on her as her fingers worked the ribbons.

'You don't like me.'

He grimaced. 'It isn't a matter of like or no'. I find you an...' He stopped. 'An inconvenience I could do without. You'll bring me trouble.'

'I will do my best not to.' The sooner they parted company, the happier they would both be.

Her dress and cloak were still damp, but much more bearable than they had been. Lord Glenarris gave her no more attention while she dressed, which gave her the opportunity to secrete her money away without him noticing. She would need every penny she had now she had further to go. The dire circumstances she was in crashed down upon her. She was further from France than when she had started out. She gave an involuntary sob that caused her companion to jerk around to face her.

'It's nothing,' she said.

He looked doubtful, but began to dress. His shirt was long and loose, reaching almost to his knees, and the slashed neck was open deep enough to show his collarbone and the hollow at the base of his neck. He shrugged a padded jerkin over the top and laced it loosely. He then lay on top of his *brat* and gathered it around his waist, stood and draped the ends over his body, gathering and belting it, bunching and folding with a deft hand. Marguerite watched, fascinated by how the cumbersome fabric obeyed his hands. The sleeves of his shirt were pushed up to the elbows. He had good arms, lean but toned and with a light feathering of fine hair on his forearms that made her fingers twitch at the thought of stroking them.

He stopped midway through tying a curious-looking dagger to his front with a leather belt and glared at her. 'Is there something wrong with what ye see?' he asked brusquely.

'Oh, no,' Marguerite breathed. That sounded unbecoming and far too honest. 'Your clothes are different now. You look…'

She ran her eyes over him. A light beard had grown in the two days since he had left Stirling and his hair was uncombed. Seeing him now she would have sworn he was not the same man. She stopped, unable to express the words in his language and unwilling to speak them in her own.

'Aye, well, ye ken we're wild men up here. The pomp and glamour of a royal court is of no use to us in the Highlands.'

He sauntered over to her and leaned against the trunk of a tree so that he towered over her, one arm raised. She had to crane her head to look at him properly. He was tall and she had assumed when she first saw him that he would be sinewy beneath the doublet and high-collared shirt, but the body that had pressed against her in the night had been lean but muscular.

'You're not in Stirling any more, my lady.'

His eyes glinted with danger, but, far from terrifying her, a thrill rushed through her that she was unprepared for. His words opened a door and let in the reality of her situation that she had refused to think about the night before. She was further from home than when she had started out. If she thought too hard about the task facing her she would crumble and cry, and that was the last thing she intended to do in front of Ewan Lochmore.

'How fortunate I won't be here much longer.'

She placed her hand on the same tree trunk, close to his. He shifted slightly and his hand dropped downwards a little. If she reached her fingertips up Marguerite would be able to touch his thumb. What would he do then, this surly creature that sense told her she should run from, while every instinct told her to do the opposite?

'And how exactly do you intend to solve this problem, given that you're not where you thought you were?'

Last night he had laughed when he told her how badly she had gone wrong. There was no hint of laughter now as she searched his expression. There was little concern for her plight either. He might have been enquiring how she would fix a broken basket.

'Take me to the town you sent your men to. I shall find servants—a maid and a groom will suffice—and make my way back and I won't have to hide between boxes and sacking while I do it.'

'You'll return to Duncan?'

'No. To France.'

'You'll never get that far safely. How do you know you'll hire someone trustworthy?'

'I got this far,' she snapped.

He craned his head, looking at their surroundings with exaggerated slowness. Dappled sunlight glimmered through the dense leaves and played across his face and hair, mingling the brown with gold.

'Yes, you're doing very well at getting to France.'

'I do not want your opinion,' Marguerite said. 'This is not your business.'

He pushed himself away from the tree and folded his arms, fixing her with a look of pure annoyance. 'It became my business when you stowed yourself away my cart, my lady.'

His point was a fair one and he had been remarkably calm about what she had done. He could have shouted or beaten her, or left her to freeze in her wet clothing, but he had done none of those things. He walked away, but twisted round with an odd expression on his face.

'How did you know how to set a fire?'

It was not what she had been expecting. 'My brother taught me when we were children. We used to make dens in the woods and stay in them until the stars came out. You see, I am used to being outdoors.'

She smiled faintly at the happy memory. Lord

Glenarris's eyes crinkled at the corners and he grinned.

'I used to do similar with mine.'

He had a nice smile. It lit his usually serious face and lent him an appeal that was often absent. The solution to Marguerite's problem suddenly became as clear as mist lifting over the glen.

'Lord Glenarris?' She took a hesitant step towards him. If she had imagined a saviour it was not this crude Highlander whose unconscious touch stirred her so alarmingly, but her choices were severely limited.

'You told me I should make friends. I think I can trust you.'

'Why do you think you can trust me?'

If she thought about it too hard she didn't know. He'd been rude and surly and didn't bother to hide the fact she irritated him. It was a feeling in her belly rather than her head. She looked him in the face. 'Because you gave me that advice. And because you didn't attack me last night.'

His brow knotted. 'You have very low standards if that is all it takes to earn your trust.'

'Low, or realistic?' she asked. 'My point is that I was going to hire a man and maid, but I think I would prefer someone I can trust. Will you take me to where I need to go?'

He looked incredulous.

'To France?'

'Not that far, just to somewhere I can board a ship. I'll pay you.'

'I don't need your money and even if I did I'm not traipsing halfway across Scotland with you! I have responsibilities I must perform.'

His expression became careworn. Marguerite, who had spent so many months offering solace to her mother, could not bear to see him looking so sad. Forgetting her own predicament, she reached out a hand and placed it on his upper arm.

'I can see you are troubled. I am deeply sorry I have added to them.'

He gave a start as she touched him, but recovered and placed his hand over hers. He gave it a brief squeeze.

'You didna' mean to, my lady. I do know that. If I took you all that way back—which I won't— it would be to return you for your wedding. You have your duty, too, however unpleasant it might seem. We can't run away from what we're bound to do.'

Tears smarted in Marguerite's eyes. Instead of blinking them away, she let them well up in the vain hope that it might stir Lord Glenarris's heart. They had some effect because his face softened. 'Won't you change your mind?'

He raised a hand to her cheek, but drew back at the last moment.

'I'm sorry, but, no. I'll see you safely to Druinunn and help you find someone *I* trust. That's all I can do.'

It would have to suffice, though now she had thought of the Earl acting as escort and protector it would not be banished. She wanted no other companion on her journey home. She nodded reluctantly.

'I'll settle for that.'

Chapter Nine

Half the morning had gone before they reached the town. It was not actually raining and the hills were purple and green in the insipid sunlight. Druinunn was small. Hardly deserving of the description of town. The road wound lazily down into the glen, giving Marguerite an excellent view of the long, main road that ran through the centre and beyond. A scattering of buildings on the outskirts grew denser as they neared the centre of the town where four streets met at a market square. The only buildings of any size were a small church and the inn at the furthest end of the street, where Lord Glenarris should have spent the night.

Marguerite was not optimistic about finding the servants she needed, but Lord Glenarris had said he would help her and she believed him to be a man of his word. He might even change his mind about taking her to Leith if she could not find someone who met his approval. He had remained silent since refusing Marguerite's proposition and she had been happy to ride behind him lost in her thoughts.

It was market day. The square was filled with stalls and carts. People and animals milled about the square.

'Good news, we'll break our fast well and find you a servant quickly,' Lord Glenarris said. His tone was brighter than Marguerite had heard for some time. She wasn't sure whether the thought of food or being rid of her caused him the greatest happiness and truly she didn't care.

Four horses stood out incongruously among the working animals. They waited outside the inn in the custody of a small boy with bare feet. The best was a young chestnut gelding with a white blaze and a pale mane that Marguerite knew by sight. The blood drained from her body until she felt hollow and faint.

'What ails you now?' Lord Glenarris asked impatiently. 'Let go.'

She looked down to discover that her hands were gripping tightly on to his waist.

'The horse. It belongs to Duncan.'

To his credit, Lord Glenarris didn't try persuade her she was wrong, or argue the fact.

'How did he find you here?'

'I don't know. He boasts of having ears in England and France as well as Scotland, but I thought I had been so careful to slip away. Someone must have told him.'

There was no sign of Duncan. He must be inside the inn. All was not lost. Marguerite freed her leg and attempted to struggle down from the horse, but Lord Glenarris seized her around the waist.

'Be calm, you'll get hurt if you hurl yourself off like that.'

He held her close to him, preventing her escape.

'Let go!' Marguerite pleaded. 'He mustn't find me. Is this your doing?'

'It is none of my doing. How could it be when I only discovered you last night? Now, stay still.'

Caught at an awkward angle and sliding sideways, she had no choice but to wrap her arms around his neck. They were face to face, for all the world like a pair of lovers about to kiss. Marguerite raised her eyes to his and noticed how his eyelids flickered, pupils growing wide. His fingers spread wider at her waist, causing shivers to spread out along her sides and back. She held his gaze as he stared back at her, intending to appear brave, but could feel her legs quaking.

'Please, I beg you not to reveal me to him.'

He glanced towards the horse, then back to

Marguerite and his expression grew hard. 'Don't fret. I won't let him find you.'

He lifted her back into the saddle with ease and walked his horse into an alley before lifting her down. He did not release her immediately, but bent in close, bringing his face close to hers. She licked her lips nervously and gave him a smile. He brought his hand to her cheek so that his fingers brushed the hair that fell across her ears and tilted his head to the side. Their lips were within kissing distance and she wondered if this was the price she would have to pay for his silence. She would do it if she had to. His lips curved in a smile that was dizzyingly sensuous. Marguerite found herself imagining what they would feel like. Hard and bruising as he crushed her mouth, or soft and tender, slowly drawing her lips between his? Whatever he did, she decided it would be more pleasant than when Duncan had forced himself upon her. She felt an unexpected pang of disappointment when he simply released her.

'I'll keep you safe,' he murmured. 'Trust me.'

He took her by the hand and led her back round the corner into the market square. An elderly woman and her middle-aged daughter were sitting on a low bench beside a stall piled high with skeins of wool. They wore black cloaks and caps, had drop spindles in their hands and a large basket on the ground.

'Good morrow, mothers,' Lord Glenarris said, bowing with a flourish. 'My wife is newly with child and feeling faint. May she sit with you awhile? She'll work for her seat.'

The women looked puzzled, but when a coin flashed in the Earl's hand they moved up and let Marguerite sit between them. One handed her a pair of carders and a hank of wool.

'Now, Maggie, my love, stay there while I complete my business. Keep yourself warm.' Lord Glenarris pulled the hood of her cloak up. He stroked her cheek, leaving a trail of heat in the wake of his fingertips.

Maggie! My love! Marguerite's mouth dropped open in astonishment at the over-familiarity. He winked at her and sauntered away, whistling, leading the horse behind him.

From her position between the old women, Marguerite was perfectly positioned to see what took place. Lord Glenarris tipped his head forward and ruffled his fingers through his hair, causing the thick tangles to stand out from his head. He loosened the *brat* that he had so meticulously arranged until it sagged around his shoulder and fell in untidy drapes. He pushed his sleeves up, once more revealing his well-shaped forearms, and stopped walking as he reached the boy holding the horses.

'Are ye selling or buying?'

The child gaped at him.

'They're fine animals for a lad like you. Did ye thieve them?'

The child began protesting loudly and before too long Duncan appeared from within the inn, followed by three lumbering men dressed in brown. Marguerite wanted to run, but could not move without drawing attention to herself.

She had placed her trust in the Earl and he had gone straight to Duncan. His soft words and gentle touch had seemed so unusual in a man that she had been fooled into thinking him an ally, but he had no intention of helping her.

Marguerite gave a soft moan and the grandmother passed her a jug of milk, which she drank from gratefully. It meant that when Duncan looked around the square, his eyes passed right over her, dismissing her as a villager and beneath his notice. Her heart stopped pounding a little. Perhaps Lord Glenarris was not about to betray her after all. Either way, she had no choice but to wait and watch what was about to take place.

'Duncan McCrieff! Why are you here?' Ewan made his voice genial and surprised. He patted the chestnut gelding on the neck. 'Is this handsome animal yours?'

McCrieff looked him up and down and sneered. He put his hands in his jerkin, thrusting his chest forward like a strutting bantam in a farmyard.

'Did you sleep in a bush last night? I've been looking for you, but your men denied you were there. I see they were right.'

'Aye, I did.' Ewan made a show of straightening his *brat* and brushing his unruly hair. He rolled his neck from side to side, feeling a crick he did not have to feign.

'My horse grew lame so I was forced to sleep by the road. I'm trying to catch up with them. Angus! Jamie! Show yourselves! We're closer to noon than sunrise.'

He bellowed towards the inn and before long his companions appeared, greeting him as if they had been parted for weeks, not a night. Angus and Jamie glared at two men who were lounging on barrels by the door. Ewan recognised one of them as McCrieff's English brother-in-law and fury almost knocked him sideways. Duncan had brought an Englishman into Scotland at this time!

'You're a long way from Stirling and this isn't McCrieff land.' His voice became accusatory. 'What could a McCrieff ever have to say to a Lochmore that would compel him to cross the country to do it?'

McCrieff glared. 'I'm looking for my bride.

She went missing on the same morning you left. Did you take her?'

'Your French lass? Take her? Are you accusing me of abducting her?' Ewan did not have to feign the anger that coursed through his veins. When he had left Mademoiselle Vallon he had been undecided whether to return her after all, but Duncan's bullish expression was tipping the balance rapidly. He reached for the dagger at his belt and drew it. A fight in the market square was not his preferred option, but if it came to it he would not hesitate.

'Enemies our clans may be, but you'd better have good reason for that accusation or I'll have your blood.' He circled round so he was facing Marguerite Vallon and Duncan had to turn his back on her to keep Ewan in view.

'She has no friends in Scotland, but I saw her speaking to you on a number of occasions,' McCrieff said.

'You accuse me on the basis that we spoke once or twice!' Ewan threw his head back and laughed, though the thought that he was the only ally the poor woman had made his belly twist with grief. His laughter caused bystanders to turn their heads. Some began milling around to see what was happening.

'Did you help her abscond?' McCrieff snarled.

'Abscond?'

Ewan grinned widely at Angus and Jamie, and risked a glance at Marguerite Vallon over Duncan's shoulder. What little he could see of her face beneath her hood was pale. She was biting her lips in a manner that would ruin them. They should only be bitten by a lover and gently at that. The thought quite distracted him for a moment.

'Was she abducted or did she run away from you?' He strode closer to McCrieff. 'Has she abandoned your marriage before it has even taken place? Why would she do that?'

McCrieff bunched his fists and lowered his head and Ewan saw embarrassment flit across his face. 'I am uncertain why she left, but she may have taken something I said in jest as serious.'

'Is it my assistance in finding her you're begging for?' Ewan said warmly, throwing his arms out wide. He was enjoying this playacting now. 'Lochmores and McCrieffs have our differences, but I'll gladly help if you need it.'

'I don't want your help!' Duncan spat. 'Did you help her leave Stirling?'

Ewan spread his feet wide and leaned forward. 'I will enter the Kirk right now and swear before the altar that I did not assist your woman in leaving the castle. Do you wish for proof that I don't have her?'

He ordered his men to bring the cart around and threw the covering back with a flamboyant gesture to reveal the neatly stacked boxes and barrels.

'Do you see any woman in white either hiding herself or bound and taken against her will? Would you like to search inside the boxes? Perhaps I've hacked her into pieces and stowed her in the wine cask?'

McCrieff shook his head. Once more he looked about him, but saw no one dressed as Ewan described. The lass at the wool stall in a dress of green and dark cloak did not even draw his attention. How fortunate she had changed her clothing before she fled. Ewan stifled a grin, as it occurred to him that fortune had nothing to do with it. Her departure had been planned with impressive thoroughness and his estimation of her raised.

'The last time I spoke to your intended bride before I left was the previous day when she impressed upon me how much she hates our country,' Ewan said. 'Look to the ports.'

'I've sent men in all directions,' McCrieff gloated.

Ewan's stomach knotted. Getting the lass to a port in safety would be harder than anticipated. 'I'm honoured I received your personal attention.'

Eyes and ears, Mademoiselle Vallon had said. Ewan narrowed his gaze and strolled close to Mc-Crieff, a daring idea coming to him.

'The only person I spoke with that day was Robert Morayshill. We spoke about an uncertain future for Scotland and those who may help her or harm her cause for their personal gain. You would have found it most interesting, I'm sure.' He glanced pointedly to the Englishmen who loitered behind Duncan. 'As might your companions.'

McCrieff's shoulders tensed and his mouth twitched. He drew his sword and Ewan knew he had scored a hit with his insinuation. It was not proof, but was something to mention to Morayshill, who could decide whether to act on the information. He drew his own blade and moved towards Duncan with a growl.

'We're not on McCreiff land here. Lochmore neither. Do ye want to start a fight on another clan's land? Shall we go back to Stirling together and declare what has passed here?'

There was silence for a long moment. Ewan bared his teeth and squared his shoulders. Duncan sheathed his sword.

Ewan kept his held out. He jerked his head towards the gelding. 'Look for your woman elsewhere and stay away from me.'

'If I discover you're lying…'

'You won't.'

With a look of pure hatred at Ewan, McCrieff called his men to him. He swung into the saddle and they galloped back in the direction of Stirling, sending townsfolk scurrying out of the way of their hooves.

Ewan stared up the road for a long time until he was sure McCrieff would not return before he strolled back to the women at the wool stall and knelt by Mademoiselle Vallon.

'Are you feeling better now, Maggie?'

'I...'

He grinned at the old women. 'Why he would think I have anything to do with his betrothed's absence is beyond me, when I have a beauty right here,' he said.

He gazed at Marguerite with a look of affection and stroked her cheek. Her eyes widened in surprise and she blinked rapidly, thick lashes fluttering in a manner that caused a shiver to run down Ewan's spine. The old woman gave them both a warm smile. He pulled Marguerite to her feet and realised she was trembling all over. Her wide mouth twisted down. Impulsively, and ignoring all convention, he gathered her up and held her tightly. She did not remain stiff as she had the night before, but wilted against him. He kissed her lightly on the forehead and led her to the cart, doing his best to ignore the heat that rushed through his lips.

'Now, lassie, there's nothing to worry about.'

'There is.' She sniffed. 'I don't know what to do. I'm all alone.'

'You're not alone.' He unwound his arms and tilted her face upwards. Her eyes were wide and full of despair. 'I lied to him to protect you.'

'Did you?' She looked at him doubtfully and he grinned. He had not spoken a word that was untrue, though he had avoided answering some questions and evaded others.

'In spirit, if not in fact,' he amended.

'You were very cunning,' she said. There was admiration in her voice. 'I feared you were going to tell him I was here and challenge him to fight.'

'I'd have fought him if it came to that, but I told you I wouldna' give you back. The truth is, I do not know why you ran from him, but I do not condemn you for it and I will not return you to him.'

'You may have fooled him now, but why did you tell him I was going to France? Now he will be watching the ports.'

Her voice became shrill. He held her tight, crushing her to him with a powerful embrace she could not have broken free of even if she had tried. He noticed she made no attempt.

'He said he had men there anyway,' Ewan pointed out. 'He's no fool and I think he's a spider with a large web.'

She groaned in despair. 'He will stop at nothing to find me.'

She sagged against Ewan with her arms limp at her sides. She seemed unable to stop the trembling that had taken hold of her. He drew her closer, acutely aware of the contours of her breasts and belly brushing against him as he held her so intimately. She rested her head against Ewan's chest. He stroked his hand over the silken mass of hair and murmured soothing words into her ear until she stopped trembling.

The scent of earthiness from the forest floor filled his nostrils, along with a hint of rose that had somehow survived in her hair and an undertone of sweetness that was her skin. He breathed deeply, finding it intoxicating. She raised her head suddenly and their cheeks brushed. He blinked, caught in the act of what might seem a violation.

Her breath was gentle on his cheek and when she turned her head their lips were almost touching. Only his sense of honour prevented Ewan closing his mouth over hers and tasting her as he longed to do. She lifted a hand to his shoulder, her fingers stroking the edge of his *brat*.

'Will you help me find someone to take me back to France now? I need to leave quickly.' He saw entreaty in her eyes and beneath that a hint of helplessness.

'Wait awhile,' he said. 'You haven't eaten yet and you don't want to risk catching up with him as you travel.'

She glanced towards the road and shuddered, then dabbed fiercely at her eyes. Ewan realised with dismay she was blotting away tears. He followed her gaze, half-expecting to see Duncan McCrieff riding back, and a knot of anxiety thumped in his belly. He could not leave her now, but equally he could not travel on to Leith before returning to Lochmore. It was nigh on two hundred miles in total.

'I won't leave you in the care of someone I don't know, but I can't take you back to France, or even to Leith, I'm afraid. I said I have responsibilities I must fulfil,' he said. 'Let me think.'

He released her from his embrace and she stepped away with what Ewan hoped was an air of reluctance. She did not push him for an answer. He slipped her arm under his and began to lead her through the market place. He saw no one he would trust to hold his horse, let alone take care of this beauty. An idea had been forming that he had done his best to ignore. If he carried through with it he would indeed be guilty of stealing away McCrieff's bride. Sense warned him not to. His conscience cried out that he could follow no other path.

Chapter Ten

Ewan bought oatcakes and milk as he thought of what he needed to do and how to balance that with what Marguerite needed. They sat side by side on stools outside the inn to eat. She devoured hers hungrily, tongue skimming around her lips to catch the crumbs with a precision and swiftness that transformed Ewan's legs to water. Spending time in her company without trying to kiss her would be a trial. But he could see no other option.

He sat back against the wall, stretching his legs out, and looked at her. Now was his last chance to change his mind, but the sight of her trying to control her trembling lip and blink back tears tore his conscience and heart to shreds. They shared no common grief, but the loneliness that exuded from her reached inside him to the black knot where his own grief had nested.

'I cannae take you back, but I can take you with me. I'll take you to Lochmore.'

'To your home?'

Her eyes widened. She glanced away modestly with lashes fluttering, then quickly looked back at him with her head on one side; innocence incarnate. His heart pounded. He would have to tell her what effect her unconscious habit might have on a man less scrupulous than him. He wondered if she had already discovered the result unpleasantly in Duncan McCrieff's arms.

'It's the wrong direction, but from there you can find a boat to take you round the coast, or you can travel back across the country when some time has passed. I don't mind which.'

She reached into the bag that she was wearing across her body. 'How much will your services cost?'

He took her wrist. 'I'm not a hired man. I don't want paying.'

She looked down at his hand encircling hers and flexed her fingers. They were long and slender, with neat, rounded nails, and the pulse in her wrist grew faster beneath his fingers. He wanted to run his thumb over the soft mound at the base of her thumb where the skin was creamy and soft, to see if it caused the rhythm to increase. Aware of how his own blood was quickening, he placed her hand in her lap.

'You'll be my guest. Consider it my contribution to the Auld Alliance to see a daughter of France safe.'

'Why are you helping me when I've caused you so much trouble?' she asked suspiciously.

He could have answered any number of ways, but struggled to articulate any of them and to make sense of some. The knowledge he was thwarting a McCrieff. The way she had faced him with courage when he discovered her. The fact she had paid for the stolen cheese that first night.

He leaned his head back and stared at the sky. 'When I was seven my brother, John, and I found a deerhound bitch who had whelped. We stole a pup and took him home. My father made us return it, but the mother would not touch it. It was our fault and our father said we must keep him and care for him.'

He stopped and smiled to himself. This was the first time since their deaths that he had been able to speak of his brother and father with such ease. That he had found pleasure in recalling the memory, even. That for the first morning since his father had died he had woken with his mind on something other than the heavy load of responsibilities. She was proving a useful distraction.

'We thought it would be easy until he grew

hungry, widdled on the floor and howled half the night until I took him into my bed. I realised I'd been overconfident, but I had said I was going to keep him so I did. He became my responsibility. You became my responsibility when I deliberately lied to your fiancé to protect you.'

She looked at him sharply. 'Are you comparing me to your dog?'

He winced at her tone and ruffled his fingers through his hair, giving her an embarrassed look.

'It isn't the best comparison, I'll admit, but I promise I will see you are safe.'

'Then I thank you for your offer of aid. I accept.' She smiled and her cheeks dimpled. 'I promise *I* won't howl in the night.'

Implying she would not need to be taken into his bed? He wondered if she was deliberately making the comparison so that he did not start to harbour any expectations. From the way she shut her mouth firmly and her cheeks took on a blush of rose that matched her lips he suspected she had just realised what she had said and had not fully thought of it. Now he was unable to rid himself of the image of her in his bed, eyes glowing in ecstasy and emitting a high-pitched howl of pleasure as he coaxed her to the brink of reason.

'We need to make a start if we're to put distance between us and Duncan McCrieff.' He stood jerkily and held a hand out to help her rise. She ignored it and rose without help, patting her skirts down briskly.

'What happened to your dog?' she asked. 'Do you still have him?'

'This was almost twenty years ago, my lady! He ran off when the blood rose in him and fathered half the strays in Kilmachrie.' Ewan grinned. He held an arm out for her to take. 'But I loved him and looked after him until he left of his own accord.'

'I promise also that I will not stay for twenty years,' she said. She dipped her head and slipped her arm under his, and Ewan had to stop from blurting out she would be more than welcome to do so.

They walked back to the cart and Ewan told his men what he had decided. The look on Angus's face was fearsome and Ewan felt Mademoiselle Vallon draw back. A talk with Angus was long overdue. He ran his eyes over her, taking in the rich cloth and the fine nap of her cloak.

'Even without your white gown you stand out. We'd better find you something better to wear,' he said. 'Jamie, take Mademoiselle Vallon with you and see if you can find something more suitable for travelling. Buy food for the four of us for the next day or two while you're gone.'

He reached for his purse, but found her hand

on his forearm. Cold and slight, her touch seared his bare skin nevertheless. He looked into her eyes and saw the determination he was beginning to recognise.

'I do not need your money. I will buy what we need.'

Grudgingly impressed, he passed her into Jamie's care and watched them head off into the crowd, two young people talking together. His twenty-six years felt like a century on his shoulders. He wondered if Marguerite saw him as aged as Duncan. He wondered why he cared.

Angus was frowning. 'One night, you said. One night with the woman. Now we'll have her on our hands until Lochmore Castle. What were ye thinking? What did the two of you do last night for her to have such a claim on you?'

Nowhere near what he had wanted to! Ewan couldn't shake the memory of the way their bodies had cleaved so perfectly as they slept and had spent the journey to Druinunn burning with curiosity to discover how well other parts of their anatomies would suit each other. A slight resentment that he had not even as much as tried to kiss her fired his temper. He would tolerate a great deal of impudence from Angus, but the slur on his character and Mademoiselle Vallon's reputation would not go unchallenged.

'Have you forgotten who you're speaking

to, Angus?' Ewan spoke sharply. He raised his chin and placed his feet apart, adopting the pose Hamish used to take. 'I am Earl of Lochmore and my decisions will not be questioned.'

Angus turned crimson. His fists clenched and Ewan half-expected he would storm off, or worse, deliver one of the blows with his forehead that could stun a man half his age. He'd received the back of Angus's hand in childhood often enough when he'd been caught disobeying rules, but he was not a child now and he was Angus's laird.

Ewan held his stance, despite the tension that raced through him. It was the first time he had called Angus to heel and the first time Angus had openly contradicted him. His father would have expected unquestioning obedience from his clan and wouldn't have been past knocking a couple of heads together to make his point. But Ewan wasn't his father and hadn't yet earned that right. He dropped his pose a little into a slightly less challenging stance.

'I would welcome your counsel, however, my old friend.'

Angus nodded slowly and Ewan observed a hint of approval and respect bloom in his eyes. 'Aye, my lord. I forget myself. I beg your forgiveness.'

'You have it.' Ewan held a hand out to Angus,

who clasped it firmly and bowed his head. Ewan was aware he had passed some unspoken test.

'In truth, it isn't anything I planned or wanted, but I have taken Mademoiselle Vallon under my protection.' He sighed.

'Why did ye do it?' Angus asked. 'I'm no' questioning your decision, just curious. You could have sent her back with that McCrieff cur and put him in our debt.'

'Hardly honourable behaviour,' Ewan said, frowning. 'You heard McCrieff bluster and threaten, but you didn't see her fear.'

Or feel the trembling of her slight frame when she beseeched me so plaintively, he added privately. He shook himself free of the memory of Marguerite Vallon almost swooning against him in the alleyway, with her black eyes piercing him in desperate appeal.

Angus gave him a leering smile. 'An earl needs a countess, I suppose. Stealing a McCrieff bride would see you pass into clan legend and would seal your reputation.'

'I don't intend to marry the lass!' Ewan exclaimed. He'd bed her quicker than a click of the fingers if he'd met her in one of Glasgow's taverns and she was not a McCrieff's woman.

'Whatever he said to her must have been terrible if it caused her to take such drastic measures. I'm not sure he believed I'm not involved. I fear he might return or send watchers. He might not start a fight in the middle of a town, but in the wild I doubt he'd hesitate.'

'Aye, he could. It's risky for us all now if he does. I dinnae like it, but you're Laird and I'll abide by your will.' Angus drew his lips back in what could pass for a smile. 'I suppose hiding her under the sacking in the cart isnae acceptable.'

Ewan grinned. 'Sadly not. I think we must treat her with a little more courtesy than that. She already thinks us savages and I'd rather not confirm it.'

'Why do you care? You'll be rid of her before long.' Angus scowled.

Ewan didn't answer. He shouldn't care what she thought, but the warmth that had glowed in her eyes when she praised his cunning at fooling Duncan McCrieff had made him rejoice. While he was riddled with uncertainty over whether or not he would be accepted by the Lochmore clan, Mademoiselle Vallon had placed her trust in him. He was determined to prove that faith was not misplaced and he wanted see that expression again as it had caused his heart to miss a beat.

'Well, perhaps not quickly enough,' Angus continued. 'You wanted to be home quickly and now we're tasked with travelling at a speed a woman can sustain. A woman like her will be too frail to travel far each day.'

'She'll have to manage,' Ewan said with a shrug. He frowned. 'I should have told Jamie to buy velvet cushions and silk hangings to keep her happy. She'll no doubt be wanting fine trappings as she travels, a genteel lady used to the court.'

'No, I won't!'

Ewan started as her voice came indignantly beside him. Jamie and Mademoiselle Vallon were standing close by. She held a large bundle beneath her arm. She swept closer and stared at Ewan. Her eyes blazed and her cheeks were red. Ewan wondered how long they had been there and if she had heard their exchange regarding marriage.

'Remember, my lord, I slept for a night in your cart among your luggage and another on the ground. I need no fine carriage or feather bolster. You do me a disservice to imagine I would scorn your kind offer so insultingly.'

She rummaged in her bag and held out a handful of coins, some copper pennies and some silver *placks*.

'I told you already to keep your money,' Ewan snapped.

'No. I wish to pay. You said I would be your guest, but if that is how you mock your guests I reject your hospitality. I will pay you for your troubles or I shall walk away now.'

Her jaw jutted forward and she looked angrier

than Ewan had seen her before. He remembered the sturdy boots she wore beneath the elegant gown, the way she had tramped after him around the grounds of Stirling Castle and the fact that she knew how to light a fire. The delicate and refined blossom was tougher than he had presumed on first meeting and he had insulted her more than he intended.

He had no intention of taking her money, but he wasn't prepared to argue over it now. 'Very well. But I'll take them on the understanding I'm your bodyguard, not your servant.'

He picked out a few of the coins, leaving her two of the *placks* and something that must be French he didn't recognise. He slipped them into the deerskin scrip that hung from his belt. She'd get them back when they reached Lochmore Castle.

He switched to French to answer her so they could speak privately.

'Forgive our mockery, but do you understand how you'll be travelling? We have almost a hundred miles to go. It won't be easy. As we get further from Stirling the land becomes harder and settlements further apart. We might well end up sleeping under the stars again and the weather can be crueller than it has been.'

Trepidation crossed her face. She drew her hands beneath her cloak and glanced down at her feet, but looked back at Ewan so quickly he'd not had time to take his eyes off her. She fixed him with a look that almost stopped his heart in its intensity. Her expressive eyes were black coals that burned with an internal fire. Her lips were an asymmetrical bud of deep red that called out to be kissed. Fingers of flame danced over Ewan's flesh, caressing his neck and working down across his spine and belly. He reached out to touch her shoulder and draw her to him, but she pulled away, tossing her heavy black hair behind her.

'I do not care about hardship. I will sleep under the sky and walk the whole way across your mountains if necessary. I would walk five hundred miles to escape my marriage. I would walk double that!'

'You won't have to go that far,' Ewan said gently. She'd given him an idea though.

'Can ye ride a horse?'

'With ease.' Her uneven mouth widened into a smile that transformed her from the frightened girl into a woman of stunning beauty. Aware that Angus and Jamie were watching the exchange but unable to follow it, Ewan switched language.

'We don't want to risk Duncan McCrieff coming back and meeting us. Angus and Jamie, you will travel along the main road with the cart as planned. Mademoiselle Vallon and I will take a different route across the country. We'll travel by horseback.'

He gave her a smile. 'We'll be quicker that way and if your betrothed comes looking for you again he will not find us.'

Mademoiselle Vallon shook her head, her eyes growing wide with shock. She clutched her bundle to her chest and bowed her head modestly. 'Lord Glenarris, I cannot travel alone with you. That would not be respectable.'

'But travelling with three men ye don't know would be,' Angus growled. She shot him a look of dislike.

'Angus, go see if you can buy a horse suitable for a woman to ride,' Ewan instructed, keen to part Angus and Mademoiselle Vallon as soon as possible. 'Be quick, I want to be gone before noon.'

'Wait!' Mademoiselle Vallon reached into her bag once more. She drew out a small wooden casket and opened it. Ewan caught a glint of gold and a flash of ruby before she snapped the lid shut and wondered what she had in it. She held out a silver ring with a pearl set into the centre.

'Will this pay for a horse?'

Angus and Ewan exchanged looks while Jamie whistled in surprise.

'It'll more than pay, but it'll draw enough attention that if your betrothed comes back and asks someone will remember it. I suppose that canna be helped, though.'

Angus stalked off.

'I wanted to hire a woman as well,' Mademoiselle Vallon said. 'I need a maid.'

Or a chaperon. Ewan shook his head. 'That'd be harder to come by than a horse. Slower to travel as well.'

She looked nervous, drawing her cloak close around herself and stepping away. She was reluctant to travel alone with him. That was fair enough. He didn't particularly wish to be alone with her again either.

Because, since waking with her in his arms, he very much did: alone and somewhere private, preferably with a good mattress and feather bolsters and an afternoon to spare. Not his woman and not his right.

'Given that you've already run away from your marriage, I doubt you're too concerned with your reputation. I have already told you I have no intention of touching, you so your virtue is safe. If anyone questions us we'll say you're my sister.'

She gathered her raven locks into a bunch and twisted it about her hands, then pointed to Ewan's light brown hair. 'I do not think we look like brother and sister.'

Ewan rolled his eyes, growing tired of her protests to what seemed to be a perfectly sensible solution. 'Then I'll say you're the unspeakably expensive French whore I've purchased,' he snapped. 'Will that satisfy you?'

A look of disgust passed over her face before she lifted her head. Her eyes were flint. 'If you intend to mock or shame me you're wasting your time. Say what you choose, my lord. Just ensure we travel away from Stirling and Duncan McCrieff. That is what I am paying you for after all.'

Ewan ground his teeth. He filled the time waiting for Angus to return by packing a pannier with clothing and food. A sheepskin might provide shelter so he strapped it to the back of his saddle and belatedly added a cooking pot. As he unlocked the chain-bound chest that contained his books and valuables, he sensed Mademoiselle Vallon peering over his shoulder.

'You have books? What are they?'

Books he had no use for now he had left Glasgow and the law behind him. He twisted his head round to see her face lit with interest. Maybe she was surprised he could read at all. He shut the lid with a bang. He'd escort her and take her money—or at least pretend to—but he wasn't intending to share any of himself with her.

'Did I ask what *you* have in *your* bag? No. So don't pry into my affairs.'

They stared at each other in silence, animosity heavy in the air until Angus returned leading a sturdy black pony with three white fetlocks and a tangled black mane.

'The best I could do,' he said with a shrug.

The pony had wild eyes and a beaten old saddle, but Mademoiselle Vallon apparently didn't care. She took the reins from Angus's hand, thanked him and swung herself into the saddle, sitting astride. She stared down at Ewan, rearranging her skirts modestly.

'Shall we go, Lord Glenarris?'

He nodded curtly, bidding farewell to Angus and Jamie. Side by side in silence he and Mademoiselle Vallon trotted out of town and towards the hills. It would be a long few days before they reached Lochmore Castle and as far as Ewan was concerned they could not pass quickly enough.

Chapter Eleven

Travelling in the wrong direction, on an obstinate pony, in the company of a silent and surly man was not part of Marguerite's plan. Lord Glenarris rode beside her, but she might as well have been travelling alone for all the company he was. He sat back in the saddle, his posture relaxed as the great black horse moved beneath him. All signs of the well-dressed nobleman she had encountered in Stirling were gone. His immense gathered *brat* hung carelessly from his shoulder, revealing the plain jerkin and yellow linen shirt he wore beneath. It almost hid his legs completely where the hem swung down low below his waist, but occasionally Marguerite caught a glimpse of laced boots and long, well-shaped legs.

She spoke to him once or twice, but his answers were short and brisk. His eyes never met hers and his face was solemn. He wore a sword buckled to his waist along with a curious-looking dagger that added to the sense of wildness. Daunted, she did not dare make any further attempts at conversation, but kept her eyes on the route they were taking away from the town and high into the hills. At least with every curve of the road they were getting further from the likelihood of Duncan finding them.

It seemed unlikely *anyone* would find them, given the scarcity of villages and the increasing wilderness. The road became a track, the track a path and sometimes barely that. Marguerite rode in silence and looked at the country that seemed an unending landscape of steep hills with dark pine trees in thick clusters.

It was almost sunset, but they were still not in sight of a village and Marguerite began to fear another night in the open. For all her boasting of being willing to sleep under the stars, a bed would have been welcome.

'There!'

It was the first time Lord Glenarris had spoken to her all the long afternoon and the sharp exclamation made her jump. Her heels dug into the pony's belly, causing him to toss his head in protest and flinch. Lord Glenarris reached down and took hold of the bridle to steady the pony, hushing it. He ran his hand over its forelock and back down the mane just as Marguerite reached out to stroke up its neck. Their fingers brushed and for a brief instant Lord Glenarris's ran over Marguerite's, covering her hand. He made eye contact for the first time since leaving Druinunn, holding her gaze with an expression that sent her stomach plunging down inside her.

'Have ye thought of a name for that beast?' he asked.

'Grincheux,' she replied. 'It means grumpy.' The name would equally well have applied to her human companion. She kept the thought to herself.

'Are ye tired?'

Marguerite thought about claiming that she could ride for hours more, but he might take her at her word and sense won out.

'Yes.'

Lord Glenarris rose in his saddle and leaned towards her, pointing ahead and down the hill. 'We're nearly where we'll spend the night.'

'I can't see an inn,' she said.

'There isn't one. We'll sleep in the croft by the burn.'

He took her hand and guided it until she picked out a small, stone building a few miles in the distance. It nestled in the dip where two hills met and flattened, and was most definitely not an inn. She wrinkled her forehead.

'What is it?'

'A shelter for shepherds. Travellers use them at times. It won't be lavish, but we'll be under a roof and warmer than last night.' He tilted his head and gave her a deep stare, his face unreadable. 'Unless you'd prefer to repeat that experience?'

And sleep wrapped in Lord Glenarris's strange garment? In his arms? She could almost feel his breath on her neck once again and smell the heady scent of him. A tremor ran the length of her spine and she snapped her head round to look him in the eye.

'That will do fine,' she said coldly.

She became aware he was still holding her hand. She tugged gently and he uncurled his fingers, allowing her to slip free, before taking up his reins again.

'Let's ride. I want to be out of this saddle.'

He spurred his horse into a trot, his face set once again into a solemn frown. His horse could travel faster than Grincheux and she knew he was holding back, so he might be irritated by the speed they were making. Marguerite urged her pony forward. It ignored her before grudgingly increasing into a trot and finally into a canter. She gave the pony his head and pitched past Lord Glenarris, who had not been expecting her burst of speed. It was not long before the Earl was alongside her, keeping pace with ease. They glanced across at each other. Marguerite noticed his face had lost the sombre expression and his eyes were bright.

She risked a smile that he returned, transforming him into someone altogether more appealing. He raised an eyebrow and cocked his head towards the distant hills. She nodded. He gave a grin that was full of challenge and daring, then, with a whooping cry, he broke into a gallop, heading off into the distance. With an answering call Marguerite urged her mount forward. She could not hope to keep up, but with the Earl leading the way, her hair and cloak trailing behind her, and the knowledge that Duncan was further away with each passing mile, she felt happier than she could recall since leaving France.

He was waiting at the shelter, which Marguerite discovered was a low, sturdy building of grey stone with a single entrance. A small stream to the left gushed over moss-covered stones before collecting in a small pool. Lord Glenarris's horse was drinking there and Marguerite rode over before dismounting. Grincheux thrust his head in, drinking deeply, and Marguerite looked enviously at him, feeling the same thirst.

'Will it be clean?' she asked.

'The burn? It's the purest, coldest water you'll drink.' Lord Glenarris strolled over. 'It comes down from the mountains. Drink from the flow, not the pool.'

He strode a little way uphill of the horses, filled his hand and began drinking. After only a moment of hesitation Marguerite followed him and discovered he had been speaking the truth. The water was so icy it hurt her belly, but was more refreshing than she could have imagined. She put her hands together and gulped down more, sighing with pleasure, then ran her fingertips across her brow. She looked up to find him staring intently across at her, but when she stared back and smiled he looked away and rose to his feet.

He refused all Marguerite's offers of help as he unsaddled the horses, built a fire and began preparing a meal of some sort of root vegetable, oats and a small lump of lamb. Nor did he speak to her. She investigated the hut and found an assortment of thin straw mattresses that had been piled on top of each other. She did not look too closely as she divided them equally and dragged them to each end of the small room. They would have no privacy, but at least she would not need to sleep as close to him as she had the night before. The Earl came inside, noticed how she was arranging the room and his lips jerked into a caustic smile.

'At least here it doesn't matter that you don't have a maid to uphold your reputation.'

He dropped his bags down beside one and Marguerite's bundle by the one she was kneeling beside and left. She unpacked and repacked her new clothes, taking little comfort from his words. Reminding her she was alone in the wilderness with an unfamiliar man was an odd way of offering consolation.

The stew filled Marguerite's belly, but that was all that could be said for it. Without being asked, she took the bowls and rinsed them in the pool. Lord Glenarris acknowledged her return with a nod, then went back to staring at the black sky. He was sitting with his long legs crossed and had pulled his great *brat* over his shoulders to keep himself warm. His fingers were locked together and he looked as deep in thought as he had when they had met in the castle grounds. A frown caused a crease between his eyebrows and a solitude emanated from him that reached to Marguerite and squeezed her heart with invisible hands, teasing her own loneliness to the surface.

She had intended to go to bed, but did not yet want to be alone.

'May I join you?'

He waved a hand at the ground beside him. Marguerite sat close to him. She drew her knees up to her chest and pulled her cloak around her to keep as much heat in as possible. His shoulders tensed and the muscles in his throat tightened. He clearly did not welcome her presence. She should move further away, but the evening was growing cold and the fire was already dying. The sky above them was clear and the stars looked like tiny diamonds on a gown of black velvet.

'It is beautiful,' she murmured.

He didn't answer, but he blinked rapidly and continued to gaze upwards. Grey clouds were gathering in the distance, obscuring the stars in the direction Marguerite thought they were travelling towards. Today's fine weather had only been a respite and another day of rain looked likely. She gave an involuntary shiver.

'Will it rain tomorrow?'

He still did not look at her, but gave a gruff cough and stretched his legs out.

'Aye. Most likely.'

His surliness had gone on long enough and Marguerite had reached the limits of her tolerance. She rose up on her knees and faced him, frowning.

'Why will you not speak kindly to me?' she demanded.

'You aren't paying me to be sociable.'

'How much would that cost? Do you have rates?' She raised her hand, spreading the fingers out. 'A penny for a smile? A groat for a kind word?'

That raised a smile at least, though it vanished as quickly as lightning flashing across a noon sky.

'If we are to travel together, it will be more pleasant if we can be friendly,' she said.

He turned to her finally and gave her a long look, sharp blue eyes fixing on her with an expression that made her skin flutter. He closed them and leaned his head back, resting against the wall of the hut with a sigh.

'Forgive me if I am not talkative. I have thoughts that weigh on my mind.'

His voice was heavy and he sounded weary.

'Will you share them with me?' she asked.

He clenched his jaw so tightly she could see the tendons in his throat standing out. 'No.'

'But I have added to your troubles.'

'Frankly, yes, you have.'

His honesty was unexpected. Impulsively, she reached a hand out and touched his shoulder to console him. He flinched and she withdrew it.

'I am going to bed,' she said.

She rose and bobbed a curtsy. He stayed seated, but bowed his head slowly. She backed through the low doorway, only turning away when she had to make sure she did not bump her head. She lay fully clothed on the thin mattress with her cloak wrapped around her and faced the wall. Much later she heard him come in. She feigned sleep and he settled on to his mattress at the other side of the room, grunted a couple of times and fell asleep.

Rest didn't come so easily for Marguerite. She shivered and rolled about, and lay awake for far too long, musing grumpily on the fact that she had found rest easier the night before in the unfamiliar arms of the Earl.

It had not been a good night. Marguerite wasn't rested. She wasn't clean. She ached and was hungry. She rolled over and opened her eyes. Lord Glenarris's mattress was empty and she could hear him moving about outside, whistling softly. While she had some privacy she pulled her new clothes from her bag. She could be clean, if nothing else.

She stripped to her linen shift and bunched the fabric, using it to scrub her body briskly, then threw it in a heap and reached for her fresh one. She stood upright and raised her arms, bunching the shift to pull over her head.

A silhouette blocked the light from the door and a cry of surprise filled her ears. She spun to face the door in time to see Lord Glenarris spinning on his heel, arm raised as a shield over his face and leaving in a hurry. Marguerite squealed.

She ducked down, covering as much of her body as she could with arms and shift, but he had already gone.

'My lady, I'm sorry. I didna know!' From the direction of his voice Lord Glenarris was standing just outside the door. 'I would never have...'

'Go away!' Marguerite gave a soft moan of dismay and curled into a ball on the mattress in a belated and unnecessary attempt at hiding herself. He had seen her naked. How could she ever face him after that? Her only hope was that the light had been so poor she would have been in shadow and he would not have been able to really see her.

'I'll ready the horses,' he called. His voice was unnaturally high and nonchalant. 'Join me when you've... When you're... Come out soon. There are oats to eat.'

Oats! As if that mattered! Marguerite pulled the shift on and tugged it down, wondering if spending the rest of her life in the hut was at all possible so she did not have to look him in the eye. She fumbled her way into the ankle-length shirt and the deep blue dress she had bought in the town and her dark mood lifted a little. The dress fastened down the front from neck to waist with pairs of laces, but the wool had been cut and sewn so it pulled in at the waist without needing the reams of braid her French gown had. After her closely fitting gown, the clothes felt oddly loose around her breasts and waist, but comfortable none the less. Riding would be easier without the stiffened stomacher, tightly laced waist and narrow sleeves. She tried to remember how the women in the town had worn their hair and headdresses and did her best to copy them, but in the end simply plaited her hair and let it hang down her back. She pulled her new shawl around her shoulders, pinning it on the shoulder as Lord Glenarris did. Feeling apprehensive about what he might say, she slipped out of the hut with her bag held tightly in front of her.

Lord Glenarris was attending to the horses, fastening rolls of luggage on to the saddles. He did not look up when Marguerite emerged. He was very obviously avoiding looking at her at all because he waved a hand behind him and pointed in the direction of the cooking pot.

'I've left you some porridge if you're hungry,' he mumbled.

The back of his neck was pink and Marguerite realised that he was as mortified as she was at what had happened. Knowing that made her feel slightly better. She forced the oats down though they were cold and so tasteless they made her want to gag. He seemed to have an unending supply and she resigned herself to them being an ingredient of every meal. She resolved to keep watch for any berries or plants that looked edible as they travelled.

When she had finished she could postpone facing Lord Glenarris no longer. With her head high in the hope of retaining a scrap of dignity, she strode over to him. Whatever he said, she would endure it.

'I am ready to leave.'

He turned slowly and, Marguerite noted with amusement, with his eyes down as if he feared she might still be naked. It gave her an unaccustomed feeling of power that she could cause such a reaction in him. She found it surprisingly invigorating.

'You can look at me now.'

He raised his head obediently. His eyes widened and he broke into a delighted smile.

'Well, don't you look bonny, lass!'

Was that good? Marguerite assumed so from the expression on his face.

'You've got it almost right except for your *arisaid*. May I?'

He darted forward and made an adjustment here and there, tugging the shawl so it was held in place over her breast rather than shoulder. He stepped back, surveying her, and she dipped a curtsy, oddly pleased at the effect she had on him. At least he had made no mention of what had happened in the hut and it seemed he was not going to. She walked past him and took up her reins.

'Thank you, Lord Glenarris. Shall we leave?'

'It occurs to me that if we're to travel together we may as well call each other by name,' he said as they mounted their horses. 'I am Ewan.'

'You may call me Marguerite.' She held a hand out and he lifted it to his lips.

'You need a Scottish name to go with your new clothes.' His eyes danced. 'That's Margaret in my country.'

'Then I shall be Margaret.' As an afterthought she asked, 'Is Maggie short for that?'

'Aye. Though we should wait until we know each other better still before I call you that.'

He clicked his tongue and the horse began to walk off. Marguerite couldn't help wonder how much better they would grow to know each other.

They did not climb into the hills, but kept to the edge of the large lake that Ewan called a loch for the rest of the day. The journey should have been easier, but the clouds grew more threatening, rolling across the sky leaden with the threat of rain. The wind blew down from the mountains in bitter gusts that reached beneath Marguerite's shawl. They made her shiver despite the thick layers of wool she wore and, though she tried her hardest to hide her discomfort, she knew the Earl must be aware of how hard she was finding the journey.

Ewan, as she must now remember to call him, was slightly more talkative than he had been the day before, riding alongside where he could and directing her eye to the wide-winged eagles that soared overhead. Later he even provoked an argument that lasted half the afternoon by suggesting Marguerite only supported the cause of the widowed English Queen Margaret because they shared the same name. She was surprised he remembered they had spoken on the subject, but threw herself into her defence with enthusiasm.

'She is a widow, grieving for her husband, and the mother of a young child,' Marguerite concluded. 'Of course she is going to wish to keep her son close by her. No parent would do otherwise.'

It did not occur to her until later that he was doing his best to distract her from the hardships they faced. He succeeded, because by the time they had settled their argument it was growing dark. She stopped talking when she realised Ewan was climbing from his saddle.

'Where are we?'

The loch was still and silent with mist hanging over the water giving it a ghostly air. There was no sign of a hut, much less an inn, and the trees that almost met the water grew densely.

'I'm afraid we'll be spending the night outside once again,' Ewan said. 'We'll go inland a little to find more shelter.'

They led their horses through the trees until Ewan stopped in a small clearing. Once again they dined on oats cooked with water, but with slices of salty cheese Ewan produced with a flourish from his saddlebag. They ate in silence, both too exhausted to make conversation and craving sleep. Ewan had removed his sword and the odd-looking dagger and had drawn his great *brat* up over his head. Marguerite pulled her shawl around herself in similar fashion. She peered out from beneath the heavy folds.

'You look cold,' Ewan said.

'I did not imagine I would ever miss a simple hut.' She tried to laugh, but her teeth chattered. She wrapped her shawl tighter round herself and huddled against the tree. Ewan shuffled close beside her. He unwound his *brat* and, as he had done before, wrapped it tightly around Marguerite, then his hand found hers and he squeezed gently.

'Your hand is frozen!' he remarked. He took both her hands between his and began rubbing them in firm circles until Marguerite's fingers grew warm. She flexed them and gave him a shy smile. 'Thank you.'

He kept hold of them, drawing them to his chest, and Marguerite found herself leaning closer to him, drawn by cords she could not see or feel. Ewan inclined his head towards her. Even seated he was taller than she was. Marguerite had to tilt her head back to keep his eyes in view, but her gaze kept returning to his mouth. His lips were no longer tightly pressed together or as severe as she had grown used to seeing. Now they were relaxed and slightly open, curving into a smile that lent them a measure of sensuality she had not seen before. When Duncan had demanded she kiss him, she had been overcome with revulsion. Now there was no distaste. She licked her lips and parted them in anticipation of something she had never imagined she might willingly do and closed her eyes with a gentle sigh.

Nothing happened. She opened her eyes to discover Ewan was sitting back, frowning once more.

'How old are you?' he asked sternly.

A blush crept down the back of Marguerite's neck and round over her chest. He hadn't kissed her. She should feel relieved that he was as honourable as he had promised to be, but all she could think of was what his lips would have tasted like.

'What day is it today?' she asked.

Ewan raised his eyebrows. 'The twenty-fifth of the month.'

'Then I am eighteen.' Her stomach lurched. She held up a hand, two fingers raised.

'For two more days, at least. My birthday is on the twenty-seventh.'

'You'll be spending it somewhere a lot less comfortable than Stirling, I'm afraid,' he remarked, grinning.

The enormity of what she had done crashed down upon her. She folded her arms tightly across her chest, defending herself against something she no longer needed to, and looked into the glowing embers of the almost-dead fire. Somewhere, Duncan was still searching for her. Somehow she had to evade him long enough to get to France.

A sob welled up and she swallowed it down. Ewan reached out hesitantly and patted her on the forearm, then let his hand rest there.

'I'm sorry, that was tactless of me.'

Marguerite blinked back tears and put her hand over his, drawing strength from his tentative attempt at comfort. Obviously emboldened, he put his arms around her. He drew her to his chest and she was surprised at how natural the gesture felt.

'I should find you somewhere better to sleep,' he murmured against her ear.

He'd misunderstood. He thought she was a silly girl almost weeping because of discomfort. Once the danger of tears had ceased she expected him to release her, but he rearranged his brat, slouched down and drew her deeper into his arms.

'Don't think I'm crying because I fear hardship!' She looked at him defiantly. 'I just remembered my marriage was to take place on my nineteenth birthday, but I will not be spending it in a bridal bed.'

She would not cry at that thought. 'I'd sleep on heather rather than that. On rocks and mud.'

She blinked fiercely to hold back the tears, but she was so weary that one or two breached the barrier. Ewan reached out and wiped them from her cheek. He took her hand and squeezed it. The gesture was presumably meant to be reassuring, but so close after the kiss that had not happened it sent her skin fluttering as if she had plunged into the burn fully clothed. She squeezed back, lacing her fingers between his, and heard his shocked intake of breath.

Ewan pulled the sheepskin over them and held her close. A sense of warmth and safety stole over Marguerite. She should be ashamed of her behaviour. Marriage, and the acts that accompanied it, was something to be dreaded and endured. If the tales her sisters had told her was not proof enough, the brutal kiss Duncan had forced upon her confirmed it. Yet here she was, almost encouraging a stranger to take the liberties she had denied her rightful bridegroom, and regretting when he did not. She was ashamed, but that didn't stop the images that filled her mind. Would lovemaking with Ewan be something to fear when he was capable of such tenderness? Even if he didn't wield his power as cruelly as Duncan would have, or her sisters' husbands did, she would risk pregnancy and death in childbirth. She fell asleep wrapped in the warmth of his embrace, wondering if a night in his bed would be worth the danger of pregnancy that it would inevitably entail.

Chapter Twelve

Marguerite woke feeling rested, ready to begin the day. She had fallen asleep lying straight, but woke with the curve of her spine pressed against the fullness of Ewan's torso and her thighs and buttocks pressed against his groin. His arm was wrapped tightly around her and his hand had settled in the hollow curve of her belly below her breasts. The rhythm of his breathing made his body rise and fall, and each breath he drew in caused his chest muscles to push against Marguerite's shoulder blades. The breath itself blew across her cheek, bathing it in warmth where the rest of the air was cold and damp.

Marguerite's hair fell over her face, tickling her nose, and she sneezed. It was impossible to keep it in or remain motionless. Her entire body convulsed, causing her back to arch and her buttocks to grind against Ewan's crotch. He stirred, a ripple of life spreading through his body, but he did not waken. His fingers spread wide over the softness of Marguerite's belly. Worse still, his head rolled forward on to her neck and he gave a soft moan.

'Are you awake?' she asked, horrified to think he might be aware of what he was doing. He had said she was safe from him. He said nothing, but made a little crooning noise in the back of his throat.

No, he was asleep, which was precious little comfort to Marguerite. He muttered something unintelligible into her ear and began to nuzzle against the nape of her neck. The scratch of beard growth and the soft warmth of his lips against her bare flesh somehow combined to produce the most deliciously alarming effect on Marguerite. It was an entirely new sensation and tickled. It wasn't unpleasant. In fact, it caused Marguerite to clench her toes in guilty delight as his mouth brushed across the sensitive skin.

To indulge the glorious sensations that were assailing her was far too tempting. She should wake him, but she was intrigued by the way her skin was warming and becoming more sensitive, not only where his lips skimmed, but spreading outwards and internally as well. Without thinking, she leaned her head back to allow him greater access.

Ewan found her ear. He nuzzled against it and

tugged gently on her lobe with lips that were at the same time firm and soft. To permit him this intimacy bordered on debauched, no matter how many layers of shawl and *brat* and linen lay between them. Marguerite spoke his name sharply, but was astonished to hear it come out as a husky gasp. Ewan mumbled against her neck and the hand that had been resting on her belly strayed upwards to her breast. The slow trace of his fingers across the thin linen was deliciously wicked.

The scraping of his fingers across her nipple, combined with the insistent pressure on her ear, sent a throb of heat through Marguerite that was almost too much to withstand. Invisible cords tightened all the way down her spine and pulled at the cleft where her legs joined. Was this why women dreaded marriage, if this assault on the senses that left her quivering and begging silently for more was common? She managed to swallow the gasp of shock as her body convulsed, but only just.

'Lord Glenarris, wake up!'

Marguerite succeeded in twisting round to face him with one arm pressed flat against his chest. She called his name again and watched as he began to wake up. His eyelashes fluttered and he yawned widely. She had nursed her mother for long enough to recognise someone waking from a heavy slumber. At least she knew he had not been intentionally groping her while feigning sleep.

His eyes, when they opened, were heavy with desire and the lips that had so recently been causing Marguerite to writhe with pleasure curved into a sensuous smile.

'Lord Glenarris, stop that at once.'

'Stop what?' He gazed at her blearily. His brow knotted in puzzlement, then dipped further in irritation.

'There's no need to shout,' he growled. 'What's the trouble? Are we being attacked?'

His eyes became alert and his arms became rigid, tensing for danger almost between heartbeats. It was impressive to see.

'Nothing like that,' she said.

He glared at her. 'Then why are you yelling in my face?'

'You...' She dropped her gaze, acutely aware that she had been the one to take liberties, not him. 'You were...touching me.'

Ewan pushed himself to his elbows. 'Ah. Well, in that case I dare say you're justified in shouting.'

He threw the sheepskin back, letting an unwelcome blast of cold strike Marguerite. He froze and dragged the sheepskin back over his waist. He gave her a strange look over his shoulder and stood up, crossing to the other side of the now-dead fire.

'I didn't mean to, though. A man can't be held responsible for something he does in his sleep. If it is any comfort, it probably wasn't you I had in mind.'

Probably. It wasn't much comfort. Marguerite pulled the *brat* tighter around her body. She couldn't help wondering whom he had been thinking of as he touched her with such tenderness. How many women had Ewan Lochmore woken with and had they been treated to the same attentions while he was half-asleep? And, more importantly, why did the thought of being one of them inflame her with such ferocity? She pulled her shift back into place. She felt like a harlot and neither of them had done anything to warrant it.

Ewan was deeply troubled. He had no knowledge of touching Marguerite as he slept and had no idea what form this inadvertent violation had taken, but from the way she tensed whenever he came near her, he believed she was telling the truth. He'd been dimly aware of her squirming against him as he drifted awake and he had woken with the evidence of his desire for her uncomfortably visible.

Neither of them had mentioned the morning before when he had walked in and seen her naked, and he was determined not to be the one to do so. Perspiration gathered at the nape of his neck and the small of his back as he remembered the full breasts and pale limbs that met where dark down hid her most intimate place. He'd been able to think of little else ever since and had suffered pangs of guilt that, when he had comforted her, half his mind had been on undressing her and offering her a distraction from her troubles that would be of an entirely carnal nature. The mere thought made him weak with desire that the memory of her body pressing against him did nothing to quash.

She sat wrapped in his brat, gazing up at him with eyes that were watchful, yet inquisitive, and tracked every movement he made. He turned his back, not wanting her to suspect what the sight of her sitting there did to his composure.

'I'm going to bathe.' A soaking in the icy waters of Lomond would quench the fires. 'You'll be safe while I'm gone if you don't stray.'

Amusement passed over her face and she laughed, her eyes creasing at the corners in a manner that made Ewan want to do anything to make her smile again. She stood, wrapping the *brat* around her shoulders, and came towards him.

'Ewan, I will be safe and I am used to watching for danger. I have long been used to spending time outside my father's house. I would walk for the whole day alone and never come to harm.'

He patted her shoulder. A poor substitute for the urge to skim his hand down her back to rest it in the warm contours of her spine or trace it over the flatness of her belly. Her lips twitched into the uneven smile. She leaned in towards him, then stiffened and drew back. Her eyes never left his and her cheeks flushed. Whatever he had done in his sleep had not left her unmoved. The thought made him swell again.

Wordlessly he strode down to the loch barefoot. He stripped, left his *leine* on the shingle and plunged into the loch naked. He swam out until his skin began to tingle, then dived deep, rising with a gasp and drawing deep breaths. He stood waist deep to scrub himself down until he felt more in control of his body.

When he returned, Marguerite was sitting on the blanket still wrapped in his *brat*, her knees tucked under her to one side. She had left him half of the cheese on the cloth and had something in her hands. Ewan's sword and jerkin were where he had left them before going to bathe, but the small dagger was no longer neatly placed alongside it. Marguerite was examining it with interest.

Anger flushed Ewan's cheeks. She'd interfered

with his belongings without asking! He padded closer on bare feet until he was standing directly behind her.

'What're you doing?'

She jumped at the sharpness of his question and raised her head to look at him. She had the grace to look a little guilty.

'I—I was looking at your dagger. Forgive me, I did not mean to pry, but it is a very unusual design. I was curious.'

Ewan's anger subsided a little, replaced with a hint of amusement. It was a common style of dagger, but to Marguerite it would be unusual enough to be worth remarking on, especially given the interest she was trying to deny. He'd enjoy a little revenge and teach her not to meddle with his belongings.

'My ballock knife, you mean?'

Ewan squatted beside her, grinning as a look of puzzlement settled on her face.

'Your baloque knife?'

Marguerite repeated the unfamiliar words, her accent sending a frisson of delight through Ewan's belly and straight to the part under discussion. Marguerite examined the knife once more. She ran her finger in a slow figure of eight over the smooth oval lobes of the guard at the bottom of the hilt with a languor that made the breath catch in Ewan's throat. Was she truly so innocent of men that she had no idea what the shape represented? She was only eighteen, and a virgin at that, but even so…

He tried not to imagine her fingers running over his body with the same light touch, but could not rid himself of the thought once it had taken root there, exciting him and threatening to rouse his member from the slumber he had only recently succeeded in lulling it into. The sooner they reached home and he could be rid of her the better and he half-wished he had not begun teasing her.

'That's what it's called,' he explained. 'Because of the shape.'

She stared at him innocently, questioningly.

'You know. A man's…' He cocked his head downwards, indicating with his eyes towards his lap. Marguerite followed his gaze. For an instant she looked confused, then her eyes widened and her mouth dropped open in understanding.

'Oh!'

She whipped her hand away from the knife as though it was white-hot. Ewan suppressed a grin at her reaction. She dropped her head, face hidden beneath the fall of glossy, black hair.

'I did not know that!' she said, mumbling.

'Aye, I could tell that. Better give it back to me, if you're done examining it, that is.'

She stared at him and he raised an eyebrow,

nodding encouragingly. She reached out hesitantly, picking the knife up by the bell-shaped pommel between the tips of her fingers as if she could no longer bear to touch it. She held it out to Ewan without looking at it. Avoided looking at him, too, or at least determinedly not looking at the relevant part of his anatomy.

'I'm not sure it warrants handling with quite that level of revulsion,' he said, grinning. He closed his hand over hers and grasped the hilt firmly, tugging it from her grip. Her pale complexion was starting to grow rosy across the line of her cheekbones. He held it out, the length of the hilt comfortably nestling in the palm of his hand, the blade pointing up his arm. He felt a little sorry for embarrassing her, though not enough to resist adding one last tease.

'Are you sure you wouldn't like to hold it properly?' he asked, grinning again. 'They're not made to the measurements of the bearer, in case you were wondering.'

'I was not!'

Her head came up as she snapped her answer. Her mouth jerked into an expression of loathing that Ewan had never seen before.

'You disgust me. I will go bathe now.'

She swept her clothes into her arms and stalked away in the direction of the stream, her back rigid and her hands bunched tightly into fists at her sides.

Ewan sat back on his heels and watched until she had slipped between the trees to the water's edge. He chewed his lip thoughtfully as he stowed the troublesome knife at his belt, adding his sword. Her reaction had been unexpected. Yes, his comment had been a little crude, but not overwhelmingly so.

He was worried by her reaction. He resolved to spend the next night sleeping far away from her, even if it mean sleeping without any blankets to warm him, rather than risk his body giving in to the urges he fought to control when he was not in command of it.

She had not returned by the time Ewan had rolled and stowed the blankets. He began to feel irritated that she was wasting so much time, presumably sulking. Cold water would revive her spirits and cool her temper quickly enough. When she had still not returned in the time it took to eat his portion of cheese he began to grow concerned. She could not have come to harm. Could she? The loch was too shallow for her to get into difficulties unless she swam out and as far as he knew they were alone.

But what if they weren't? If Duncan McCrieff had somehow tracked them, then seeing Marguerite bathing alone and not anticipating an attack would be the perfect time to reclaim her. Mc-Crieff was not the only threat. A lone vagrant, or a band of travellers, could try robbing her. Most black-hearted curs would not hesitate to attack a lone woman.

Ewan's scalp prickled. He hastily retraced his steps to the stream, drawing both his knife and sword ready in case he needed to strike.

Marguerite was sitting on the bank, facing the water. She was fully clothed, fortunately for Ewan's composure, and unharmed. Relief cooled the perspiration that had broken out down his spine and made him shiver.

She looked around and gasped in alarm, hands coming up protectively as he appeared. He lowered his weapons and her shoulders dropped. She turned back to the water and hugged her knees.

'What are you doing? We need to go.'

She ignored him. Ewan's jaw tightened.

'Lass? Maggie? Did you hear me?'

'I heard you.'

She looked straight into his eyes and Ewan was astonished to see the lower lids were moist with the start of tears.

Astonished, and a little ashamed.

He'd seen her almost weeping enough times since he had pulled her out of the cart, but this was the first time he could attribute the tears to his actions alone and he could not bear it. His hand came up instinctively—protectively—to wipe them away. She jerked her head back.

'Why are you—?' he started to ask.

She snorted loudly, cutting him off coldly before he could finish the question. She unwound her arms from around her knees and pushed herself to her feet. With one hand she gestured at the knife Ewan was still holding out.

'You will not need your knife.'

There was only a hint of hesitation before the final word, but Ewan marked it.

'I'm sorry I offended you earlier. I did not intend to.'

'Offend? No.' She sniffed and shrugged. 'You men are all alike. With your revolting symbolic knives. You care only for fighting and drinking and what you force women to do for your pleasure.'

'Force! That's a strong word and a serious accusation.'

Ewan thundered at the unfairness. He had never forced anyone and he'd resisted Marguerite's flickering interest with more difficulty than he'd expected. Fortunately, his brain caught up with the implication behind her words. He added it to the memory of her handling the ballock knife with such dislike once he had pointed out the nature of what it represented and the unease with which she had first permitted him to hold her as they slept. His conscience woke and kicked the inside of his belly. He wisely closed his mouth and sheathed the knife in one smooth movement. She straightened her skirts briskly, running her open hands from waist to knee, then tugging the bodice into place evenly between her rounded breasts. It felt invasive even to witness such intimate adjustments when they were discussing matters of assault and coercion, but Ewan could not tear his eyes away.

She noticed where his gaze had strayed. Her eyes grew cold and hard. Ewan could hardly bear the change.

'You said we needed to leave. So let's leave.' She walked slowly towards him and every hair on his body prickled with anticipation, but she carried on past, stopping to look coldly at him once she was safely out of his reach. He ran and caught her by the arm. She spun around, face contorted in anger.

'Let me go!'

He released her, and held both hands up to demonstrate she had nothing to fear. 'Don't walk away from me!'

She tossed her hair back and glared.

'Did McCrieff force himself on you?' Ewan demanded. His eyes blurred with hatred. He'd return to Stirling. He'd hunt McCrieff down and dismember him. He'd hang his testicles from the wall of Lochmore Castle. 'Is that why you ran?'

Her face crumpled, her mouth twisting into a grimace.

'You do not command me to answer in that tone! I don't wish to speak about this. I want nothing to do with you.'

He had mocked her as crudely as if he had pulled his member out and waved it at her.

He held his hands out, then withdrew it, clenching his fist out of her sight. He yearned to offer comfort, but understood that to touch her would be to shatter the fragile friendship they had begun and which he had so stupidly kicked around the floor like a sheep's bladder. He reached out to hold her, but hesitated lest she fear he was about to commit some violation and dropped his hands to his sides.

'Tell me, please, why did you leave Duncan? What did he do to you?'

'Why do you want to know?'

'Because the way your face closed down made my stomach plummet and I can't bear the thought of you in such pain.' He held his hands out, palms upwards, and spoke softly. 'Will you share it with me?'

She held his gaze. 'You share none of your troubles with me.'

She made a fair point. She had made over-

tures of friendship the night before that he had ignored. Keeping his problems to himself suddenly
seemed unimportant and the need to understand
what she had endured was overpowering, but he
said nothing, fearing that to begin explaining his
heartache would see him unable to cease.

She shook her head in disappointment and
walked back to their camp ahead of him. Ewan
sighed, rubbing his eyes before following her.
The sun was barely up and his soul already felt
battered to pieces.

Chapter Thirteen

They rode in silence, keeping the loch on their left side. Marguerite rode on his left, which gave Ewan the opportunity to stare at her as often as he could. If she asked, he would say he was watching the road that followed the other side in case he saw anything untoward. She kept her eyes forward and never as much as glanced at him. He was uncertain whether her reticence was due to his blunder or because she was tiring of the journey. She looked as weary as Ewan felt, and slumped in her saddle, showing none of the enjoyment in riding she had shown the previous day. He admired the fortitude she had shown, but was growing worried that another night sleeping in such conditions would see her becoming ill. Coming this way round Loch Lomond had been a mistake. He should have taken her along the well-travelled route with crofts and inns even if it meant Duncan McCrieff chancing upon them.

* * *

They stopped earlier than Ewan had intended to that evening when they happened upon a *steid* at the head of the loch. It had been drizzling for hours and the clouds were becoming blacker when the cluster of small houses appeared through the mist. The certainty of a proper mattress in the dry was too good to pass up.

'We'll have a bed tonight,' he said to Marguerite with a grin. She nodded and raised a small smile.

She spoke for the first time as Ewan knocked on the door of the largest of the four houses. Her voice was even lower and huskier than usual, tinged with anxiety that made Ewan want to hold and comfort her.

'We don't know them. Why will they allow us in?'

'The laws of hospitality,' he said. 'No one will turn away travellers somewhere are remote as this. Feuds have been started for such.'

A thin woman in a drab, green dress opened the door. She peered suspiciously at Ewan and Marguerite. Ewan bowed and spoke rapidly, explaining his name and purpose.

'Who's she?' The woman glanced at Marguerite, who was standing meekly at his side with an uncertain smile on her face. She would not have been able to follow their speech, but must have guessed the question referred to her.

Ewan paused, recalling how he had taunted her by suggesting he would call her his whore. He flushed at his crassness.

'She is my wife,' he said firmly. From her sharp intake of breath Marguerite understood that. She looked at him, then back at the woman.

'I am,' she agreed.

The woman's face relaxed and she opened the door a little wider to admit them into the small house. She introduced herself as Moira and screamed a handful of names. Before long five children, equally ragged as their mother, appeared. Moira gave brisk orders, cuffing the oldest lad around the head for good measure. By the time Ewan had attended to the horses, Marguerite was sitting on a stool, drinking a cup of milk. Three small girls cooed in admiration at her long black hair, risking an occasional stroke. Ewan gazed on enviously, fingers itching to do the same. He caught her eye and smiled.

'You're the most beautiful thing they'll have ever seen,' he said in French.

She blushed scarlet and gave her attention to the children as she played clapping games and sang songs in French to them. She seemed to have no fear of singing in small company and her deep melodic voice stroked Ewan's temper as sure as if her fingers were stroking his brow. The two boys sat at the table to listen while pretending not to and Ewan drew them into a game of jacks. Moira nodded her head in time to the rhythm as she stirred the pot over the fire.

'Give us the one you sang in Stirling,' Ewan suggested, when she came to an end. 'The happy one.'

'No sadness tonight,' she murmured, settling her skirts. 'Will you join me?'

He shook his head. 'It would be unfair on our hostess to curdle her milk with my voice.'

'I believe there are no wildcats here anyway.'

Her eyes crinkled with laughter at the private joke and briefly the room contained only them.

'I will join you, however,' Ewan said. He moved closer to the fire and stretched out at her feet. She did not stiffen as he leaned back alongside her, but allowed her hand to fall into her lap close to his shoulder. She began to sing the song he had requested and the world became a softer, happier place for Ewan.

News of their arrival spread because before long other groups of women and children arrived. A lone man arrived as night fell. He was a ten or more years older than Ewan and moved with a deliberate, ponderous manner of moving that made Ewan wonder if he was slightly touched in the head. He dropped two brace of rabbits on to the table and grunted. His wife was a pretty, heavily pregnant woman with intelligent eyes. Ewan wondered whether her situation had caused her to marry a man who seemed half-witted. Living so remotely there would not have been many to choose from, of course, and now Scotland had lost so many sons there would be fewer still.

With a slow smile the man produced an earthenware bottle and poured two drams. As the man returned the bottle, his sleeve fell back to reveal a recent wound running from wrist to elbow. He saw Ewan looking and pulled the neck of his *leine* to reveal livid bruises across a collarbone that looked misshapen from a recent break.

'Flodden,' the man said.

A moment of understanding passed between them and nothing more needed to be spoken, though Ewan felt like the basest fraud to have not admitted he had not been there. He shared a toast with the man to lost friends and they both tipped the cups back, followed by fits of loud coughing as the harsh brew burned their throats and bellies.

'Uisge beatha,' Ewan explained to Marguerite, holding out the refilled cup towards her. 'It means water of life and right now I'd say it has improved mine beyond telling. Try it.'

She sniffed it and wrinkled her nose before pushing it away. 'I think I would be sick.'

Despite the moment of melancholy he had shared with the man, it became one of the most pleasant evenings Ewan could remember for many years. When his head began to nod from the effect of the *uisge beatha* Marguerite reached out and stroked the hair back from his brow. Feeling bold, he rested his head against her skirts and let himself dream.

He sat at Marguerite's feet, his heart quickening whenever she glanced at him, sharing tales and drinking with good people. He wished he could fix the moment to a canvas to bring out whenever his heart filled with grief. He'd willingly give up his Earldom for the chance of such companionship even in a house as poor as this one, but perhaps he wouldn't have to.

He had never thought about marriage, but Angus had been right when he said an earl needed a countess. Ewan would have to wed and produce the next Lord Glenarris. A match with a woman from a neighbouring clan to strengthen alliances or create new ones would be most sensible, but why not a French alliance? If Marguerite was not to marry Duncan, she would still have to wed someone and he passed the rest of the evening dreaming idly of enticing Marguerite to stay in Lochmore as his bride. He would deal with the consequences of offending the Mc-Crieffs as and when it arose, but with a dozen reasons for enmity, he did not care about adding one more. And what better way to raise his status as laird than to steal a McCrieff bride?

When the children were rounded up and bundled off to bed behind a curtain at the far end of the room they snatched a moment of peace. Ewan gazed at Marguerite, not knowing what to say that could adequately express his enjoyment of her company. She smiled down at him.

'You should tell them about the coronation,' she suggested.

'What would these women care for who sits on the throne?' Ewan replied, more harshly than he intended. He'd been thinking of words of love and her mind had been on politics. 'They may care if their new laird will be a fair man, but I don't think they'll care who is Regent or King.'

Marguerite looked shocked at his tone. Ewan took her hand.

'Forgive me. But look how poorly they live. They've lost their men and will be worrying how they'll survive the winter and clothe their children,' he explained.

He sighed. The intrigues of the court seemed a world away now. These people didn't worry over Morayshill's traitor, or whether ambitious men took foreign brides. Ewan thought of the pouch of alms money he had to deliver to his tenants and wished he had more. He was unsure which clan these people belonged to, but hoped whoever it was intended to treat them fairly. A determined light filled Marguerite's eyes. She crossed the room to where her bag had been stowed and delved inside, producing a jumble of linens and other clothes that she spread on to the table.

'What are you doing?' Ewan asked.

'One of these gowns will make smocks for at least three children,' she told him, passing a pair of fine wool stockings to Moira. Ewan tried not to think of Marguerite wearing them, or of himself teasing them off and exploring the soft skin beneath because the image caused him to break out in a sweat.

Much later than was sensible to be going to bed Marguerite and Ewan lay facing each other side by side on a pallet before the dying fire where the children had been ordered to drag it. The peat burned low in the hearth, casting light on to their faces and turning Marguerite's glossy raven locks into glowing ribbons of midnight red. Marguerite's hands were beneath her cheek and, though her eyes were tired smudges of purple, her expression was serene. He would have looked at her for ever. Not reaching out and touching her, not drawing her into his arms, not kissing her was unbearable.

'What are you thinking?' she asked unexpectedly in a whisper.

'That you were very generous to give away your clothes.'

She gave him a smile of such indescribable sweetness Ewan's heart melted.

'I can buy others when I reach France,' she said.

A heart that had so recently melted should not be able to shatter, but Ewan's did. They were travelling to Lochmore Castle, but while that was his final destination, it was not hers. That was all he had been thinking of and he had somehow forgotten that Marguerite was not intending to stay longer than necessary. The thought made him unutterably sad.

'When I first saw you in the courtyard I thought you were a *glaistig*,' he murmured. 'A ghost.'

'Why?' She looked astonished and a little amused.

He laughed, remembering the expression of shock she had worn at the time. He had been shocked himself, he recalled.

'You appeared from nowhere and were so pale, dressed all in white with your dark eyes staring into my soul. I did not realise you were mourning then. I thought your white clothes were from beyond the grave.'

Ewan closed his eyes and when he opened them it was to discover she was still watching him. Her eyes had such a depth of sadness in them that his own began to sting in response. Marguerite lay silently, watching and waiting for him to continue.

'I'm mourning, too. For my father.'

'I guessed that,' she said softly. 'At Flodden? I can't imagine how terrifying the battle must have been. Were you with him when he died?'

She would not judge him unfairly. Lying close, in the near dark, Ewan could finally allow himself to admit the truth to her.

'I knew nothing of his death until afterwards.' He could have left the story there, but now he had started unburdening himself he could not stop the guilt and rage bursting out. He pressed his fingers to his temples then ran them down his neck to his shoulders, massaging them in small circles.

'I wasn't there at all. For five years I have been studying law at Glasgow. I feel more at home with a quill in my hand than a sword. Father thought it would be useful to have a son versed in matters of law. He had no time for such things himself, but he could see the country is changing. It won't be enough to settle disputes with the sword for much longer. When the clan members were summoned my father didn't call on me to join him in the battle. He took my brother instead and left me in Glasgow. I would have been useless to him.'

He closed his eyes and muttered darkly, admitting the fears that had plagued his nights.

'I fear I'll be a sad disappointment as Earl. I'll fail his memory.'

'You won't fail. Fighting isn't everything. Think how cleverly you managed to keep Duncan from finding me and you saw I hated having to perform and were kind enough to stop me.' She took his hand.

'Cleverness is all well and good when they want someone to arbitrate over the theft of a sheep, but will that be enough to lead them into battle or keep them safe from attack? I'm afraid you've chosen your travelling companion poorly, Marguerite. I should never have agreed to take you with me.'

'Why did you? The other night you called me an inconvenience,' she reminded him.

His guts twisted. 'That was rude of me. Put it down to lack of sleep.'

'If you wish.' She gave him a stern look that made him shiver with delight. 'No tales of pups now. Tell me the truth.'

He was quiet for a long time and rolled on to his back, staring into the eaves. 'I didn't like the thought of you trying to find your way home alone. That was the truth. But deciding what to do with you gives me a distraction from what I should be doing. What I'll have to face when I get home to Lochmore.'

'So your tales of rescued pups was a story?'

He gave her a sidelong look.

'Not a story. But not the whole truth.' He sighed and raked his hands through his hair. 'I wasnae expecting to become Earl. Travelling with you gives me the time to think about it. You are an inconvenience, but a pleasant one,' he assured her, giving her another smile to show he meant no insult.

'Thank you. That is a more honest truth.'

She was looking at him with such compassion that he felt himself growing weak under her gaze. She ran her eyes over his face slowly. Ewan could almost feel her gaze on his limbs as surely as if her hands were caressing him. He was left with the impression she was picturing what he was like, not only beneath his clothes, but also beneath his flesh and into his soul itself.

'I have not chosen badly.'

Her fingers were still cold and he wondered what it would take to warm them properly. He closed his fist over her hand. 'Will you tell me now what made you run from your wedding? Please?'

'I doubt a man would see anything wrong in what he did.' She spoke with such disgust that

Ewan struggled to imagine what debasement she meant. She closed her eyes and distaste twisted her face. He could hardly bear to hear the words to confirm what he suspected.

'He made me kiss him.'

'A kiss? Is that all?' Ewan had been imagining rape, degradation, a beating. He shook his head, incredulous and relieved. 'You ran away from Stirling and caused all this trouble over a kiss.'

She gave a snarl and snapped her head up. Her eyes were hard. 'It was not *just* a kiss. It was stolen and humiliating and it hurt. When he spoke of what a wife must do he laughed. He said he would enjoy it.'

'Aye, well, you are supposed to enjoy it,' Ewan said. He bit his tongue, realising as he spoke that what Duncan McCrieff enjoyed might not be what this innocent young girl would like.

'Both participants,' he added.

She lifted her eyes. 'Have you done it?'

'Aye,' he replied cautiously. 'Most men have.'

Her lips twisted into a grimace as he presumably confirmed every base thought she had of him, but her eyes were hungry, with pupils so wide their blackness enveloped him.

'It is your fault that I cannot rid my mind of these thoughts that plague me!'

She was trembling. Ewan leaned back, unsure

what exactly he was being accused of and unaware of anything he had done to provoke such ire.

'Thoughts of what?'

'Of kissing and more.' Ewan's heart sang at the idea this radiantly beautiful woman might have contemplated kissing him.

Marguerite covered her face with her hands. 'When you touched me this morning, while you were still asleep... I liked it. I didn't want you to stop.'

'That's nothing to be ashamed of,' he murmured. His throat felt parched. He moistened his lips.

'Kiss me,' Marguerite murmured.

He almost choked. 'What did you say?'

'Please, Ewan.' She stroked his cheek, searing his skin. 'Show me it isn't something to fear.'

'What is there to fear?' he asked in bewilderment. In his case, only a heart that could break with need to obey her request.

She sniffed. 'To a man it means nothing, of course. There is no threat to you.'

'Are you worried you'll lose your reputation?' Ewan asked.

'I'm worried I will lose my life,' she replied quietly. 'Women die in childbirth, but what risk can there be in a kiss? I trust you. I know you would not force more from me.'

Ewan's heart speeded up, drumming a march

with such intensity he thought it might burst free of his chest.

She stroked his cheek. 'I want it to be you.'

'You don't really mean that.'

'I do'

She might as well be a lamb announcing she trusted a wolf.

'You're asking a lot?'

'Am I? Is kissing me such a great trial?' Her voice was more sob than words. Her eyes were wide and beseeching, rimmed with pink from the tears she had shed but full of hunger and fear. Ewan raised his to the ceiling, wondering what purgatory he was in to be asked such a thing when he'd thought of little else for days. He stroked her arm.

'Aye, lass, I'll kiss you. But once only.'

She bit her lip and it took all Ewan's self-control not to seize hold of her and devour her. His hand was trembling as he took hold of her chin, tilting her face to his. Her eyes were trusting with only a flicker of apprehension in them. He intended the kiss to be light and quick. Nothing more than a brotherly skim of the lips: a small indication that kissing could be enjoyable to ease her mind.

He touched his lips to hers briefly, then drew back, but Marguerite came into his arms. She placed her hands on his shoulders and craned her head up, arching her back and pressing her mouth hard against his. She began to move her mouth wildly. She had no idea what to do and Ewan wondered what Duncan McCrieff had done to make her think this was what kissing should be.

Ewan pulled back, spread his fingers over the contours of her cheekbones and held her still.

'Not like that.'

This time, he kissed her with all the depth of passion he had been suppressing, controlling the pressure and speed. Marguerite parted her lips and began to move them with a steady measure that complemented Ewan's. A melody to his rhythm. She tasted so sweet Ewan forgot his resolve to be brief. He captured her bottom lip between his, lightly tugging until she opened her mouth a little more.

He sighed and closed his eyes, giving himself over to the pleasure and wondering who was teaching whom. She twisted closer, hooking her bare foot over his. It was cold and broke through the fog of lust Ewan was lost in. A warning beacon lit in the part of his mind he still had control over. If he allowed her to embrace him—and embraced her back—he would be in danger of going far beyond kissing and that was something he could not permit himself to do.

He drew away.

'I think that will do, don't you?' he said in a ragged gasp.

She gave a small sigh of disappointment, lips still parted, full and ready to be kissed again. Ewan wanted to rage at her. Lying on a bed with a man she had kissed with unfettered passion and giving him a look of such heavy-lidded sensuality was like a doe stepping into the path of a hunter and beseeching him not to loose an arrow. He remembered his first awakening of lust and the confusing, overwhelming turmoil of emotions that had riddled him. It had been for his mother's maidservant and he had been torn between wanting to bed her to satisfy the burning need to possess the woman who drove him to distraction and wanting to avoid her at all costs. Now those same desires were bursting forth within him again, obliterating all other sentiments. If the urges were reciprocated, it was going to make the journey much more complicated, but Marguerite looked at him with such entreaty his resistance was melting once more. He placed a fingertip on her bottom lip and pushed it gently to join the upper one.

'Before we do anything we cannot undo,' he said firmly, drawing his hand away.

The distracting lips turned down. 'I understand. I know men can't stop when they are roused to passion.'

'Oh, don't believe that. Some choose not to, but we can stop. It isn't enjoyable, however. Especially when a man is lying close to a woman as beautiful as you and his body is giving him commands it takes a great deal of strength to disobey.' He sat up and tucked the blanket over Marguerite, giving her a rueful grin.

'For that reason I shall find my rest elsewhere. Sleep well, Marguerite.'

He spent the night on the floor beneath the table.

Chapter Fourteen

Marguerite woke late the next morning, roused by the sound of children wanting their breakfast. She stretched out her arms wide. She had the mattress to herself, and flushed with guilt when she recalled how Ewan had spent the night on the floor. She opened her eyes and looked over to where he had taken himself, but he was already awake and sitting at the table. Their eyes met and his gaze lingered on her as she looked up at him from the pallet. He brought her over a cup of milk and a hard oatcake, holding it out to her with a grin.

'You look better rested than yesterday. That's good. I let you sleep longer than I should have.'

'You didn't have to do that.'

'I know. But you looked so peaceful I hadn't the heart to disturb you.'

She took the cup. Their fingers brushed and fire raced along the length of her arm like a brand along her skin. Her breath caught, remembering the overpowering heat that had flooded her as he kissed her. She bowed her head and sipped the warm milk, conscious he was still watching her.

'We have a long climb ahead of us today,' Ewan said. 'I'll leave you to dress.'

He went to speak to Moira behind the curtain that divided the room. Marguerite pulled on her clothes and folded her remaining linens back into her bag, but pulled out her jewel casket. She called Ewan to join her. She had kept the contents secret, but after they had shared confidences in the night she did not mind him seeing what she had. She opened the box to display the treasures within. Ewan gave a low whistle and dipped his finger in to inspect the pieces.

'This is worth a lot.'

'My father is a rich man,' she reminded him.

'You've been carrying these around wrapped in your stockings since Stirling? D'you not think it might have been wise to tell me before now?'

'I saw no reason to tell you. I told you I could pay for my passage and you see I speak the truth. Some are keepsakes from my mother and others would have been part of my dowry,' she said. 'What should I choose that they would be able to exchange?'

'Maggie, you've already given them your clothes. Anything here will be more than they could need.' He reached out to shut the lid. She seized his hand to prevent it.

'Ewan, let me do this. Anything I have left will be gifted to the convent when I enter it, but I want to leave these people something to ease their lives.'

'A convent? That's what you plan to do?'

'I nursed my mother and ran my father's household. I like being useful. I can tend the poor and sick there.'

He looked shocked and reached out a hand to her arm, as if intending to hold her back. It occurred to her that they had discussed only her plan to return to France, not what she would do when she arrived.

'And that is your reason? Could you not do that elsewhere?'

'Perhaps I could have once, but now I have disgraced myself and my family. I have no other option, nor do I want one.' She bit her lip, hearing the regret that she hoped he did not notice. She had known her path since she fled from Duncan, but while travelling with Ewan it had become tangled and twisted.

'All I desire is a life of peace.'

Liar, her body shouted. She desired so much more than that in the form of the man standing before her with sorrow in his eyes. She fixed her gaze on the jewel case. Ewan sighed and picked out a slender gold choker with five pearls hanging from it.

'This, but the gold only. They'll be able to cut it when they're in need.'

He drew his vulgar-handled dagger and walked to the table. Now that Marguerite knew what the design represented she could not look at it without blushing, while feverish with curiosity to discover how accurate it was. She wanted his lips on hers, his hands on parts of her she should blush to contemplate. The kiss had opened her eyes to what delights existed and she burned to discover more. One kiss might have been too far, but she wanted more.

Ewan cut the pearls from the choker and dropped them into Marguerite's hand, closing her fingers over them. He ran his thumb slowly over the ridges of her knuckles, then further down across her wrist where the pulse beneath began to race.

'You're a good woman, Maggie.'

If he knew what she was contemplating, he would not say that.

'Give it to her, please,' she said.

Ewan spoke to Moira, who rushed over and embraced Marguerite pouring out such fervent thanks that Marguerite became embarrassed and was glad when Ewan took her arm with a quiet 'come now, Wife, we must be going' and they left the small houses behind them.

The path that begun the long climb upwards was steep and rocky. They rode side by side at first, then one behind the other, but when they were unable to do even that they were forced to dismount and walk. Their spirits were high despite this because Marguerite's saddle now had a rush basket attached to it containing a small pot of honey, four fresh eggs, warm oatcakes and a rabbit to be roasted that night. Ewan even managed to hide his obvious exasperation when Marguerite queried whether he had paid for what Moira had given them.

'Aye, lass, I wouldna' take what they have without leaving them something, though they'll be able to buy a hundred rabbits if they liked.' He looked ahead, pointing to the peaks in the distance that were silhouetted grey in the morning light. 'Save your breath for walking. You'll need all your strength.'

The mountains were forbiddingly high and the sky was cloudless. The day would be warmer than the one before.

'Are we crossing those?' Marguerite asked.

'Not right across the top. We're crossing the pass into the next valley and we'll meet up with the road once we're down and past the top of the loch.'

'The road from Druinunn?'

'The road from everywhere south. We can be at Lochmore Castle within three nights and in the meantime there will be more inns and *steids* for us to sleep in so we won't have any more nights in the forest or on floors. We'll both be glad of that.'

He smiled, but she couldn't return it.

'What if we meet Duncan?'

'We're unlikely to do that. If he had followed Angus and Jamie he would be a day ahead of us at least. It's a good thing.'

He stroked her arm. Since the night before he had done that more often, finding reasons to touch her in some way, and she had responded with small gestures of her own. He had not spoken of what Marguerite had induced him to do, or made any complaint about what must have been another uncomfortable night.

When they stopped after two hours of climbing and Marguerite tried to arrange the folds of her *arisaid* around her waist and tried to mimic the way Moira wore hers, she could see him studying her from the corner of her eyes.

She knew she should feel ashamed of what she had said and done, but whenever such feelings threatened to appear they were immediately beaten into submission by the memory of Ewan's lips on hers. It had been glorious; soft yet firm and leading her into dizzying pleasure she had not even suspected could exist. She had believed kisses involved only mouths, but last night her entire body had responded to Ewan's touch. If Duncan had kissed her like that, she might never have fled Stirling at all.

Then she remembered the hard look in Duncan's eyes and the cruel manner in which he had mocked her reluctance. He might force her to his will, but he would never be capable of wielding power over her with such thrilling gentleness as Ewan had done. It was fortunate indeed that he had shown more control than Marguerite had. Now at least she had one secret, stolen memory that she would look on with fondness for the rest of her life to take with her into the cloisters.

He handed her a bottle and she drank the cold, sweet water. Nothing had tasted so good. She licked her lips and passed it back to him. He took it wordlessly, his face wearing the forbidding expression she had not seen for days.

'Why are you going to spend your life in a convent?'

Marguerite caught her breath. How had he guessed what she was thinking of so unerringly?

'I do not wish to return to my father's house,' she said. 'I think he will be angry with me for what I did, but even with his forgiveness it contains too many memories of my mother. My eldest brother is at court, the next one has a wife I do not like and my younger brother intends to become a priest so spends all his days praying in the chapel. It isn't the same home I left.'

He shook his head. 'That's not what I meant. Why a convent at all? You're so young to shut yourself away for ever.'

Not so young. Today was her birthday. It should have been her wedding day, too, and the fact that she had only just remembered made her want to laugh out loud.

'It is quite usual in France. When I was thirteen I would have entered a convent as my sisters did until they married, but my mother could not bear to part from me so I stayed at home and took lessons with my brothers. When she fell sick she wanted me to nurse her so I did not go at all.'

'Why not marriage, I meant. A husband in France.' He shrugged. 'Or in Scotland even.'

'I have just left one bridegroom. Even if another man would have a woman who behaved so disgracefully and ruined herself, I do not wish to be married,' she replied curtly.

She walked back to the horse and began adjusting the bridle with a pretence of concentration so she had an excuse to hide her face. She knew the moment he came to stand close behind her. The rich musky scent that she had smelled on his clothes and skin when they lay close drifted to her nostrils, causing the hair on the back of her arms to stand on end. She was certain she could feel the heat of his body, even though such a thing seemed unlikely. He took the bridle from her hand.

'Not all men are like Duncan McCrieff.'

His eyes were full of fire that was alarming in its intensity. The desire that had awoken at his kiss began to flicker inside Marguerite once more. She pushed it down, but recalled the way he had opened his heart to her the night before.

'I have seen too many women suffering to believe you. My sister Françoise told me so much of what is required of a wife. I could not bear it happening to me.' She dropped her eyes.

'What happening?' he asked, puzzlement writ clear on his face.

'Cruelty. She said he would whip her at times. Not in response to any wrongdoing, but because he enjoyed it. She said it made him more vigorous when he made love to her.'

Ewan gave an angry, animalistic growl. 'I wouldna' describe that as lovemaking.'

'She said when he touched her breasts it was as though he were milking a cow, tugging until she could barely keep from crying out. I once tried to speak to him, but he threatened to beat me, too, and now will not admit me to his home so I have not seen her for two years.'

'He sounds like an oaf who should have stuck to his cows,' Ewan snarled. He lifted her chin with a finger, staring earnestly at her. 'I'm sorry for your sister, but hers is not the only husband. Can you not think of any happy marriages?'

'My sister Marie's was not *un*happy. Her husband was a fat old man, but he treated her kindly and only required his rights once a week.' She felt tears welling and swallowed, carrying on in a thick voice. 'She gave thanks to all the saints when she became pregnant because he no longer touched her.'

'And is she happier now?' Ewan asked.

'She died a week after giving birth. She bled and bled and didn't stop. Her daughter died, too.'

'Oh, lass. Oh, Maggie, I'm so sorry.'

'Even my mother, who was fond of my father, was worn out with so many pregnancies that she had no strength to fight the canker that grew in her womb,' she whispered.

The tears came now. Marguerite could not hold them back any longer. Ewan drew her to his chest almost before the first juddering sob passed her lips, wrapping his arms around her back and holding her tight. She leaned against him, weeping in loud, messy gulps, not caring what he thought of her lack of control as he rubbed his hands in long firm strokes down her spine and made soft noises in her ear. Once she swore she felt a kiss on her head. She was soaking his jerkin and *leine* with tears, but when she eventually lifted her eyes he did not look angry with her—in fact, he wiped her cheeks with his thumbs to rid her of the last trace of them. It was such a kind gesture that her heart cracked. How had she ever thought he was a savage creature when he was capable of such tenderness?

She noticed then that his eyes were red-rimmed and slightly puffy. He had been weeping silently while she cried and she had not noticed. He had lost his family through violence and was as alone as she was. Remorse flooded her. She stroked his cheek as he had done to her so he understood she realised what he had been doing. He leaned his cheek into her palm, his eyes growing heavy with longing that was mirrored in her heart.

'We are not so different in our grief,' she said, tilting her head back a little. 'We can offer each other comfort.'

His expression changed, his eyes becoming guarded. 'I said once only. Don't temp me to break my word.' He laced his fingers through hers and drew her hand down. 'We should waste no more time lingering here. We have a long way to go before we reach the pass and the day is growing late.'

He strode back to his horse and began leading it away. Marguerite followed in silence, watching his lean frame, but he never looked back at her. He wanted her, she could tell, and she had been unwise to put herself in his path in such a shameless manner. The anguish of her desire for him was almost greater than the heartache of her loss. To tempt him into another kiss would be foolhardy and only end in misery for both of them, but wouldn't it be worth that risk? Wasn't Ewan himself worth it?

The path became so steep that for most of the afternoon Marguerite's thoughts were entirely taken up by making sure she did not stumble and with trying to keep breathing. Ewan had become the taciturn man she had first known, only enquiring occasionally if she was managing.

'I'm just pleased I am not wearing my court dress,' she gasped, tugging her *arisaid* down over her waist so the wind caressed her torso through the layers of linen. 'I don't think I would have been able to draw a single breath otherwise.'

Ewan grunted and carried on walking. He slowed his pace a little so she was not so far behind, but even then she struggled to keep her footing. Marguerite felt wretched and tired. Her shift was damp with perspiration that made it cling to her thighs and her overskirt tangled between her legs as she walked. She was thirsty and hot and spending her birthday clambering over rocks in the company of a man who was doing his best to ignore the attraction they both clearly felt. The only thing that stopped her from sitting on the heather and weeping was the knowledge that she should have been spending the day being married to a man who made her skin crawl.

By the time they reached the peak her head was aching and she was almost in tears from exhaustion, a headache and an ill temper. A small stream bubbled out of the peaty ground and trickled over rocks. Marguerite dropped to her knees beside it. Ewan joined her and they drank their fill before leading the horses to it. Ewan sat against a large rock, stretching his legs out. He patted the ground at his side.

'Sit by me, we can afford to rest awhile.'

Marguerite obeyed. The rock wasn't broad enough for them to both lean against. Ewan put his arm around her shoulder and drew her near so she leaned against him instead and closed her eyes. Gusts of chilly wind buffeted her, but she did not care. They dried the stickiness from her neck and cheeks and cooled her aching head.

'Look at where we are,' Ewan said.

Wearily she opened her eyes again and looked at the view for the first time. The sight snatched away what little breath she had left. The mountain peaks rose to their backs. To the left was the winding path they had climbed up, with Loch Lomond far below. To the right another loch wound like a wide silver ribbon into the distance at the bottom of a long valley with steep mountains on both sides. Pines and oaks covered the bottom of the mountains while higher up the rock was barren green and grey scrub. The country stretched on and on, a rainbow of blues, greens and greys.

'It's magnificent,' she breathed. 'I've never seen anything like it.'

Ewan gave her a grumpy look and spoke severely. 'Finally you have found something to like about my country.'

'I like a lot of things!' she protested before she caught the glint of humour in his eye. He was teasing. She laughed and his eyes sparkled.

'What else do you like?' he asked, swiftly twisting to face her and giving her a keen look that made her heart flutter.

'I like my horse. I like the mountains. I like my dress,' she said playfully.

'That reminds me. I have something for you.' He rummaged in the pouch he wore and instructed her to hold out her hand. She obeyed and he pressed something small and soft into her palm. It was a length of ribbon that looked like the one Moira had been weaving.

'Before you ask, I paid Moira for it,' Ewan said. His eyes glinted then softened. 'Happy birthday.'

'You remembered!' Tears pricked Marguerite's eyes. Ewan gave her an odd smile.

'Aye, well, I can keep a thought in my head for two days at a time.'

'Thank you!'

'I'm sorry it isn't something better,' Ewan said. 'If you'd told me before I left Druinnan it was your birthday, I could have been better prepared.'

'Oh, no! I love it!' she cried.

Marguerite closed her hand over the ribbon, which had suddenly doubled in worth, in case the wind caught it or Ewan tried to take it back. She could not believe he was apologising for one of the sweetest things anyone had done for her. Her heart surged with affection.

Impulsively she leaned over and kissed him lightly on the cheek. He tilted his head and caught her lips, transforming the intended peck into a proper kiss. Marguerite's mouth hardened. She tried to remember how he had taught her to move in unison with him. She relaxed her lips and pressed her mouth to his for the briefest of moments.

They drew back and stared at each other in silence. Marguerite became aware of a rhythmic drumming and took a moment to realise it was her heartbeat that had doubled in speed. Ewan was watching her warily. She had not expected her stomach to twist with such disappointment when Ewan had ended their kiss the night before and left her to lie alone. Her fear of submitting to a man had vanished completely the instant he had kissed her. He had been entirely in command of her and if he had not drawn back she would have drowned in the pleasure. Now she could not bear that he might leave again when her whole being craved his lips on hers once more.

She met his eyes, parting her lips. Spurred into action by this simple, unspoken signal, Ewan's hand came behind her head and he pulled her back towards him. She was ready for his lips to claim hers, but unprepared for the force with which they met.

He kissed her hard. There was none of the hesitant gentleness of their first kiss or the measured way in which he had guided her through the second. This was urgent and intense. A clash of overpowering lust that was designed to satisfy his needs as much as her curiosity. His lips pulled at hers with a wildness that she relished. She cleaved to him, tasting him, wrapping her arms around his neck to keep him close.

She wasn't sure when they tumbled from

seating to lying, but somehow they were on the ground, heather cushioning them, their legs entwining, fingers clutching wildly wherever they could find bare skin. Ewan's hand closed over her breast with a gentle squeeze that made her dizzy. She moaned and ran her tongue the length of his neck, tasting his skin. He gave a deep-throated growl and pushed against her. With a shock Marguerite realised he was fully aroused and how close to the precipice she had allowed herself to step. She pulled away, trembling, and fighting the voice of her body that demanded she allow it the sensations it craved.

He raised his head and his eyes were loaded with desire that matched hers.

'I can't.' How she found the words to deny them what they both wanted she would never know.

His expression changed to one of understanding and acceptance. He drew his hand back from her breast and pushed himself on to his elbow.

'I know.' His voice was laden with regret.

'I can't forget what Françoise told me.'

'Oh, lass, I told you, it doesn't have to be like that. I would never hurt you.'

'I know,' she said, realising how deeply her trust had grown. 'It isn't you.'

'I know that, too.'

She felt his arms loosening. He was going to

leave her and she would die from the need that consumed her. Not a death of body, but of spirit. She gripped the neck of his *leine* in both hands and pulled him back down.

'I want to.'

She clutched him again, running her fingernails down the firm muscles of his back and round to his belly. The hardness that was pushing against her leg swelled. Her whole body pulsed in response and she lifted her face close to his, whispering against the corner of his mouth, 'I want *you*.'

The muscles in Ewan's neck tightened. He muttered something beneath his breath that she could not catch, then looked deep into her eyes.

'Maggie...' His voice was commanding. It made her melt, turning her limbs to water while fire flared inside. 'Let me go, or we'll do something that can't be undone.'

'I should never have made you kiss me because now I can't bear knowing there is something more, but I don't want to have a baby,' she said, tears springing to her eyes. 'I don't want to die.'

'Not all women die.' Ewan drew her close, wrapping his arms around her. The hot, earthy scent of him made her want to weep with frustration and need. 'A woman with the strength and courage to sleep in the wilderness is tougher than that. I swear I won't get you with child, but there are other things we can do. I'll stop whenever you tell me. Do you trust me?'

'Yes.'

He eased her back and she closed her eyes, realising that there was nothing that could, or would prevent her from doing what they both wanted. Ewan ran the tip of his forefinger down her hairline until he reached her ear. Gently brushing her hair behind the lobe, he circled the fingertip around, grazing the soft skin in the hollow behind her ear with his nail. The urgent pull deep down inside her began to spread further. When Ewan had nestled against her while she was asleep it had been diverting enough, but the pleasure he coaxed from her when he was awake and acting intentionally was enough to make her weak with an ache that she had to satisfy or lose her mind.

He continued skimming his fingers down and round her jaw, replacing them with his lips each time he moved on to another part, then brushed the flat of his thumb over her mouth. She opened her lips, running her tongue tip over his thumb and heard his quick gasp of pleasure. She bit down gently and he gave a surprisingly high and vulnerable whimper as he drew it away.

Ewan closed his mouth over hers, nipping at her lips. She kissed him back, her head beginning to spin. She ran her hands over his torso and under the heavy folds of his *brat*, tracing the shape of his buttocks. His hand moved down, inching her skirts up until he touched her naked thigh. When his hand discovered the hot opening between her legs she almost forgot to breathe.

His palm rested over the soft mound of hair while a finger circled the nub that was now so sensitive that his touch was almost too much to endure. She clawed at him, bunching up his brat so nothing lay between them and grasped the part of him that was hard and ready, feeling it swell in response to her touch. Ewan gave a strangled gasp and slid his fingers inside her, tipping Marguerite over the edge of reason as muscles tightened that she had not even known she possessed.

He looked into her eyes, asking a silent question. She mouthed *yes*.

He settled between her thighs, taking his weight on his elbows. He began slowly in long, smooth movements, but before long the rhythm grew faster, his thrusts harder. Marguerite ground her head back into the heather and arched her hips to meet him as he sank into her over and over, causing further and deeper waves of pleasure to engulf her. When she sensed him trying to pull free she rose up to meet him, hands clawing at his buttocks to draw him in again, refusing to end the bliss that consumed her.

Ewan gave a last cry that started powerfully and ended in a low moan. His body grew rigid with one final, fierce thrust. She felt him withdraw, felt his hand slip down once more between her legs. Then she was crying aloud as Ewan had, the touch of his hand bringing forth a swell of ecstasy that spread out through her core leaving her drained and trembling.

She knew he had tried to hold back and she had not let him. The troubling consequences of that were something she would have to face later, but for now she was unable to do anything beyond give in to the heaviness of her limbs and sleep in Ewan's arms.

Chapter Fifteen

Marguerite slept. Ewan dozed with one arm over her to keep her warm. Or perhaps to prevent her vanishing, like a dream melting at sunrise. Clouds rolled lazily across the sky.

They should be leaving. They should never have remained here so long, but events had not exactly gone as Ewan had expected and now he had a slumbering woman, warm and soft, with her sweet-scented head in the crook of his arm. Ewan could not remember feeling such peace before and he was content to relax and recover from what had been a very enthusiastic half-hour and let Marguerite do the same.

He tried to remember back to the first time he had experienced that all-consuming release and how it had left him as weak as a newborn pup. Lovemaking still left him drained and drowsy, and content for the world to carry on around him. A hundred McCrieffs could appear over the mountain and Ewan would be incapable of even raising his sword.

He glanced down at Marguerite, scarcely able to believe what had just happened. She lay on her back, eyes closed and mouth slightly open. Her hair had come loose from its braid and fell in heavy tangles around her. One bare thigh was crooked up and Ewan tugged her skirt down to cover it. The sight excited him beyond all reason.

Marguerite was beginning to wake up. Ewan felt the slight change as she tensed. He considered it strange that he was so well attuned to her after such a short time together. She rolled on to her side and faced him, her eyes like twin pools of ink. Boldly, he stroked her cheek and at once her face crumpled into an expression of distress that was a knife in Ewan's heart. For him their lovemaking had been more wonderful than he could have possibly expected, but she regretted it, as he had feared she would.

He had offered Marguerite enough opportunities to stop and had been sure she truly wanted to do what they had, but now he found himself full of guilt. He should not have left the decision to her. He should have shown the strength he had shown the night before, but his resistance had been pushed to the limit. He had found her lips easier to break free of the previous night in Moira's cottage than the hands that brought him to such heights of desire and the body that responded to his touch so eagerly. He drew his hand back from her cheek, opening his mouth to apologise, but she clutched his hand, holding it to her face. She smiled despite the tears that were gathering.

'Is it always like that?' she asked.

Ewan hesitated, reluctant to tell her of the hundred different tempos and shades of lovemaking he longed to share with her. 'Did I hurt you?' he asked.

'No,' she said in a trembling voice. 'All I knew was what my sisters told me. Oh, my poor Marie, poor Françoise. They never knew it could be so sweet or thrilling.'

She fixed her dark eyes on him.

'Thank you. For…for everything.'

'You are thanking me?' he asked incredulously.

She blushed and gave him a shy smile and Ewan knew he was a lost man.

'I thank you because now when I enter the convent I shall have the memory of something exquisite to keep with me.'

Ewan's heart lurched and his stomach tightened. 'You're still going to do that?'

'Why, yes. My plan has not changed.' She looked puzzled. 'Did you imagine I would return to Duncan now I know there is nothing to fear from making love?'

Ewan passed a hand over his eyes, feeling rather foolish. He wasn't sure what he had thought.

'Not to him, but you could consider a better match. Are you still determined not to wed?'

Her eyelashes fluttered and she stared past him into the heather. 'The best marriages are rare. My husband could be a cruel man.'

'Or he could not.'

'Duncan would have been,' she said, shivering.

'Aye, I think you're right there,' he agreed.

She stroked her fingers along his jaw. The intimacy was unendurable. He wanted her to stop. He wanted her never to stop.

'I was scared of the physical side,' she whispered, resting her head on his shoulder and laying her hand across his chest. 'I could bear living children, or I might die like my sister did and so many women do. Now I know there is nothing to fear, but no man will have me. To leave Duncan but marry another man would be a grave insult. I do not regret my choice. Please believe me.'

He did believe her—more was the pity. Ewan had bedded more than enough women, but none had answered him with such passion or abandonment as Marguerite. If he had been given the choice there and then of a hundred different partners or Marguerite alone for the rest of his life, he would not hesitate for an instant. He couldn't find the words or trust his voice to explain what it had meant to him so he simply laced his fingers through hers and held her hand tightly. He believed he might have found the Countess he needed.

'What must you think of me for behaving so wantonly!' Marguerite said. She leaned back against him and sighed. 'I am quite ashamed of myself.'

Her expression said otherwise. The hand that strayed to his chest and spread wide across his heart indicated she was not sorry at all. She rested her hand in his lap and he felt himself spring to life again. Her eyes widened, full of desire and impishness. Ewan's conscience began to demand he listen to it and stop now before they began again, but another part of his body was also speaking and he knew which would win if she touched him again.

Anxiety flickered in his belly. He'd reassured her he would not get her pregnant. He had intended to break free before his end came, but she had held him so tightly and her touch had dizzied his senses so greatly that he had been lost before he was able. He could not let that happen again. Next time he would be stronger. It did not surprise him that he was already thinking of a next time, or that with the way she was gazing at him, eyes full of intent as she ran her fingers over the folds of his brat, that *next time* was rapidly becoming *now*. He covered her hand and held it firmly. She flashed him a look of reproach.

'Do you not want me now?'

He faced her, running his hand over her upper arm. She half-rolled on top of him, her eyes radiant and her lips already forming into a bud that he yearned to taste once more.

'Maggie,' he said, 'you are the most infuriatingly desirable creature I have ever seen. I burn to touch you. I have since the moment I saw you when I thought you were a spirit, insubstantial and beyond my reach, but you're not. You're real and alive and you drive me to distraction. You have no idea how hard it was for me to leave your bed last night. How hard I have to strive to keep my hands off you.'

'Yes, I do, for I feel the same.' She slipped her hands around his shoulders, under the neck of his shirt to touch the bare flesh of his back, and put her lips close to his mouth. Her scent filled his nostrils and his mouth twitched to capture the taste of her.

'We need to stop this.' He sighed. 'Once was unwise. Twice would be reckless.'

'I feel reckless,' she said, stroking her hand

along his arm and sending pulses of excitement coursing through Ewan. 'I like being reckless.'

She really did, he realised. After all, she had stolen away from the castle more times than he knew, spent the afternoon in his company and then stowed away in his cart, prepared to find her way back to France. She was not the timid creature he often thought of her as, but had an impetuousness that excited him. She was still determined to return to France; that was clear enough and his throat tightened with anguish at that thought. The time had long passed when he had seen her as an inconvenience or a distraction.

He was beginning to care for her and the pit of grief that he had fallen into since hearing of Hamish's and John's deaths had been slowly shrinking. If he allowed himself to fall in love with Marguerite, he was not sure his heart would survive a third loss.

Take care, he cautioned himself.

'What of your reputation?' he said.

'While we are here who is to know apart from us?' she whispered. Her husky voice reached deep inside Ewan and woke all the senses he was trying so desperately to ignore. 'After this there will be nothing but memories for me.'

Care could go to the devil! She wanted him. He wanted her. Why should they not give in to what they both craved?

Ewan rolled over so they were lying side by side, fully touching.

'Here and here alone,' he murmured. Marguerite began to rake her hand down his back. Blood heated Ewan's face. He felt himself swell and harden. He was ready to take her now, but held back. The first time had been so fast and frenzied they had not even removed any clothing. He grew hot at the thought of seeing all of her, touching all of her, tasting all of her. He intended to take his time and show Marguerite how much pleasure could be gained through a slow discovery of what the other enjoyed. He reached down and caught her wrist, lifting it to his lips and pressing them over the pulse. Still holding her hand, he eased her on to her back and when she raised her head he captured her lips, leading her back down as he kissed her.

'The best thing about the *brat*,' he murmured against her ear as he reached down to unbuckle his belt, 'is how easily it can be removed.'

Her giggle of delight was music to his ears and the gasps of pleasure that flowed shortly afterwards would live in his memory for many years to come.

Afterwards they lay together, wrapped in the *brat* and a jumble of clothes, both sated and weary.

'Ewan, do we have to leave soon?' Marguerite yawned, twisting round to face him. 'Only, I don't think I can ride my horse just yet.'

The sky was cloudy but rain free and they were sheltered from the wind. To leave would mean to leave Marguerite's arms, which he could not bear to do.

'It will delay us, but if you're happy to we can sleep here for the night.'

'I'll sleep anywhere if it is in your arms,' she said, her eyes full of promise.

Talk of horses reminded him that he had completely disregarded them. Reluctantly Ewan dragged himself away from Marguerite. Fortunately they had discovered the stream and were still there. Naked and barefoot, he unsaddled Randall and Grincheux and tethered them to a bush. Marguerite watched him as he walked back and forth with an odd smile on her lips that Ewan could not interpret. He slipped back beneath the *brat* and took her in his arms, letting her body warm him.

'Ewan,' she murmured as she rested her cheek against his neck. 'I think your knife handle is not at all true to life.'

He kissed her, moving his lips over her skin to the soft spot at the base of her hair. She craned her neck like a cat so he could reach better and began to tease her fingers down his belly. There would be precious little sleeping done tonight.

Sleep had come for them eventually. Wrapped around each other, perfectly content and perfectly warm despite the cold wind. They stayed slumbering so long past the dawn, in fact, that it was late morning by the time they finished the slow descent on foot and reached the beginning of the road at the base of the pass alongside the loch.

'Are we on your land now?' she asked him as he helped her mount the pony.

He rested his hand on her thigh, trying to forget the way it had been wrapped around his waist the night before, as he answered.

'Not mine. This land belongs to the Laird of Clan Campbell, Earl of Argyll. We've another two days before we're home.'

They were half a day later than they should have been, but Ewan would not have exchanged a moment in Marguerite's arms to be back in Lochmore immediately. All the same, Ewan travelled with a growing sense of unease. There was only the one road to follow now and if Duncan had come this way again it was possible he might encounter them. Ewan would have nowhere to hide Marguerite from him this time and, though he was reluctant to shed blood, he would spill

Duncan's entire supply before he let Marguerite be taken from him.

He mounted his horse and fell in alongside Marguerite in a quick trot. The road was good and they would make up some lost time, as long as he was able to resist Marguerite when they stopped to eat.

'We'll travel through Argyll's land before we come to mine.' Ewan brightened, remembering that Struan MacNeill lived close by. They would pass his manor house in the village of Ballinorchy by nightfall and, with luck, would find a welcome fire and bed there for the night.

'We'll be on my land tomorrow,' he explained. 'Do you recall I have been granted new holdings? We reach the lower edge of those before we come to Kilmachrie and Lochmore.'

A small furrow appeared between Marguerite's brows. 'I remember. Duncan was angry that you were given the land belonging to the Earl who died. He told me it had been promised to his cousin Donald.'

A chill raced down Ewan's spine. 'Promised? When?'

She shrugged, sending her hair rippling across her shoulders. 'I do not know. Before the battle, I assume.'

Ewan said nothing. How could Duncan have known that McNab would die during the battle? How could anyone ensure a particular man would die? Unless, of course, someone was passing information and an account of who should fall victim on the battlefield. Ewan had been so caught up in keeping Marguerite safe that he had forgotten to think about the identity of the spy. Now he was surer than ever that Duncan was the man he sought. The way he had reacted in Druinnun when Ewan had mentioned Morayshill, the fact he was planning to visit Berwick, his boast to Marguerite of eyes and ears everywhere: everything pointed to him. It would be Ewan's duty to bring him to justice but first he had to return home.

He felt for the pouch of alms money in his saddlebag and tried his best to ignore the guilt that flickered in his belly. Families were waiting for him to bring what they needed. He had lingered too long enjoying himself with Marguerite while his tenants and clansmen waited for their Earl. Though his heart begged him to ride beside Marguerite in a leisurely fashion he broke into a gallop, trusting her to follow.

Lochmore Castle and duty called.

As Ewan had hoped, they were welcomed at Struan MacNeill's home that evening. Ballinorchy huddled between the end of the loch and the base of blackthorn-covered hills. The castle was a tower keep, similar to Lochmore Castle, but Struan's family lacked the wealth to extend it as Ewan's ancestors had and it remained a squat tower with a hall on the lower floor and a pair of rooms for the family on the upper floor.

Struan greeted them in person. He clasped Ewan's hand, but frowned as Marguerite passed up the staircase in the company of his young wife, who was promising Marguerite hot water and fresh linens. Janet had definite ambitions regarding Struan's status and did her best not to turn her pert nose up at Marguerite's travel-soiled skirts and *arisaid*. Struan waited until the women had left before speaking.

'Unless I'm in my dotage and mixing faces, that's Duncan McCrieff's missing bride.'

'Aye, it is Mademoiselle Vallon.'

Struan's face darkened. 'Are you addled? Mc-Crieff nearly tore Stirling apart hunting for her and swore death to the man who had stolen her and dire retribution on the maid herself.'

A chill froze Ewan's limbs at the idea he had considered returning Marguerite to the brute.

'I didna know till too late that she had stowed away or I'd have taken her back. I took a risk by bringing her with me to your home and I'd thank you not to give her away. You know Mc-Crieffs have long hated Lochmores, but they're no friends to the MacNeills either. Our clans both owe allegiance to the Campbells and the Mc-Crieffs have fought against them in the past.'

'*Dinna fash*. If he comes searching again, he willnae find her from me,' Struan said. 'I believe he passed on his way to Castle McCrieff, but I was off in the high fields and missed him.'

Ewan sucked his teeth. If Duncan had gone to Castle McCrieff, he must have given up his search for Marguerite. He was closer than Ewan liked to Lochmore Castle, but would be occupied with his uncle.

Struan eyed him darkly. 'Be wary, Ewan. Donald McCrieff is said to be in high fury over the McNab grant of land and vowing revenge. If he decides you've stolen Mademoiselle Vallon from his cousin, it will add to the insult.'

Ewan debated briefly sharing his suspicions that Duncan was the traitor Robert Morayshill sought. He decided against it. Why involve his friend in dark dealings if he didn't need to?

Struan had a wicked glint in his eye. 'The lass is pretty, which must have made your journey a little more interesting. You did say you were looking for a woman, but I didn't expect you to steal one.'

Ewan's neck grew hot. He didn't like what Struan was implying and caution warned him to hide his ever-increasing infatuation. 'Pretty or not, I could have done without her bursting out from among my luggage,' he said curtly. 'Mademoiselle Vallon will be returning to France as soon as I am able to be rid of her. She's been nothing but trouble to me.'

A sound made him turn. Janet and Marguerite stood in the doorway. There was no point hoping she had not heard his words because her expressive eyes were tight with misery.

'Thank you for your hospitality, Master MacNeill,' Marguerite said, curtsying to Struan. 'I shall be leaving your country at the earliest opportunity. I have already wasted far too long here when I should have been returning home. As Lord Glenarris says, I have been more than troublesome to him with very little compensation.'

Ewan greeted her formally, bowing over her hand and calling her Mademoiselle Vallon. She curtsied, but her eyes slid past his. She ignored his proffered arm and walked to the table alone. Ewan followed miserably. How could she know that the prospect of her leaving filled him with a dread far greater than any relief?

Chapter Sixteen

⚭⚭⚭

The food was more plentiful and better than the sparse meal Moira had offered them, but the night was not as relaxed. Marguerite acted as if they were strangers to each other, sitting at the furthest corner of the table from him. It was a far cry from the closeness they had shared in Moira's small cottage and much less than the intimacy of the night before. He was realistic enough to know that once they reached Lochmore Castle the closeness they had shared would be nothing more than a memory, but he had hoped it would last beyond nightfall.

Struan talked for most of the evening, telling them of the increase in tensions that had arisen between local septs since only half the men had returned from Flodden and families were struggling. He tried to explain the long history of the clans and their rivalries to Marguerite, as if she would be interested in feuds stretching back decades.

'But why do you fight?' Marguerite interrupted. Her eyes were cold, reminding Ewan of the disdain with which she had viewed Scotland when they first met. He tried not to feel the annoyance that surged inside him. He had wondered that himself oftentimes. Raids were a regular part of life. With borders so close together, memories long and tempers made fiercer by ale, it did not take much for one clan to offend another. A group of Lochmores would descend on a McCrieff village or vice versa on some pretext. There would be a brief skirmish, with heads and fists or clubs and swords playing a part depending on the nature of the men and offence. Honour would temporarily be satisfied, compensation agreed and matters ended. A knot of anxiety filled his belly. Clan Lochmore would be expecting him not only to mediate in these quarrels, but, if necessary, to take arms and lead them. When Hamish had sent him to study law that had been so there was an extra arrow in the clan's quiver, not for Ewan to become the sole one.

'It's the way it has always been,' Ewan explained. 'I don't even know how the hatred between Lochmores and McCrieffs started. Over lands granted or spoils unfairly divided, I imagine. A woman or livestock might have been taken.'

Marguerite looked down her nose at him. 'You equate women with sheep, Lord Glenarris!'

'Not at all, Mademoiselle Vallon.' Ewan lifted his chin. 'Sheep are much more useful than a woman.'

She frowned, then softened slightly. 'You're teasing me.'

Ewan raised his cup at her and smiled as the coldness between them thawed slightly. They shared a private moment that made him shiver inside. 'A little, but there's truth in it, too. Sheep give a man wool and meat.'

'Livestock is a man's livelihood,' Struan explained. 'Often his only way of putting food in his family's bellies. A woman doesn't do that.'

'She roasts his lamb and weaves his wool into blankets for his bed,' Janet broke in. 'She gives him children. In the best marriages she comforts him and soothes his worries.'

'Aye, she does that,' Struan agreed. He took Janet's hand across the hearth and kissed it. 'She keeps him awake half the night, then gives him a soft place to lay his head.'

A lump filled Ewan's throat at the sight of their obvious affection. He found himself unable to meet Marguerite's eye lest she see the emotions that were ravaging him. A soft place to lay his head. Arms to comfort him and lips to drive him to ecstasy. He'd seen glimpses of them all too briefly with Marguerite, but never would again. She was beyond his reach and if he did not harden his heart it would break.

'Mademoiselle Vallon, it is growing late. I wish to be back at Lochmore Castle before nightfall tomorrow so I intend to leave early. Perhaps we…' He paused and collected his thoughts, not wanting to suggest he had any expectation of sharing her bed. 'Perhaps *you* should retire?'

She opened her mouth, then closed it abruptly. 'Of course, Lord Glenarris. I shall bid you goodnight.'

She rose and curtsied to Struan and Janet. As she passed Ewan hurt flashed across her face. He managed to control himself long enough to watch her vanish up the staircase, wanting nothing more than to follow her. Janet retired shortly afterwards, leaving the men alone.

Struan sighed. 'You're walking a dangerous path, friend.'

'I told you, I'm not scared of what McCrieffs vow to do when they're in their cups.'

Struan gave him a pitying look. 'I wasnae talking about them.'

Ewan swallowed the last of his wine and banged his cup on the table. 'The sooner Mademoiselle Vallon is back in France, the better it will be for all.'

'Yes, I can tell from the way you stare at each other that you're already looking forward to the day you part.'

When Ewan eventually went upstairs Marguerite was lying on her truckle bed facing the wall. Ewan's had been placed at the opposite side of the room, beneath the window, but he crept over to stand beside her. Her hair fell over her face and in the darkness he could not make out her features.

His heart lurched with the almost physical pain of not touching her. Struan and Janet would have no knowledge of what went on outside the heavy curtains that surrounded their bed. There was nothing to stop Ewan slipping into Marguerite's bed as he wished to do. Nothing, except from the chill that had developed between them. He turned back to his own bed, shrugged off his *brat* and climbed under his covers. Marguerite rolled over with a sigh, but Ewan could not tell if he had disturbed her peace or if she had been awake all the time and pretending to sleep. He had started the morning deliriously happy with Marguerite wrapped in his embrace. He ended the day alone and miserable, trying to convince himself that the distance between them was for the best.

* * *

When they met soon after the break of dawn, Marguerite was wearing her stiff-bodiced French dress with her hair captured beneath a linen cap and veil. It might not have been a signal that she was putting Scotland behind her and looking to France, but Ewan took it as such. She greeted him with the newly renewed formality that matched her choice of clothes, curtsying deeply and keeping her eyes down as if they were strangers.

'Good morning, Lord Glenarris.'

'Don't do that,' Ewan snapped. 'Haven't we travelled long enough together to greet each other as friends?'

'I had thought so,' she murmured with a downward twist of her lips that made Ewan desperate to kiss a smile back on to them.

He took her by the elbows, lifting her upright to face him. Through the close-fitting sleeves of her dress Ewan could feel the soft contours of her arms. Her dress was tighter than the loose Scottish dress she had worn and showed off her slender frame in more detail than Ewan remembered it doing. Now he knew precisely what lay beneath the stiffly laced bodice and waterfall of skirts he could think of nothing else beyond the silken creaminess of Marguerite's skin. He spread his fingers wider and Marguerite gave a little shiver. The longer they were together the harder it would be to part.

'We'll be in Lochmore before nightfall if we ride fast, but you don't have to come that far,' Ewan said. 'Struan is sending a servant to Stirling with a letter. I am sure he will escort you back to where you need to go if you choose. Duncan has passed by here to Castle McCrieff so you are in no danger of meeting him.'

Marguerite was silent for far too long. She looked at Ewan with eyes brimming with challenge. 'Would you prefer me to do that?'

'Do what makes you happy,' he said, not wishing to induce her to make any decision. 'I only suggest it so you don't have to make an unnecessary journey.'

She gave him a slight smile and his spirits raised. 'I would like to see your home before I return to France as I have travelled this far.'

Ewan moistened his lips, but at that moment Janet entered the hall. Ewan and Marguerite sprang apart and Marguerite became engrossed in straightening her veil. She arranged her *airsaid* over her shoulders and smiled at Janet, now looking a curious mixture of Scottish and French.

Ewan held out his arm and she slipped hers through it.

'Then let's be on our way.'

* * *

Ewan really did intend to go straight to Lochmore Castle, but Marguerite's change of clothing meant she could not ride with the ease they had become accustomed to. It was hardly surprising, given how the stiff bodice pinched her waist to nothing, and though she made no complaint, she grew pale and fell behind frequently until Ewan was forced to draw Randall into a gentle trot that she could keep pace with. He did not mind, in truth, knowing that these hours spent riding alongside the loch would be the last they would spend together. In the end he could not resist one final detour as they crossed into Lochmore land to his favourite place. He spent a stolen hour sitting on the edge of a stretch of white sand by a small loch and watched the gulls fly lazily overhead with Marguerite at his side.

'It smells of the sea,' Marguerite said, inhaling deeply.

'This is Loch Mora. It's saltwater,' Ewan explained. 'If we sailed along it we'd reach the Firth of Clyde, but we follow the hill over the top of this loch all the way to the sea where Lochmore Castle stands.'

'The sea. Of course. On the west coast. Something else you have taught me.' Marguerite's eyes shone with amusement, then softened. She gave him a smile of such sweetness Ewan felt his heart was being ripped from his chest with the longing for her that was overwhelming.

'You don't mind that you came so far out of your way?' he asked.

'If I had not, then I would not have seen the sights I have. I would not have done the things I have done.' She reached for his hand. 'Thank you for all you have done for me and shown me. I have lived more with you in this past week than I ever had—or will again. I shall miss you when I return home.'

He had no words. They would have to part, but he would treasure the time they had spent together. He raised her hand and briefly touched his lips against the back before pressing them into her palm. That was all he dared to do. He was surprised he was not visibly shaking at her touch and if he gave in to the impulses that were fighting to be heard he would end up bedding her on the shore.

'Let's get going. We'll be eating roast mackerel and sleeping in a proper bed tonight.'

His ears caught up with his mouth and he bit his tongue. Not *a* bed. There was no question they would be sharing a bed. If Marguerite noticed his slip, she chose to ignore it.

It was thanks to that detour that they did not reach Castle Lochmore until dusk. It was thanks to this that Ewan received a warning that prevented him riding straight into danger.

A blood-red sunset turned the sky over Loch Arris to flames, but as they rounded the foot of the hill and finally came upon the flat marshland that surrounded the spit of land where Lochmore Castle stood Ewan realised there were true fires outside the walls.

'Bonfires,' Marguerite murmured. 'Are they celebrating the harvest?'

Ewan's heart stopped. He swore, sitting up in his saddle, the blood draining from his face. He shook his head mutely. There should be no fires here, only dark, peaceful fields where sheep and cattle grazed.

He did not know which enemy had surrounded his home, but Lochmore Castle was under siege.

Something was wrong. Ewan grew tense and his face drained of all colour. He hurled himself from the saddle, unsheathing his sword with a snarl as he began to run down the road, leaving her alone.

'Ewan, stop!' Marguerite dismounted and chased after him. The stomacher of her dress bit uncomfortably into her waist and prevented her drawing breath. Cursing the restrictive dress, she picked up her skirts and ran after him.

'Wait for me,' she pleaded. 'Please!'

He stopped at her cry and she would have collided with him if he had not shot his hands out and grasped her around the waist to hold her back from him. Even this touch was enough to turn her into a quivering mass of lust, but Ewan's lean face was twisted in anger and his eyes were wild with despair.

'What's wrong?' she panted. She clutched his free arm to prevent him from leaving her.

'Can't you see?' He shook his hand free and waved it towards castle.

Even though it was some distance away, Marguerite could make out sturdy walls, above which a tall, square tower rose, silhouetted against the darkening sky. The flames Marguerite had taken for lights of the castle were outside the walls.

'Those are no welcoming fires. My home is under attack!'

Marguerite's legs became straw. A gentle wind would have blown her away. She took hold of Ewan's shoulders, cleaving to him for strength.

'Duncan?' she whispered. 'He's found me!'

'It could be.' Ewan eyed her darkly, sending a chill through her. He snapped his head up. 'Or mayhap this has nothing to do with you. Yours are not the only affairs of concern in the world. I think you forget that sometimes.'

He had been confusingly and heartbreakingly switching between aloofness and warmth since they had arrived at Struan MacNeill's home, causing Marguerite to feel the first regrets that she had allowed her passion to override her sense. Now more than ever his expression chilled her.

'That isn't fair!' she exclaimed, stepping away.

'Isn't it?' Ewan's face was grim, reminding her of when they had first met and he had seemed to hate her. 'I delayed my return to Lochmore because of you. I should have been here.'

Marguerite dropped her head. She was unable to deny the truth in what he said, yet his accusations scorched her heart.

'If I had been here, I would have been able to prevent this,' he said. His voice cracked with anguish and Marguerite could not bear it. She rested her hand on his cheek.

'You don't know that!' she whispered.

'You think I could have done nothing? That I would have been useless?' His jaw tightened beneath her fingers. His voice was low and tore into her heart.

'I didn't mean that!' She stamped her foot, wondering if he was deliberately misunderstanding her. 'I mean you would have tried, but you might have been hurt or killed. Now you are safe. You don't have to fight.'

'Should I run away like you did?' he asked angrily, staring down at her with his blue eyes that were chips of ice. 'We can't all evade our responsibilities.'

Marguerite gasped in shock at his cruel words. She dropped her hands and spun away from him, staring instead out to the castle and the sea beyond. The small fires were dotted about the wide, flat expanse between them and the castle. No wonder he was furious and despairing. She could not blame him. The sound of steel scraping from a scabbard made her jump. Ewan, standing behind her, had drawn his sword. She flinched and saw his eyes flash with irritation. They seemed remarkably good at offending each other, as if the intense closeness they had shared had opened a doorway to other, angrier emotions.

'Don't look so frightened,' Ewan said. 'I need to get closer and see what is really happening. Stay here.'

Marguerite opened her mouth to protest and demand he take her with him. Sitting alone in the dark when an enemy might be close terrified her, but what right did she have to object when she was the reason for his troubles?

'Be safe,' she whispered.

He grimaced. 'I'll be back as soon as I can.'

He pulled his *brat* over his head and crept away, leaving Marguerite with the horses. She sat on the bracken and hugged her knees, trying to glimpse him, but he kept to the thick tangles of bracken among the trees and she lost sight of him far too quickly. She could not get comfortable. Midges attacked in droves until she pulled her *airsaid* over her head and the laces of her gown felt too tight and uncomfortable. Her gown was designed for sitting on chairs or dancing, not squatting among wet undergrowth.

The moon moved slowly from one side of the tallest pine to the other and she began to fear Ewan was not coming back. Her imagination created a thousand horrific situations in which he succeeded in entering his castle and forgot he had abandoned her, where he revealed her whereabouts to Duncan, or, worse, that he was captured or killed.

The imagined loss of him was almost too much to bear when their fragile friendship had shown hints of turning into something deeper. She was beginning to despair and had succumbed to the tears that made her eyes swim when Ewan appeared at her side and dropped on to the ground so silently she cried out in alarm. He flung an arm around her shoulders and pressed a finger to her lips. It served to silence her, but also to remind her of the way he had traced the shape of them with a touch as soft as a feather as they had made love. She hurled herself at him, wrapping her arms around him and burying her head on his chest. He rocked, caught off balance, and embraced her back.

'Maggie, what's wrong?'

Through her sniffs she told him some of what she had feared. He laughed gently before growing stern and holding her away to face him. 'Do ye really think I could forget you? Or that I'd hand you to that bawbag! What do you take me for?'

She bit her lip and shook her head, guiltily wondering why she had ever doubted him. He had never failed her yet. She noticed how weary he looked, how gaunt his lean face had become. She found some bread left over from what Janet had given them and passed it to him, along with a skin of wine that he drained with vigour.

'What did you discover?'

He groaned. 'It's bad. They're McCrieffs. At least thirty of them, probably more, but I couldna get close enough to be sure. I didn't see Duncan. You are safe at least.'

'I don't care about that,' Marguerite said firmly. 'What are we to do?'

'We?'

'Of course!' She looked into his eyes. 'You helped me and this is my fault. If I can do any-thing to help, I will. Just give me the word.'

'Ah, lass, I'm sorry for what I said earlier.' Ewan leaned against her. She stiffened, but as his hand settled on her arm she relented a little. 'It was said in anger more than truth. I don't blame you for this. It was my choice to travel with you and most likely I couldn't have prevented it.'

'There must be something we can do,' she murmured, covering his hand with hers. 'Can we somehow steal past them and make it as far as the gate?'

'No. Aside from the fact that I'm not going to walk you through a camp full of drunken McCrieffs, we canna get in that way without being seen and I won't risk trying to get the gate open.' He began pacing back and forth.

'I have an idea, but it might be a risk. There is a tunnel that leads from the cellars beneath the oldest part of the keep to the seashore. We call it the Water Gate. It was built for circumstances such as these, I suppose when my ancestors needed to leave without being seen. I plan to ride to the village along the coast and take a boat. We can be there within an hour. When the tide turns I'll row to the beach behind Lochmore Castle and try to get inside.'

He gave her a smile. 'The villagers are Clan Lochmore so you'll be safe there.'

Marguerite gave him a stern look. 'Your plan sounds excellent, apart from one thing. I do not wish to be left in the village. I will come with you.'

Ewan frowned. 'Maggie, don't be foolish. It's far too dangerous.'

She put her hands on her hips and jutted her jaw out. 'I'm not a simpering girl who can't do more than walk around a knot garden without becoming faint. Have I not proven myself capable of enduring difficulties since I left Stirling? I have slept beneath the open sky, climbed mountains and bathed in lochs without complaint.' He still looked doubtful. She took his hand.

'Besides, if you get into the castle it doesn't mean you can get out again. I'm safer with you and I'm not letting you abandon me.'

He laced his fingers through hers; making her skin flutter like a thousand moths brushing against her. 'You've borne everything well. I cannot argue with that. Very well, you come with me if you choose. Be warned, though, the current is strong and if the tide is against us we could be drawn out to sea. We leave now.'

Chapter Seventeen

Riding along the coast involved returning the way they had come and it was late by the time they reached the village Ewan had spoken of. The stone cottages sat in a row along the bay, hugging the rocky shore. There was no harbour or even a jetty and boats of varying sizes were pulled up on the shingle, their existence only evident from the eerie creaking of the wood as the wind caught them. The village lay in darkness, but Ewan rapped softly on the door of the furthest cottage and muttered something in an accent so thick Marguerite couldn't understand a word. Eventually it opened a crack and someone evidently appeared because Ewan began speaking faster and gesturing towards the boats. The door slammed and Ewan returned presently.

They left the horses tethered at the shore. Marguerite carried the panniers while Ewan untied a small boat and had dragged it to the furthest end of the beach where jagged rocks met the thick woodland. He was silhouetted against the sky, a tall, slender figure tensed and watchful.

She crunched over the shingle to join him. He placed a hand on either cheek, turning her face to the moonlight and examining her.

'You're tired. It isn't too late to stay here,' he said. 'I cannae think of you getting hurt.'

She stifled another yawn. 'I shall go where you do. I've followed you this far.'

'Thank you.' He grasped her hand, squeezing it reassuringly before dropping it all too quickly for Marguerite's liking. He held the small boat steady. 'Best get in. I'll push us off.'

Ewan did not speak as he rowed along the coast and round the headland. His only sounds were increasingly weary grunts of exertion as he drew the oars back. Marguerite kept a watch towards the shore as the small craft lurched on the waves, but if any enemy was watching them they were too well concealed. She hoped for both their sakes the boat was not visible and all Ewan's effort would not be in vain. Ewan steered the craft to shore after what seemed like hours and brought the boat into a bay protected by an outcrop of jagged rocks.

He took his boots off and jumped from the boat to drag it alongside a low natural jetty of rock with iron rings set deep. Marguerite took the oars and tried to steady the craft as Ewan moored it, but her sleeves were too tight and she was unable to lift her arms as high as she needed to. She sighed in frustration.

'I think we're safe,' Ewan said. 'McCrieff land is on the headland on the opposite side of the sea loch. If they had thought to station men here we would have known about it by now.'

'Is that likely?'

'I don't think they would bother. There's no way over the rocks up to the castle unless they want to scale the Devil's Seat.' Ewan wrapped his arms around Marguerite and lifted her over the edge. She put her hands around his back to steady herself. His *leine* was damp to the touch as she ran her hands over his shoulder blades. They were in almost total blackness and she could not see his expression, but heard his sharp intake of breath before he lowered her and she found herself standing on soft sand. He released her slowly and stretched his arms upwards, gesturing towards a jumble of boulders topped with a flat rock that stood imposingly at right the end of the beach.

'Let's find the tunnel entrance,' he said. He took her hand and led her up the sand, her feet slipping on the uneven ground and her hem trailing. She pulled her hand free.

'Wait. I want to change. I can't move properly in this dress. I'll hold you up.' She took her blue dress from the pannier and untied the laces beneath her left arm. Ewan watched. In the pale moonlight she could make out his expression of out-and-out lust. She had been about to strip naked without a second thought. Shame burned her cheeks and throat, but other parts of her were growing equally hot from desire for him.

'Do you need help?' Ewan asked in a voice as smooth as cream.

She nodded slowly. He spread his hand on her right side and began pulling the laces free, hooking his thumb between the braided holes and tugging gently. He bent his head close to Marguerite and his cool breath on her neck drew a soft keening from her throat. He looked up with eyes brimming with sensuality and slipped the fingers of his unoccupied hand to the neck of her gown, fingers playing with the ribbon that held it closed.

'Why did ye wear this today?'

'I wanted to look my finest when we arrived at your home. I did not want to disgrace you in front of your people,' she said.

'You could never disgrace me, whatever you wore,' he murmured. 'I thought you were putting Scotland behind you already.'

Perhaps she had been. The intense hurt she had felt at Ewan's sudden coldness and the words she had overheard had made her want to run from his sight and long for the day she was back in France, but now he was in her arms once again she had no intention of letting him slip through her fingers.

'It was stupid of me,' she agreed. The laces were undone and she took a deep breath of the damp, salty air. Ewan's warm fingers were playing idly with the soft hollow of her collarbone. She rolled her shoulders back. 'This is far too uncomfortable. I did not realise how constricting my country's clothes were until I put it on again. I prefer my new dress.'

'I prefer you in your new dress, too.' Ewan tugged the ribbon and began to ease the gown down over Marguerite's shoulders and arms, his eyes never leaving hers.

'I prefer you out of it even better.'

Marguerite shuddered as the night chill caressed her naked flesh. Ewan's lips curled into a smile of sensual promise. Was he really intending to make love to her now, of all times?

'We said we wouldn't after we left the mountain,' Marguerite whispered.

Even as she spoke her hands were moving to unbuckle his belt. She tugged it free and let the *brat* fall to the ground, skimming the palm of her hand over his groin and down his thigh. Ewan stayed her hand and brought his mouth close to her ear. He bunched his fingers in her hair, weaving them into the braid.

'The tunnel...' she murmured, her voice ragged with the effort of maintaining rational thought.

Ewan silenced her with a kiss.

'I don't know who or what we'll find at the other end of the tunnel,' he said in a low voice. His breath was hot, his lips firm and moist against her cheek. 'I hope that the fact the McCrieffs are camped outside means the castle hasn't been breached, in which case we'll be safe, but it could be dangerous. Whatever is waiting for us can wait awhile longer, but you're here with me now and I want you again.'

Marguerite rolled her head back, guiding his lips to the tender spot at the base of her ear where his touch made her head spin.

'I want you, too,' she gasped.

She could feel him swelling, pushing hard against her, and excitement coursed through her. She tilted her hips, angling them so that his hardness was directly between her thighs.

'Then one last time,' Ewan said. He tore his *leine* over his head and pulled her down with him on to the *brat*.

They knelt facing each other, naked in the mist and blackness. Before, they had made love in sunlight. Now there was little to see save what moonlight revealed. Marguerite ran her hands over Ewan's lean muscles, feeling her way along his arms, over his chest and down his belly and over the tight V-shape where the skin was softest to touch. He traced the length of her spine. When she arched her back he bent his head to her breast, taking her nipple in his mouth. She cried out in shock at the pleasure.

'We need to be quiet,' he admonished gently.

He replaced his mouth with a hand and kissed her deeply with lips that were salt flecked, silencing her moans. Marguerite wriggled forward until she straddled Ewan's lap. He groaned, pushing forward until he entered her. They moved in unison, faster and harder as layers upon layers of pleasure built within Marguerite. Ewan's hands moved to her breasts again, his fingers working an enchantment until she could bear the sensations no longer and the walls tumbled inside her. She arched her back and whimpered. As if Ewan had been waiting for this signal he seized her buttocks, wrenching her closer and holding her still as he gave a final, powerful thrust and sagged back on to the sand.

'Maybe one day we'll find a bed to do that in rather than under the sky,' he panted, laughing. She pressed her hand against his chest, feeling the powerful thump of his heart, elated that he was contemplating another instance after he had sworn it would be the last time. Marguerite settled into the waiting crook of his arm and Ewan pulled the *brat* over them both, sending a spray of sand everywhere.

'If I had come to your bed last night, would you have allowed me?' he asked.

'I'll never deny you that,' she said, meaning it with every fibre in her body. 'I will never regret what we do together.'

Her stomach plummeted. As much as she craved him, she would be gone before long and he had given no indication he would regret her leaving when the time came. It had been another stolen moment and Marguerite was not surprised when Ewan rolled out from beneath her and began to arrange his *brat*. He had another purpose after all. She bundled her clothes on, needing no help with the looser, freer dress.

She followed Ewan up the beach, this time without taking his hand. He made his way to what appeared to be a pile of large rocks that had fallen. Tangles of weeds and tree roots fell from the hill, half-covering them.

'Do you know where to find the tunnel?' she asked.

'Of course. I used it all the time when I was younger. My brother and I used to come here to meet—' He stopped abruptly and Marguerite almost collided with him. 'We used to come here,' he repeated quietly.

He began clambering over the rocks, leaving Marguerite speculating who he had been meeting and darkly suspecting she was not the first woman whose company he had enjoyed on the beach.

The tunnel was wet with moss and stale air, but as Ewan told Marguerite, the purpose was not for comfort. He instructed Marguerite to stay close behind him. She did not need telling twice as they moved in total blackness and she feared she might be left behind. The occasional waft of Ewan's scent was comforting in the cold, mildewed air. She held tight to the back of his belt while she dragged the other hand along the rough wall that had been hewn from rock. She could imagine Ewan as a boy enjoying stealing out for adventures and smiled to herself in the darkness. They wound to the left, then the right, climbing slightly upwards inside the rock beneath the castle.

Ewan stopped abruptly.

'What's wrong?' Marguerite asked in alarm.

She felt a gentle squeeze of his hand. 'Nothing. We're at the fork. I'm trying to decide the best way to go. The passage goes two ways. The chapel in the grounds is to the right. The cellars in the tower beside the Great Hall are to the left.

We'll go that way. I hope no one has barred the exit with wine barrels, though an open bottle will be welcome!'

They ducked through a low arch and came out into a vaulted cellar behind piles of sacks and crates. No one had blocked the exit. The moonlight that shone through the air holes set high into the wall was almost too bright after the blackness they had walked in. Ewan gave a sigh of relief, but their triumph was short-lived. Boots thudded, steel scraped and voices growled. Marguerite was seized from behind by arms that held her tightly and her bag was ripped from her hands. Ewan roared in anger as he disappeared beneath what seemed to Marguerite like a dozen assailants, unable to break free before he, too, was seized and pushed against the wall, a sword at his throat.

The curved blade was well sharpened, as Hamish had demanded all Lochmore steel be kept. Ewan drew a shallow breath, knowing that a sudden move would see his throat slit either by accident or design. He stood motionless, unlike Marguerite, who twisted in her captor's arms. Despair consumed him. Their plan had been in vain and Lochmore had fallen to the enemy.

'Move and it'll be your last act!'

The growl was familiar. Ewan's spirits rose

as he recognised Lochmore Castle's steward and fiercest protector, Connor. They were among Lochmores, but Connor's next words pierced Ewan's heart deeper than any sword could.

'We've been waiting for ye to come back, ye black-hearted whore-son!'

Is that what Connor thought of their new laird? Ewan's stomach tightened at the thought he was so unwelcome.

'Who is this doxy?' Connor said. 'Did you think we'd take an exchange for what you've stolen?'

Ewan only began to ponder what had been stolen, because Marguerite's captor twisted her arm and she cried out in pain, which banished all other thoughts. 'Ewan, stop them, please!'

'Ewan?' Connor released the pressure on the sword enough so that Ewan could speak. 'Ewan who?'

'Ewan Lochmore,' Ewan thundered. He gripped the tip of the blade between forefinger and thumb and moved it carefully from his throat. The sword dropped. Marguerite was released and rushed into Ewan's arms. She was trembling almost as violently as when she had been overcome with passion only a short while before. That she had suffered at the hands of his clansmen was intolerable to Ewan. He held her close and glared over the top of her head at Connor and the two servants who stood beside him. Half-a-dozen more Lochmore servants stood ready with swords in hands and Ewan felt a surge of pride that his people were so ready to defend themselves and his home.

'Don't you recognise your laird, Connor? What is the meaning of this?' he asked, rubbing his throat. He wiped away a trickle of blood harshly with his thumb. 'Why is there no light?'

'Pardon, my lord. We've all been beside ourselves since they attacked, not knowing what to do in your absence. We feared the passage might be breached, but it has not. We've had a watch day and night.'

Ewan's stomach plummeted and all strength left him. He clutched on to Marguerite, needing to draw sustenance from her as much as she had from him. The tunnel had been breached, but worse, his absence had caused distress to his people.

'Tell me everything,' he commanded.

At his side Marguerite shuddered again and Ewan hesitated. He could tell that Connor was eager to explain and he was desperate to learn what had taken place, but he had to attend to Marguerite. 'No, first find us some wine and bread. Bring it to…my father's rooms and we'll talk once we're settled there.'

Ewan led Marguerite by the hand through

the series of storeroom and kitchens, and up the stone spiral staircase into the Great Hall. The hall was full of men and women who worked in the castle sleeping on pallets. There were many more than usual, presumably because those who lived outside the walls had taken refuge inside. Rush lights provided a dim glow and the atmosphere was more peaceful that Ewan would expect. The floor above was divided into rooms reserved for guest accommodation and two chambers for the male and female household servants.

Marguerite gazed around at the tapestries on the walls and thick rugs in rich, autumnal colours, openly curious. Although he would love to show her his home, Ewan steered her by the arm up the keep staircase to Hamish's private quarters in the original stone keep.

The rooms on the third floor of the square tower had been the domain of the Laird of Lochmore for generations. By rights they were Ewan's now, though he felt like an intruder as he held the oak door to admit Marguerite into the panelled solar with the bedchamber beyond. Ewan had last entered this room twelve months previously on a visit from Glasgow and, though the table was free of mess and the clothes chest lay empty, Hamish's presence still filled the space.

Ewan gripped the doorway, reluctant to enter. Two deep, high-backed chairs stood close to the hearth. There was no fire in the grate, of course, but the only other place to rest was the great bed in the other room and he had no intention of taking her in there. He gestured to Marguerite to take the chair that had been Hamish's favourite, unwilling to use it himself. She looked around inquisitively, then started to speak. Ewan shook his head and waved a hand jerkily. He could not bear to answer her questions right now. She closed her mouth and huddled down into the sheepskin that was still thrown across the seat, watching him from eyes that were ringed with dark circles. She looked as exhausted as he was. He rubbed the heel of his hands over his eyes, feeling them sting and prickle with tiredness.

'I'm sorry you didna get a more hospitable welcome, Maggie.' He sighed, dropping on to the other chair. 'I should never have brought you here.'

Immediately Marguerite slid from hers and crossed to him. She knelt at his side on the rug and wrapped her hands around his waist, her skirts spreading wide around her.

'Oh, my heart breaks for what has happened here. For you.'

She sounded tearful, but her eyes blazed with fury on his behalf. Her perfect lips were drawn into an indignant pout that made them look temptingly kissable.

'You're bleeding!' she exclaimed.

She licked her forefinger and wiped it across the spot where Connor's blade had nicked him. Her touch both stung and soothed. It was characteristic of the way she infuriated and captivated Ewan by turn. He drew her on to his lap and ran his hand firmly along her arm from shoulder to wrist and back again.

'You aren't badly hurt?' he asked.

'No. It was painful only for a moment while he was twisting it.'

Ewan's temper surged at the thought she had been mishandled. He held her close. She rested her head on his chest and tightened her arms around his waist. Desire rose, but was replaced by a deeper need to draw strength from her touch. Ewan closed his eyes, his mind crackling like green timber on a fire, but the knots in his body slowly loosening as Marguerite's presence soothed his soul like nothing else seemed capable of.

They were friends again after the cruel words she had overheard, but that could not last. He told himself he should guard his heart and build a wall around it as high as that which surrounded the castle, but it was far too late for that and he knew that Marguerite was capable of breaching his defences with an ease that any invader would envy.

Chapter Eighteen

They were still sitting together when a knock at the door came. Marguerite leapt away like a cat on hot coals and was back in her chair by the time Connor entered with two servants bearing venison stew and bread, and, best of all, a large jug of hot wine.

'Now, tell me everything,' Ewan instructed as they ate.

'They're Clan McCrieff,' Connor said. 'They attacked the gate two days ago, but we think they've been slipping into the valley for maybe four and watching. They didna breach the inner courtyard—we fought them off. The servants and guards fought well.'

'I'll see they're rewarded,' Ewan said, pride in his men mingling with guilt that he had not been here to fight alongside them. Two nights ago he had been atop a mountain with Marguerite's legs wrapped around his back, with no thought for Lochmore Castle. He glanced across to see if she was thinking the same thing. Her expression was solemn and slightly puzzled, and Ewan wondered how much of Connor's thick speech she could discern. He flushed with anger that he knew was unreasonable. She was the reason he had not been here, but the choice had been his.

'They ransacked the granary and workshops and…other buildings in the outer ward,' Connor continued.

Ewan ground his teeth, noting the slight hesitation and wondering what Connor was not telling him. Hamish would have been roaring by now, pulling the truth out, but Ewan wanted to let him tell the tale in his own time. Marguerite poured a goblet of wine and handed it to Ewan. Connor's eyes slid to her and then to Ewan with an unspoken question.

Ewan's elation at hiding and bedding Duncan's bride was less amusing now she was seated in his quarters and her cuckolded fiancé might be outside the walls ready to exact vengeance, but he could not truly say he regretted his actions— any of them—and he would stand by what he had done.

'This lady is Marguerite Vallon. She will be staying a short while.' He paused, not knowing how short her visit could be if they were unable to leave the castle. He could hardly send her on her way to Leith in the fishing boat.

'Angus said you were travelling with Duncan McCrieff's woman,' Connor said.

'Angus is here?' Ewan's flesh prickled. He had imagined Angus could not have broken through the groups of men lying in wait outside, but had retreated to one of the outlying villages. 'Where is he? Send him to me, please.'

'I canna do that, Laird.' Connor's expression grew grave. 'He fought bravely, but he was badly injured. He canna leave his bed.'

Ewan was on his feet before Connor had finished speaking. 'Take me to him.'

Both Connor and Marguerite stood. Ewan took her by the shoulders and pressed gently to make her sit, but she resisted.

'Let me come with you.'

'This is Lochmore business,' he said. 'You should stay here and rest. You can use the bed in the adjoining room.'

'I don't need to rest.' Her face took on the determined look he had discovered there was no arguing with. Ewan cocked his head and she followed him back down the staircase to the lower floor where the servants lived. If she wanted to wear herself out climbing up and down staircases he would not stop her.

'Pardon my presumption, but I took the liberty

of putting him in the guest chamber rather than in the servants' hall. We're doing what we can to ease his suffering,' Connor explained. 'I would never have presumed if you had been here.'

Ewan felt the guilt rear up again. He would have been here if he had not tarried with Marguerite. He'd neglected his responsibilities far too long.

'I'd have instructed you to do the same,' he reassured Connor.

Looking gratified, Connor led Ewan into a chamber that was stiflingly hot as a fire burned in the grate and gave the room its only light. The small windows were covered with screens to keep out the noxious airs and midges and the room smelled strongly of blood and bodies. Ewan tugged at his *brat* and saw Marguerite loosen her *airsaid*.

Connor's generous nature had only extended as far as Angus using the room, not the heavily curtained tester bed. He lay on a truckle bed in front of the fire, swathed in blankets from the waist down. From the waist up he was covered in a light linen sheet.

'Angus? Can you hear me?' Ewan stood at the end of the bed, appalled at how pale and frail Angus looked.

'Ewan? You've come home?' He craned his head and tried to sit, but doing this brought forth a great wheezing cough and he lay back. 'I tried to stop them, but I couldna.'

The old man was practically weeping, his already lined face creased into deeper valleys. Ewan squatted by the bed and stared in horror at what he saw. The bruising round Angus's jaw and eyes was testament to the truth of his words and he could barely open his eyes. Ewan drew the sheet back and inhaled sharply. A gaping cut ran from Angus's ribs to collarbone. If it had been the other side, his heart would have been pierced and from the red taint on his lips Ewan suspected he was bleeding inside.

A bowl of water stood on a low table. Marguerite wrung out a square of linen and began to wipe it over his wound. Ewan reached for her hand.

'You don't have to do this.'

'He has a fever and should be kept cool. It is too hot in here. I nursed my mother when she was ill. I know what to do. Let me pay back the kindness you have shown me.'

Ewan sucked his teeth, thinking that Angus had not been particularly kind towards her. 'If I told you not to, would you obey?'

She smiled ruefully. 'Probably not.'

'Is that the lass?' Angus mumbled. 'You've not found your way home yet?'

'Did Duncan do this to you?' Marguerite

asked, her voice a sad whisper. 'I'm sorry for bringing so much trouble on to you all.'

'It wasna Duncan,' Angus wheezed. 'This was Donald McCrieff and his men. They were lying in wait for the cart. For you, Ewan. He didna know we had separated. When the servants opened the gate to let the cart in they ambushed us and breached the wall.' Angus coughed and wiped his hand weakly across his mouth leaving a streak of blood. He frowned. 'Jamie dragged me away from them before I could teach the curs a lesson. We failed you, Laird.'

Ewan looked at Angus's face. He looked older than Ewan recalled seeing him before and Ewan could understand the humiliation he was feeling.

'You didn't fail me. You drove them back and kept them from entering the inner courtyard itself. If they had done that, then Lochmore Castle would have been lost.'

Raids weren't unexpected, as he'd tried to explain to Marguerite. This was different, however. To encroach so deep into Lochmore territory and strike at the home of the Laird himself would not be settled easily or forgotten quickly. If it had been Duncan the attack would make sense, but there seemed no reason behind this.

'They didna care about the keep.' Angus coughed. His face grew even more drawn.

Ewan frowned. 'What, then?'

The granary and storerooms inside the castle wall were full from the harvest, but there was nothing worth inciting a clan feud over. Had he been right all along in suspecting Marguerite was the target? A cousin would defend clan honour, after all. He would do the same in in Donald's place. He felt a chill creep over his back and glanced at Marguerite. Her head was bent over Angus and she was methodically cleaning his wound with a quiet determination and calm he admired. Once again she was proving herself more capable than he had given her credit for.

'You don't know? Did Connor not explain?' Angus said with a wheezing moan that became a cough.

'He told me nothing,' Ewan said, exasperation mounting so that he almost shouted at the injured man. Marguerite put a hand on his sleeve, frowning and rolling her eyes towards Angus disapprovingly. Ewan drew in his frustration.

'Tell me.'

Angus grasped at Ewan's collar with a weak grip. 'It was the chapel. You must see for yourself.'

Desecrating a holy place? It made even less sense than anything Ewan could have imagined. He climbed to his feet and rushed to the door, calling for Connor. He had expected Marguerite to follow him, but she had not left Angus's side.

'I will stay for him. I can be useful here.' She dropped the linen and walked to Ewan's side. 'Ewan, I have seen fevers before and I do not think it is good. I will do everything I can to ease his suffering.'

'Thank you.' He found her fingers and squeezed gently, delighting in the way she inclined her head and half-closed her eyes at his touch.

The servant appeared at the door.

'Please bring fresh linens, more water,' she said with the authority of a queen.

They looked to Ewan, wondering whether to obey.

'Do as she bids you,' he told them.

As he left he heard her ordering the servants in a crisp voice to bring warm broth and be quick about it. He wondered what they made of this strange, small woman with the deep voice and unfamiliar accent that curled around their ears. He was still not sure what he made of her himself.

The bitter, salty air was a slap to his face after the overpowering heat of Angus's sickroom. It was all Ewan could do not to break into a run in his haste to discover what had happened. The chapel was in the outer courtyard, set close to the wall beyond the granary, and as soon as the inner gate was opened a crack he strode with Connor barely keeping pace. Ewan pushed the door open, heart thumping. By the light of the lanterns they both carried he could see signs of a disturbance. Pews had been overturned and righted haphazardly. There was large gouge in the door. The glass in the window behind the altar had been smashed and the altar cloth was crooked.

'Down there,' Connor said, indicating the spiral staircase that led down to the crypt beneath the chapel.

Ewan hesitated on the first turn of the step. His hair stood on end as the smell of dust and damp filled his nostrils, bringing back memories of his childhood. Hamish had insisted that both Ewan and John visited, accompanying them with tales of heroes long dead, to be reminded how a Lochmore chief should be fierce and fearless in battle. Ewan had always hated this place with the carved effigies of past Lairds staring sightlessly from their resting places atop their tombs.

Grief welled in him that Hamish would not rest among his kin and Ewan vowed there and then that neither would he. He would build a new chapel and new crypt for when his time came.

He descended into the darkness of the crypt. He knew their names from memory and spoke them as he passed by their graves. His grandfather and namesake, Ewan—the most recent Lochmore lay in the closest alcove to the staircase along with his wife, Morag. Beyond them, Camron and his twin brother, Colban, who had died together at Nesbit Moor, Seyton and Joan from a century before that, and at the far end the great Laird Rory and…his…

Ewan took a step forward, then dropped to his knees with a wordless bellow of anger that echoed around the silent vault. The lantern fell from his hand, plunging him into darkness. The chill of perspiration washed over his body and panic fought with fury over which would dominate his mind. It was only a brief moment before Connor followed, casting light on to the carved figures, giving them an eerie life as light and shadows played over their forms. Ewan looked again at Rory's tomb, hoping in vain he had been mistaken in what he thought he saw, but nothing had changed. The lid with its stone knight had been dragged from the top and lay shattered into two pieces on the stone floor.

The tomb of Rory Lochmore was open.

Ewan pushed himself to his feet and staggered to the lidless stone coffin. He already knew what to expect and his fears were confirmed when he saw the empty place where Rory had rested for over two centuries. He ran his fingers over the letters that named the occupant of the tomb. They were worn by time and would be practically illegible to unfamiliar eyes. Now only dust remained where the body had lain. An iron crow had been abandoned on the floor beside the two pieces of stone, its function complete. Ewan reached for it, feeling his fingers tightening around the cold iron bar.

'They only took him.' His voice sounded unnaturally calm considering the rage and confusion that boiled in his belly. 'They left her there. Why?'

'I don't know,' Connor said. 'Everything was confusion when the McCrieffs broke through the gate. We were all so intent on protecting the inner gate that we realised too late five men had come down here. Angus discovered them leaving. He challenged them, but I don't know what passed between them. He fought fiercely, but as you've seen…'

Connor spread his hands wide, shaking his head in sorrow.

Ewan leaned against Ailsa's tomb. Her hands were crossed over her breast and between them, in a slight indentation, lay a brooch. He had never paid too much attention to it, but now he picked it up, running his fingers over the unusual design of thrift flowers, crossed swords and initials R and A. There were no jewels and the metal was not rare.

'They took his brooch, but left hers. It makes no sense.'

He placed it back carefully between her waiting hands. The stone woman's eyes appeared to gaze at Ewan, but in supplication or judgement he could not say. Where was her husband now and why had he been stolen from her?

'We should put the lid back,' Connor said.

'No!' The blood pounded in Ewan's temples and his stomach threatened to empty itself. 'Not until Rory sleeps there once more.'

He could not say how long he stood at the tomb, but when Ewan took his hands from the stone they were cold and aching from gripping tight. He thought his energy had been spent, but when he crossed the courtyard a surge of rage coursed through him. He had no idea what time it was, but the horizon was turning grey and the glow of campfires beyond the outer wall had died down.

'If we rushed them now, we could drive them off,' he snarled, striding forward.

Connor seized his arm. 'Not enough men.'

Ewan ground his teeth, knowing his steward was right. Already men had died protecting Lochmore Castle. He could not send the handful of servants and workmen to their deaths needlessly.

'Tomorrow I'll speak to Angus,' he said, thinking that tomorrow was almost today. 'Now I need to rest.'

* * *

Ewan was halfway to his bedchamber when he remembered Marguerite. He crept to Angus's room. Angus was sleeping fitfully and Marguerite was stretched out beside his bed, asleep on the floor with one hand still clutching a damp linen cloth. Ewan tugged it from her hand and she mumbled under her breath.

His eyes stung, remembering he had promised a bed. He lifted her with ease, cradling her to him. As he laid her on the bed she opened her eyes blearily and put her arms around his neck. He suddenly could not bear to be alone with the thoughts that haunted him so he clambered on to the bed beside her. She rolled over to face away from him. He did not expect to sleep, but lay awake until the sun came up, his head too full of questions and fears.

He did sleep. Only briefly, but long enough to have rolled over and wrapped his arms around Marguerite. She was fast asleep, her back curled against his chest. The temptation was great to stay holding her while he still had the opportunity, but Angus appeared to be awake. He slipped from the bed.

'Hamish?'

'It's Ewan.'

Ewan bathed the old man's face as Marguerite had done, hardly able to bear the sight of the once-vibrant man reduced to weakness. When Angus died that would be the last link to Hamish and Ewan would be truly alone.

'I saw the crypt last night. Connor says you saw the raiders. What happened?'

'They told me you…' Angus was mumbling. He sounded tired and confused. The fever was growing on him. 'No right to possess.'

'*I* have no right?' Ewan's shoulders stiffened and despite himself he raised his voice. 'I!'

This was what Ewan feared. Condemnation from his clan as unworthy, but, even worse, from the other clans.

'No, Lochmores. No right,' Angus gasped. His hand became a fist, flailing.

'Tell me why!' Ewan's voice grew harder. 'I need to understand.'

'Leave him alone!'

The protest came from Marguerite. Ewan had not realised she was awake. Her eyes were black with shadows and brimming with fury. They lit for a brief moment as they met Ewan's, then hardened as she swung her legs over the bed. 'Can't you see he's ill?'

Ewan cringed as the reproach added to his mounting guilt at accosting Angus, but his need to understand the invasion was too strong to ignore.

'Don't interfere, Maggie!' Ewan stood over Angus's bed, dismissing her. 'Angus, try to remember. I need to know. The brooch was old and worth nothing, and Rory...'

'Setting old wrongs,' Angus whispered.

'I told you to leave him be!' Marguerite snapped. She crossed the room and stood between Angus and Ewan, arms folded. 'What has happened that is so bad it means you hound an injured man?' she demanded. 'Something was stolen? How can it be worth more than his peace?'

'More than a brooch was stolen.' Ewan's jaw clenched as the empty tomb and fractured effigy swam before his eyes. 'They've desecrated a tomb and stolen my ancestor.'

Marguerite's mouth became a circle of horror. She clutched his forearm. 'Why would they do something so atrocious?'

The muscles tightened beneath her fingers and he became acutely aware of her touch. 'That is what I'm trying to discover and what you are preventing me finding out.'

Marguerite bit her lip guiltily, understanding his urgency. She glanced at Angus, who was lying mutely, eyes closed. She tugged Ewan's arm and he let himself be led out of earshot.

'What?'

'When my mother...' She blinked away tears that made Ewan weak with the yearning to wipe them and erase her pain. She took a deep breath, starting again.

'His fever would not cool, however I tried, and that wound is so large. Ewan, I think he is dying. Last night he thought he was a young man again, swimming in the loch with Hamish.'

Ewan's stomach twisted with grief at the mention of his father and the anger softened slightly.

'He wept for Hamish,' Marguerite continued. 'Be kinder to him now.'

She stood before him, small and defiant, and Ewan finally gave name to the emotion that had grown from a seed to an oak—not to her—he could never do that, but to himself.

He loved her.

Ewan nodded. Marguerite returned to the bed and began to bathe Angus's burning forehead.

'Do you know why they took the body of...?' She glanced at Ewan.

'Rory,' he said, kneeling by her side and giving her a slight, weary smile.

'He disnae... They were...' Angus gazed at them from his least swollen eye.

Ewan shook his head, mystified and agitated beyond comprehension but doing his best to contain the emotions that were intolerable.

Angus gave Ewan a long, even look, focusing briefly. 'Hamish died before his time.'

'That's not an answer.' Ewan spoke evenly.

The pulse in his throat began to speed up. His patience was wearing thin, but he was mastering it. Marguerite reached for his hand and squeezed it. He didn't take his eyes from Angus, but pressed his thumb in her palm in acknowledgement.

Marguerite held a water-soaked linen to Angus's lips. He sucked thirstily.

'Do you know what Ewan speaks of?' she coaxed.

'John was heir. Knowledge for Chief alone.' Angus's eyes rolled towards Marguerite and back to Ewan. 'Father to son.'

'But not me because I was never meant to be laird.' Ewan sighed. 'He was closest to you. Did he tell you anything?'

Marguerite gave Angus a drink of water, most of which trickled down his neck.

'Once he was taken with drink. When we were young…'

'Tell me,' Ewan urged.

Angus closed his eyes. Ewan called his name sharply.

'Not now,' Marguerite said. She put her fingers on his lips, firm and warm. Desire rocked him.

'You must have other matters to attend to. Or you should rest yourself.' She didn't know he had slept beside her. 'Let Angus sleep. I'll stay in case he says anything else.'

'Aye.' He needed sleep, but could not rest when there was so much to be done. He pushed himself to his feet wearily and straightened his *brat*. He stroked her cheek, then walked to the door.

'Keep him well.'

He left her, kneeling on the floor with her hand covering the spot he had touched. Ewan went to find Connor, trying to focus on his predicament while his heart called him to Marguerite's side.

Chapter Nineteen

Angus spoke rarely after Ewan left and much of that was raving and rambling in an accent so thick Marguerite missed most of it. Only once did he seem to see her.

'You're the French bride. A McCrieff-to-be.'

'Not any more.'

'A Lochmore, mayhap in future.'

She took his hand. 'What did Hamish tell you? About Rory Lochmore?'

Angus began to laugh, which turned into a wheeze. 'Ach, Hamish… Hamish.'

Angus closed his eyes and never opened them again. Marguerite sat patiently at his bedside, trying to make sense of his ramblings. Recognising the signs of what was coming, she cooled his forehead, spooned water between his lips and pondered his words.

A Lochmore in future.

Did Angus believe Ewan intended to marry

her? She lost herself in the memories of their journey. The security his grudgingly given company gave had grown into friendship, then affection. The transformation from affection to the deeper, alarming emotion that stirred in her breast had been so gradual she had barely noticed it. It had never occurred to her that they might not have to part and he'd shown no indication that he had such thoughts, even after they had grown so close. But could she stay here?

Ewan returned that evening, looking more haggard and weary than Marguerite had seen before. If there was a time to broach the idea of her staying, now was not it. He had bathed and changed his *leine* for a fresh one and instructed Marguerite to do the same, promising to watch over Angus while she used his private rooms.

'You won't try to wake him to ask,' Marguerite cautioned.

He gave her an injured look. 'I swore not to. I keep my promises, even when it means being ordered around in my own castle by a guest.'

She could have spent an hour luxuriating in the deep tub before the fire, but returned quickly, telling herself she could not leave her patient alone for too long. A fresh dress belonging to Connor's wife was waiting for her and her jewel casket and clothes had been laid out neatly on the dresser. Ewan was sitting beside Angus, holding his hand. Marguerite ran her fingertips over the neatly arranged possessions and Ewan smiled. It had been he who had taken such care.

'As you will unfortunately be staying longer than expected, I thought it best to unpack.'

She was not sure if he meant it was unfortunate for her or for him that she would not be leaving soon, but Marguerite found herself glad she could stay longer and that Ewan would not send her back to France too soon. That she thought of being 'sent' brought her up short. She was the one who had wished to return there after all.

'That seems sensible.'

As she combed out her wet hair he watched with an expression of such longing that it made Marguerite breathless with desire. If they had not been in the presence of the sick old man, she had no doubt they would have fallen on each other without a second thought.

'How is Angus?' she asked briskly, going round to the other side of the bed.

'He's said nothing,' Ewan said despondently. 'I must know why. I won't be at peace until I do.'

'The body was centuries old,' Marguerite said gently. 'Surely they took it for spite, or because the brooch was valuable. Why does it matter?'

She meant her words to console, but Ewan glared.

'It matters because he was a Lochmore!' Ewan looked at her sternly; his eyes careworn daubs of blue among dark shadows. 'I'm the last Lochmore now my brother is dead. How can I prove myself as a laird if I canna even keep my ancestors safe?'

Marguerite bit back her reply that there were greater ways to prove his worth than discovering where old bones had been taken.

'I keep thinking about the horses,' she said. 'We've left them alone.'

'They'll be well looked after.'

'If only we could bring them here through the tunnels,' she mused.

'I don't think they're suited for rowing boats and tunnels, much less a staircase from the cellars. They're better off where they are.' Ewan grinned, showing a flash of the humour that had been sadly lacking. 'Though the tunnel was originally carved out to prevent siege and we may wish to bring them to eat after a day or two. We cannae stay under siege for long without supplies.'

He must be jesting. He would not be callous enough to eat his beloved horse. 'Why not send men out to bring supplies from the village?'

Marguerite suggested. 'They could come and go using our boat.'

'Aye, I might do that. Shall I order venison or beef for you, my lady? Sweet pears or honeyed cakes?'

Her mouth watered. 'I don't mind as long as they leave afterwards, otherwise we'll have more people than food to eat it.'

The change came instantly, but Marguerite could see the moment fire ignited inside Ewan.

'Marguerite, you're a marvel. Never mind food or horses, I can send my men to bring more men!' He seized her in an unexpected embrace. 'No one is watching the shore as far as I can tell. There are Lochmores who will come to our aid from the outlying villages. If the McCreiffs won't go of their own accord, we can attack from inside when they're least expecting it and drive them away!'

He rose with a determined look in his eye. 'I'll see to it at once. We'll have you back in France before you know it.'

Angus died the following morning. Marguerite pulled the sheet to cover the wound and crossed his hands over his chest. She shed no tears. The old man had not been particularly friendly to her after all, but he had mattered to Ewan, who had already suffered such great losses that Marguerite feared another would destroy him. She called for a servant to watch Angus's body, but determined Ewan should not hear the news from anyone but her. With trepidation she made her way through the castle, asking where she might find him.

The Long Hall was smaller than the Great Hall at Stirling, with oak-panelled walls and intricate tapestries showing scenes of battles or pageants. It was bustling with members of the household preparing for the evening meal. Despite the recent attack the atmosphere was happy and purposeful and looked a friendly place to live. Somewhere a person could be happy.

She followed directions until she reached a staircase at one of the corners of the keep and climbed upwards, wondering if she might persuade him to let her stay for a little longer than she had planned.

Ewan was standing on the battlements at the top of the tower. He glanced over his shoulder as she approached.

'When did you last sleep or eat?' she asked, shocked at the gaunt, unshaven appearance of his already lean face.

He shrugged and continued staring out across the loch and marshland. Marguerite followed his gaze, leaning over the edge of the battlement. The castle was raised on a slight hill with the inner and outer walls dropping away slightly. Distantly to the right were rooftops of the village they had rowed from. Green pines mingled with the orange and yellows of birch and oak trees, reflected in the indigo water, creating a palette of colours.

'It's so beautiful,' Marguerite murmured.

'It would be more so without McCrieffs polluting the land with their presence,' Ewan growled. He pointed to their left where the loch stretched from the sea mouth inwards, separating Lochmore Castle from another spit of land. 'They belong on that side of the loch.'

'Why have they not left?'

'I don't know. I still don't understand why they're here, but I'm content for them to stay if I'm to discover the reason why Rory was taken,' Ewan replied. 'I canna stop thinking about what they took. I need to move quickly.'

Remembering her purpose, Marguerite hung her head. 'Angus is dead,' she said quietly. 'I'm sorry.'

Ewan passed a hand rapidly over his eyes. He stared over the battlements, back straight, head high. Marguerite yearned to embrace him, but standing so straight and tense, he was too forbidding to touch. She allowed him a moment to recover before continuing.

'He died without telling me anything else.'

'Aye. And you denied me the chance yesterday to find out for myself.' Ewan's voice was bitter.

'He could have told you nothing,' she said. 'He was too ill. I don't think he knew anything really.'

'Then the answer is lost.' Ewan pointed over her shoulder. 'D'you see that largest group? Donald McCrieff is among them and Duncan is with him. *They* know why!' Marguerite reeled at the mention of Duncan, but Ewan did not appear to notice her consternation. 'Should I open the gates? Shall I go walk among them and invite Donald to tell me? Shall I suggest he bring his cousin, too?'

'No! They'd cut you down. You can't go out there!' Marguerite exclaimed. She seized his arms, worried he might do as he threatened. He looked at her hand as if he did not know what he was seeing.

Two men had separated from the rest of the McCrieffs and had walked closer to the gatehouse. Maybe it was Ewan's and Marguerite's raised voices travelling on the wind that had caught their attention. Maybe they were planning to stand in any case. Duncan McCrieff stared straight at her.

'He's seen me.'

Marguerite flung herself behind the high wall. Ewan's arms came instantly about her waist, holding her steady. He was talking, but she could not make out the words for the buzzing that filled her ears.

'Did they steal Rory in revenge for me leaving? I cannot bear to think it is my doing you have such troubles.'

Her voice came out as a half-sob. She tried to wrestle free, flinging herself towards the door to the staircase, but Ewan held firm around her waist until she stopped struggling.

'Calm yourself, Maggie,' he growled. 'I need you to be strong for me. I have to concentrate on ridding my land of those cursed McCrieffs. I canna do this if I'm thinking of you. I need a clear head.'

Guilt surged through her. She had already asked more than enough of him. She bit her lip and tried to breathe slowly. Ewan took her face between his hands and pressed his lips against her forehead, leaving a trace of heat. His temper had subsided.

'I don't think you're the reason, lass. Duncan is here because his cousin is. A clansman will rally round his Chief, however foolish his actions.'

Marguerite squeezed her eyes closed, hoping he was right, and rested her head against his chest. A body had not been stolen because she had run from Duncan.

'Have you sent messages to the villages to call your men?'

'Aye.' Ewan sighed. 'I have a handful more men, but not enough. They would have come to my father's call at least.'

His voice was bitter and full of doubt.

'And they will come to you,' Marguerite said firmly. She raised her head, staring deep into his eyes. 'They will trust in you and follow you. You're Earl of Glenarris.'

Ewan's eyes filled with uncertainty.

'That's a title that matters in court, but means little to the people who live here. I'm their Laird, their Chief, but I'm unproven. I don't know that they'll listen to a word I say.'

She clutched his hands, pulling them to her heart. 'I know that they will. If you were my Laird, I would follow you anywhere you beckoned.'

'You don't do a thing I tell you,' he said with a wry smile.

'No. But I do anything you ask.'

They looked at each other in silence. On an unspoken signal both fell into the kiss at the same time, lips meeting roughly, hands tearing greedily at each other. Lust flooded Marguerite and she pressed herself against him, feeling the hardness of his chest and limbs and revelling in the excitement that surged through her. Ewan tore himself away with a violence that was alarming.

'I cannot do this,' he groaned. 'I will not. I want you beyond all reason and you addle my senses, Maggie. I can think of nothing else when you're near me.' He raked his hands through his hair and stumbled backwards.

He wanted her, but would not allow himself to have her.

It was unbearable to see his anguish and know she was keeping him from his duty. The guilt intensified.

'Then I shall not come near you,' she cried.

She tore herself from his arms and almost fell down the stairs in her haste to be away. She could hear him calling her name, but ran down the stairs and back through the keep. Tears streaked her face and she was conscious of servants looking at her with open curiosity. She could not bear to go back to the room where Angus lay, but there was nowhere she belonged.

A familiar urge came over her that had been buried since she began travelling with Ewan. She needed to be alone and free. In haste she retraced her steps to the cellars and the tunnel. She would take refuge on the beach until she calmed herself enough that she would not hinder Ewan's attempts to find out what had happened to the remains that obsessed him. No doubt he would not miss her for an hour. He would probably not notice she was gone at all.

She made her way hesitantly through the dim tunnel towards a faint shaft of daylight, remembering which way to turn when the tunnel joined with the one leading to the chapel, and emerged on the beach. The boat was gone, taking or bringing men to aid Ewan. Marguerite strode along the back of the beach as far as she could, hitching her skirts and feeling the wind whipping round her body like a caress. When she reached the rock Ewan had called the Devil's Seat, she clambered with difficulty upwards and perched on the flat stone. From there she could see the castle wall rising high and forbidding. If there was a path it was too overgrown and when she reached the wall there would most likely be no way in. There should be a gate. She would suggest it to Ewan when she saw him next, assuming he could bear to tolerate her company.

She lay back and stared at the clouds that were gathering overhead, darkening as they rolled inwards from the sea in black and grey that perfectly echoed her mood.

She lost the afternoon and when she sat up the tide had started to come in and a fine drizzle had begun. She had to wade ankle deep from the rocks back to the beach. She was in danger of being cut off and would have to spend the night on the rock unless she hurried down.

As she stood and surveyed the waves, a small craft made its way around the outcrop of rocks from the direction of the sea loch. Marguerite could make out three or four figures rowing, but the boat seemed to be going past the beach. She waved, thrilled to see that assistance was arriving and made her way to the jetty, intending to meet them. The boat began heading to shore. When it was almost upon Marguerite she noticed something that made her heart stop. The occupants were dressed in plaid of brown and green. The colours worn by the McCrieffs. These were not friends, but spies.

Sense told her not to head towards the entrance to the tunnel. Instead she ran towards the Devil's Seat. If she did nothing else, she would lead them on to the rocks to be stranded from their boat. Cries reached her ears, accompanied by feet crunching on sand. A hand closed over her mouth. She tried to scream, but the sound came out muffled and useless. She clawed at the hand, twisting her head back and forth. At one point she managed to force her lips apart enough to scrape her teeth over her assailant's finger, but she was not freed and the blow to the head she received set her ears ringing.

'Be quiet, woman!'

A great weight of cloth was pulled over her head, tight across her face, wrapped around her arms to pin them to her side. Breathing became harder through the swathes of fabric and though Marguerite drew deep breaths, she could feel herself beginning to faint. The most sensible thing was to remain motionless and compliant, so even though terror swam through her veins, Marguerite went limp. Hands grabbed each arm, leading her forward. Blind now and having to place her trust in her captors, she allowed herself to be led on stumbling feet back down the jetty. She was lifted, then placed down at full length on the bottom of the boat. She heard the oars being taken up and then they were moving. She gave a soft moan of anguish as all hope that Ewan or one of his men would see and intervene crumbled.

Lying face up on the hard boards and rocking up and down, Marguerite fought to control the surging nausea. The idea that she might vomit into the cloth that bound her face was unbearable. She would choke and die. She had no such qualms about crying and hot tears spilled from her eyes, blinding her further and stinging her cheeks where they soaked into the cloth.

Chapter Twenty

By nightfall there were thirty more men in Castle Lochmore than there had been the day before, smuggled in through the beach tunnel. They assembled in the long gallery, fishermen and farmers carrying whatever weapon they had to hand. Lochmores all. Ewan had not rested or eaten since descending from the tower, but had spent the hours amassing weapons and discussing strategy with Connor. There were not as many men as Ewan would have liked, but thirty more than Donald McCrieff expected and they had come at his behest. Ewan ached to the bone and emptiness gnawed his belly. He stood clad in his *brat* and carrying Hamish's great *targe*, feeling the ghosts of Hamish and Angus watching in judgement. Hunger and exhaustion were trivial now.

'Thank you for coming to my call, especially after the losses we have all suffered at Flodden.' He paused as a wail of shared grief raced around the room. How could he demand more die when they had already lost fathers, brothers and sons? How could that be his first act as Laird of Lochmore? He leaned his arms on the *targe*. The shield was heavy and weighed almost as much as the load on Ewan's heart. He swilled the words round his mouth carefully before speaking again.

'Donald McCrieff has violated our home. Our stronghold. He has stolen the greatest of our Chiefs from his resting place and I want to know why.' He waited while the anticipated uproar died away.

'At first light we attack. Drive as many McCrieffs as you can into the marshland. Let the tide and sands claim them, but leave Donald to me.'

The first cheers came from the back of the room and were joined from all corners. His name was roared and the cry built in volume until Ewan feared it would be heard by the men camped outside the walls. His heart swelled and for the first time he dared to believe Marguerite's words. His clan would accept him as Chief. He just had to survive long enough to prove his worth.

Marguerite. He felt a pang of remorse. He had not thought of her since they had parted, but now his mind was filled with the image of her face twisted with pain as he rejected the kiss he so yearned to lose himself in. He joined the men at the long tables as they fell on the meal with enthusiasm, picking here and there at a dish and exchanging words, but as soon as he could he found Connor and drew him aside.

'Has anyone attended to Mademoiselle Vallon? Is she in the guest chamber with Angus?'

Ewan pictured her sitting alone with the body, but the answer to both questions was negative. Angus had been moved in preparation for burial and the chamber was empty. A rapid search of the castle found no trace of Marguerite. There was only one way she could have left. Ewan gritted his teeth, remembering her habit of stealing out of Stirling Castle to be alone.

'She'll be on the beach. I wish she would get out of this habit of roaming about alone,' he said, trying to ignore the mounting anxiety that she should have returned long before dusk. 'She'll have lost the way back to entrance.'

He picked up a lantern and made his way to the tunnel, Connor and a handful of men in tow. He expected to find her sitting on the jetty or pacing up and down looking for the passageway, but the beach was deserted. Ewan ran from one end to the other, calling for Marguerite to no avail. The tide was high on the shore and the tramping of men as they arrived had obliterated any tracks that led from the jetty to the tunnel. He found three remaining footprints at the rocks topped by the Devil's Seat. The rocks were now surrounded by water on all sides apart from the thinnest strip of beach and there were no returning prints. She had climbed up there at some point. Ewan scaled the rocks and shone the lantern in all directions but there was no sign of Marguerite. He clambered down and shook his head. Connor joined him.

'There's no sign of her at the far end. If she climbed the rocks—'

'I know.'

Ewan cut him off, unable to hear Marguerite's fate described. He sank to his knees, eyes swimming as he pictured her slipping from the rocks, caught by the tide. Had she called for help before she was swept beneath the waves? Had she fought or was her end mercifully sudden? He clutched handfuls of sand from her footprints and buried his face in them, blinded by tears.

So many deaths.

Hamish.

John.

Angus.

Each had struck him so deeply he had believed no more sorrow was imaginable, but the thought of Marguerite's emptied his soul of everything, leaving him numb. He had loved her too late and too badly. A few weeks more and she would have gone from him in any case, but the finality and cruel manner in which she had been snatched was unendurable. He had pushed her from him and she would have died without knowing how he loved her. He threw his head back and roared to the sky, not caring what Connor or the searchers thought.

'Laird, you canna stay here. You have to prepare for tomorrow,' Connor urged.

He wanted to spit his answer in fury. What did he care for tomorrow? What was a day without Marguerite alive?

Drawing strength from a reserve he did not know he possessed, he pulled himself to his feet. He was not alone. He had a clan who needed his guidance. Marguerite had said they would come to his aid and she had been right. He had responsibilities that he had shied away from for too long. He would prove to the memories of those he had lost that he was worthy of the faith they had shown in him.

Marguerite's ordeal ended sooner than she had feared. A grinding sound close to her ears told her that the boat was being drawn up on land. Marguerite was hauled upright and again lifted over the side of the boat. She was dragged a short way over rocks, slipping at one point and grazing her knees painfully. No one had spoken aloud for some time, but now her captors began muttering to each other and another voice joined them.

The cloth was unwound. Marguerite breathed in the salty air, dragging it down into her lungs with relief, resisting the urge to drop to her knees. In any case she could not have, because her two captors held her upright, each holding her by an arm, knives ready in their free hands, presumably in case she might try to run or otherwise misbehave. At the sight of the blades she decided she would do exactly what she was told.

The light-headedness began to withdraw and finally she looked around. They were still by water, but unlike the wide, sandy bay behind Lochmore Castle, they were in woodland. Four men squatted beside a fire pit with a piece of meat turning on a spit, all wearing heavy cloaks.

'Sweet Lord! Who do you have here?'

One man stood. He lowered his hood and walked towards Marguerite.

'Duncan!'

'Marguerite! Then it was you I saw on the tower this morning.' Duncan gave her a charming smile and bowed, as if he was greeting her after only a morning apart. He embraced her. 'You are unharmed?'

'Beyond what your men did to me,' she exclaimed. She tried not to recoil, but being held so close was repellent. She wriggled free of his grip before he touched her skin itself. The pleasure of being in Ewan's arms was not something that would be transferred to another man's touch.

'We found her on the beach,' one man called.

Duncan narrowed his eyes. They did not know about the tunnel, or that men were coming to Ewan's aid, and Marguerite swore they would not learn it from her.

'I climbed down over the rocks, but could not climb up again. The tide came quickly.'

'You're safe with me now and we can return home. We'll be in Berwick within two weeks. You'll prefer living in England better than this wilderness.'

Duncan reached for her once more. She stepped back.

'I don't want to.'

His eyes took on a dangerous light. 'It took me time and money to discover that you were really with Lochmore after all. I had to send men back to Druinunn to ask a lot of questions before I discovered that Lochmore had lied to me. He purchased a horse and was seen with a young woman in uncommon dress.'

'Lord Glenarris will come for me,' she blurted out. Her cheeks flamed as she spoke his name.

'Do you think so? How convenient. We had

feared we would have to wait until they starved and opened the gates.' Duncan smirked.

'What are you going to do with me?'

'I shall keep you here until Ewan Lochmore answers a message to meet him so he can have you back. Then I shall take you to him and you can watch me kill him. Once Lochmore Castle has fallen we will return to Castle McCrieff and ask my uncle to bless our marriage. He might grant me this castle as a reward for ridding him of a second Lochmore earl in only a few months of time. My Liza will have a fine dowry one day.'

He grinned at his brother-in-law, who gave a guttural laugh.

Ice enclosed Marguerite's limbs. Duncan's words contained so many promised horrors, but the thought of Ewan's death struck her most deeply. The idea of him lying bloodless and cold at Duncan's feet caused tears to spring to her eyes and made her throat close with torment.

'Why do you hate him? Because he's a Lochmore and you're a McCrieff? Because he helped me? Why did you steal the body from the crypt?'

Duncan looked confused. 'I know nothing of any stolen body.' He barked a laugh. 'Has Lochmore been filling your head with tales of slights gone by? I thought he was more enlightened than that. How disappointing. I have no time for old feuds that the clans can't even remember the cause of. He did help you, though, and for that I will not forgive him.'

His face was thunderous, the red in his cheeks rising. He drew closer to her, jerking his head to the men who held her. They released her and ambled to the fire to join the other men. Duncan slipped Marguerite's arm beneath his and drew her away from the camp. She considered breaking free and trying to run into the woods, but as she dragged her feet he tightened his grip. He led her down to the water's edge. Along the coast the walls of Lochmore Castle rose above the dense trees. They had travelled round the castle at the mouth of the open sea and were now behind the McCrieff camp.

'Lochmore accused me of treachery when we met in Druinnun. For that he should die,' Duncan told her. 'If that brings me favour from my uncle, all to the better. Do you know of what I speak?'

Marguerite shook her head, mystified. If Duncan would kill Ewan for an imagined slight, he would not hesitate to silence her, too. 'We did not speak of you ever,' she lied. 'We did not speak at all, at first. He was too angry that I had involved him in my escape and caused him difficulty. It was days before we became friends.'

Even in these dire circumstances, Marguerite could not help the way her voice softened and her lips curved into a smile at the memories she and Ewan shared. Duncan's eyes narrowed and his lip twitched.

'You became friends.' His hand slipped from beneath hers and he seized her by the arm, pulling her round to face him. 'I see you have finally left off your mourning clothes. What did you do on your journey together? What caused your grief to come to an end?'

Marguerite bristled at his words. 'I still mourn my mother.'

But she didn't as much now, did she? The heavy grief that she had once thought would weigh on her heart for ever had reduced to something that she was conscious of, but did not consume her. Her journey through Scotland in Ewan's company, the wonderful, dizzying nights they had spent in each other's arms and the shock of finding his home under siege had all served to fill her mind with other matters.

'Did you lie with him?'

Marguerite lowered her eyes. Every moment spent in Ewan's arms would be one she treasured until the end of her days. To sully it by admitting it to Duncan made her writhe in misery.

'Tell me the truth!' Duncan demanded.

'Yes, I did.' She raised her head defiantly. 'You will not want to marry me now I am no longer a virgin.'

'The state of your maidenhead does not affect the value of your dowry, but I take offence at your wanton behaviour.'

He raised his hand and she flinched.

'Don't hurt me!' She cradled her belly, thinking fast. 'I may already be carrying his child.'

'Why would that concern me? If you are carrying Glenarris's bastard that matter can easily be dealt with.'

'You would raise his child as yours?' Marguerite asked.

'Are you an imbecile? I can delay consummating our marriage long enough to see if you are truly with child, but I'll suffer no Lochmore mongrel in my kennels. Many infants do not survive more than a day.'

Marguerite's legs gave way and she dropped to the ground. She looked up at Duncan in horror.

'You would murder a newborn?'

Duncan came behind her and rested his hand on the back of her neck, squeezing firmly. Marguerite's skin began to crawl. Duncan pushed her forward until she was kneeling.

'Unlace your bodice,' he commanded. 'Oh, don't fear I am about to rape you. I've just said I won't touch you until I know you have an empty womb. I just want your laces.'

Marguerite unthreaded the laces of her dress and passed them to him. Duncan ran his hand from her neck upwards and gathered her braid in one hand.

'You are nothing more than a French whore. Giving yourself to him when you belong to me,' he snapped. 'Do you know what they did to women like you in the past?'

He drew a knife and wrenched her head back. The blade flashed and Marguerite fell forward.

Duncan had cut off her hair!

He bound the loose end of her plait with the lace from her dress. The other end was tied with the ribbon Ewan had given as a birthday gift and the sight of it brought tears to Marguerite's eyes.

Duncan handed the braid to one of his men.

'Take it to the castle at first light. Make sure you give it to Lochmore himself. I'm sure he'll recognise it and I want to know what his face looked like.' He turned to Marguerite. 'Go sit by the fire and don't even think about trying to leave. You won't manage it and I will punish you for trying.'

It was a long night. Marguerite was given a small portion of the meat, but not enough to satisfy her appetite. Duncan boiled a pot of water and cooked oats. The English men turned their nose up at the resulting slop, but Marguerite was too hungry to object to the overly salted mess. She sat shivering in the dank mist that crept around her ankles and invaded her body to the bone. When it began to rain she called to Duncan.

'I'm cold.'

Duncan shrugged. 'I have no feather bolster for you, I'm afraid.'

He pulled his *brat* over his head and rolled on to his side to sleep. Marguerite hunched down against the trunk of a tree and tried to sleep. Her mind went back to the first night she had spent in Ewan's arms. Even though he had resented her presence—and with good reason—he had behaved kindly and kept her warm and close when he must have been cold as a result. Why had it taken her so long to see past the brashness to the honourable heart that beat within him? Why had she not told him of the love she bore him?

He was the best man she had ever known and she would give anything to stay by his side. She hoped she would get the opportunity to tell him how much he meant to her before either of them died.

Chapter Twenty-One

Dawn was barely light. It rained softly and a biting wind blew from the sea. The last gentleness of autumn had gone, replaced by a hardness signalling the change towards winter. The cold suited Ewan, whose chest now contained a frozen rock in place of a heart. He dressed silently in a *leine*, thickly padded leather jerkin and *brat*, and made his way to the hall where his men were waiting.

He climbed on to the dais at the end and regarded them. Wisely he had rationed the ale and *uisge beatha*, and was greeted with clear eyes.

'As planned last night, I will leave by the main gate alone. I intend to challenge Donald in armed combat. They won't be expecting an attack. Ready yourselves for my signal.'

Ewan raised the *targe* aloft in both hands to deafening cheers. If he died, the clan might mourn the passing of a man who had been Laird all too briefly, but there were cousins here who would take his place. Lochmore would have a new laird, but he wondered if anyone would truly mourn for Ewan the man.

The main gate was unbarred, but Ewan left through the small door. The crash as it shut behind him sounded ominous in the silence of dawn. He walked along the path, sword and shield in hand, determined not to look back in case he somehow betrayed the presence of the men concealed behind the mighty oak doors.

'Donald McCrieff,' he shouted. 'Show yourself.'

He waited where the road widened into fields, ignoring the stares of McCrieff men as Donald was roused and made his way to where Ewan stood.

'I thought you'd never show yourself.' Donald smirked. 'Have you come to surrender?'

'Why are you here?' Ewan spat. 'Leave my land and take your men with you.'

Donald bared his teeth. 'You were given land that should have been mine by rights. Give up the McNab estate to me and we'll withdraw.'

Ewan gripped the sword. All this was for a parcel of land? He glanced over Donald's shoulder, looking for Duncan, but he was nowhere in sight. Would he grieve over Marguerite's death if he knew of it? Ewan's eyes sparked with tears that he blinked away. He must not think of her now.

'Where is the body of Rory Lochmore?' he demanded. 'Where is his brooch?'

'Rory Lochmore, you say?' Donald gave Ewan a sneering grin. 'Is his wife lonely in her grave without him, or is her brooch enough to keep her company? Maybe you'll meet him in the next life and you can ask him yourself.'

Ewan forced himself to breathe evenly. He hadn't expected a confession, but the description of Ailsa's grave and remaining brooch was enough to satisfy him that he had the culprit. Rising to Donald's taunts would only add to the thief's sense of triumph.

It was not as if Ewan had expected him to answer, nor did it change what he had come here to do. 'I challenge you,' Ewan said. 'Combat between the two of us, here and now. If I win, you will return the body to its rightful place. If I lose, I will surrender the McNab land.'

Donald's eyes rolled and Ewan was left with the impression he was not entirely sane. 'If you lose you'll die and we'll take Castle Lochmore. You can't hold us off for ever.'

Ewan bared his teeth, thinking of the men waiting for his signal. Lochmore Castle would not fall even if he did.

'Very well. Ready yourself.'

He raised his sword. Donald did likewise.

'Stop! I bear a message for Lord Glenarris.'

Someone was pushing through the crowd. Both fighters looked towards the ragged man, who edged closer, arm outstretched to show a small bag.

Ewan narrowed his eyes at Donald. 'What trick is this?'

Donald frowned. 'Not mine.'

Ewan took the proffered bag and pulled out the contents. A long braid of raven hair stared up at him, the ends tied together with a familiar ribbon. Ewan's body convulsed with terror and elation. He almost dropped the braid in shock, but bunched his fist as if it was the most precious object in Scotland.

The messenger's eyes were wide with terror. He pointed to the bag.

'A message.'

Ewan's fingers closed over a scrap of parchment he had missed before.

You stole my bride. I have taken her back.

The meaning was clear. Marguerite had not died. She had been taken from the beach.

From *him*.

Ewan bared his teeth. The braid mocked his relief. Marguerite was alive, but she was just as lost to him. Blackness as dark as Marguerite's desecrated locks filled his vision as he willed some other reality to take the place of this fresh nightmare.

Fury surged in Ewan's blood and he reached for his dagger with a roar, rounding on Donald.

'Are you party to this?'

'Not I. My cousin has been obsessed with that woman since she fled. I might have guessed a Lochmore would have been involved.'

The messenger was waiting. Ewan jerked a thumb. 'Go back to your master. Tell him to come here and bring the woman. I will bring down the wrath of every Lochmore from now until Judgement Day if she has been harmed.'

The man ran. Donald sheathed his sword. When Ewan raised his eyebrow, he smirked.

'I can wait. I'll enjoy cutting you down alongside Duncan.'

Ewan ground his teeth. Duncan had Marguerite. Donald was here, bearing the secrets Ewan needed to discover. When he gave the signal to the waiting men he would have to act fast, but who to take down? He could not fight them both. An impossible choice.

Presently Duncan strolled along the edge of the water, Marguerite's arm through his, as if he were taking a stroll round the gardens at Stirling. Only the tightening of his fingers about her wrist hinted Marguerite was not a willing companion.

'I found my bride, as you can see.'

There was no mass of raven hair to hide Marguerite's face and it tore at Ewan's heart and guts to see how she had been defiled. She stood silently beside Duncan, her head down.

'She says she carries your child, Lochmore! Is this true?'

Ewan's heart seized. If it were true, he could not bear to imagine how Duncan had come by that knowledge. Marguerite had said nothing to him, but he had barely given her the opportunity, as he had been preoccupied with the siege and Rory's disappearance. It was the thing she dreaded most and she had been facing the prospect alone.

'I could not say.'

Duncan bared his teeth. 'I do not allow another man to break in my horse. To deny me that pleasure with my wife is to sign your death warrant!'

The moment Ewan had delayed was here. He gave a shrill whistle and the Lochmore men spilled through the gates, screaming battle cries. They fell on the unprepared McCrieffs. Donald shot Ewan a look of hatred and threw himself into the fight alongside his men. The Lochmores were fewer in number, but defending their home and honour. They fought with a ferocity that the McCrieffs could not match, driving them towards the marshy silt of the low tide as Ewan had instructed. Ewan turned his attention to Duncan. The two men faced each other, circling around.

'You're a traitor to Scotland, Duncan. Admit it! Release Mademoiselle Vallon and surrender.'

'I'll do neither,' Duncan snarled.

'Then fight!' Ewan screamed, charging forward.

Duncan pushed Marguerite aside and the two men met with a clash of swords. Their feet slithered in the mud as they grappled, gouging at eyes and necks. Both men reached the conclusion simultaneously that swords were useless and hurled them aside. Ewan reached for the knife at his belt. His mind slipped back to the argument with Marguerite by the loch and he tightened his hand on the handle while he delivered a series of sharp jabs to Duncan's ribs with his other fist. Duncan kicked his kneecap and Ewan's leg buckled, sending him to the ground. He flailed as he fell, catching Duncan with a glancing cut across the arm that caused him to yell in pain. Ewan reached up, grasped Duncan by the shoulders and butted him squarely in the nose.

As Duncan reeled, Ewan scythed the legs from underneath him and managed to clamber astride him, hands closing over Duncan's throat. Duncan's eyes began to bulge, his already florid face turning scarlet.

'You're killing him!' Marguerite cried. 'Stop!'

Ewan was never sure if he would have choked the life from his enemy because at that moment a hunting horn sounded and a horse thundered along the road, scattering McCrieff and Lochmores men aside.

'In the name of the Holy Virgin, someone explain what is happening here!'

Malcolm, Laird of the McCrieff clan, dismounted and strode forward, adjusting his brown and green *brat*. The fighting ceased, men paused where they stood. There had been losses on both sides and in the mix of mud and blood it was hard to tell who fought with whom.

Ewan climbed off Duncan, who crawled on his knees to slump beside his uncle. Donald staggered over. Ewan faced the three McCrieffs. Bald and hawk-like, Malcolm wore his sixty years well and commanded attention with an ease Ewan envied, despite the longstanding feud.

'I return to Castle McCrieff to discover my son absent and news of a siege. Why?'

'Your son attacked my home,' Ewan growled. 'He stole the body of Rory Lochmore. I want it back and I want to know why it was taken.'

Malcolm laughed unpleasantly. 'The reason has been passed down through generations of McCrieff and Lochmore lairds, but it isn't my responsibility to tell you. That's your tragedy,

Ewan Lochmore. Why are you fighting my nephew?'

'I believe he's a spy and a traitor to Scotland,' Ewan said. He could not explain his claim to Marguerite. He didn't have a right to her by any measure.

Malcolm's eyes tightened. 'Explain quickly before I gut you for slandering my clan's name.'

'My father knew someone was passing messages to Rouge Croix in the preparation for the invasion of England. He only hinted who it was and I suspect Duncan. He has the connections and the reason to travel. I think he betrayed Scotland to the English with the aim of gaining McNab's land for your son. He certainly promoted the cause of Margaret Tudor in deciding the Regency.'

Malcolm's face betrayed nothing. Remembering something else, Ewan sneered.

'He brought his English kin into Scotland. Do you want it said McCrieffs need English mercenaries to win a fight?'

'Guard your tongue before I cut it out,' Malcolm growled. 'McCrieffs need no aid to win a fight. You'd better be sure of this before you repeat it, Lochmore.'

Ewan raised an eyebrow. 'I'd swear over the body of Rory Lochmore if you'll return it.'

Malcolm dipped his head, but Ewan saw a flash of a grin. 'A good try, but, no.'

'See for yourself.' Ewan gestured towards Duncan's brother-in-law, who had been lurking at the back of the crowd. He looked alarmed by the attention on him. Malcolm shot a look of hatred at the Englishmen.

'You have my ear,' he said to Ewan.

'It may not be enough to convict, but if Robert Morayshill is convinced by what I put before him, there should be a trial.'

Malcolm stared at his nephew, who avoided his eye. 'Is what he says true?'

'He's lying,' Duncan muttered, but his voice was unconvincing and laden with defeat.

'Duncan plans to live in England.' The three men turned to look at Marguerite, who had spoken in a rush. She pointed at her former fiancé. 'He told me he would take me to Berwick once he had killed Ewan.'

Duncan bared his teeth. 'You'd be better to keep your mouth closed, you French whore!'

She lifted her chin defiantly, while moving further out of his reach. 'You want this castle, but your daughter will not care for a dowry taken with blood.'

'It's the French woman Lochmore wants,' Duncan snarled. 'That's why they've concocted these lies. They've been rutting like deer since he stole her. She belongs to me!'

Ewan glared at Duncan with hatred stronger than he had ever felt for anyone. 'She belongs to no one but herself.'

'And what of Mademoiselle Vallon?' Malcolm took Marguerite's hand. 'Donald has a wife and Duncan won't be marrying her if what you say is true. I'm a widower and a pretty young bride would liven up my final years.'

Ewan finally allowed himself to meet Marguerite's eye.

'She can make her own choice.'

Marguerite bit her lip. If Duncan in his thirties was unappealing, Malcolm at almost double that must be more so. She dipped him a curtsy and gave him the coy smile that Ewan recognised now as insincere. She had never used it on him.

'I will return to France as I planned and, if it please you, Lord Glenarris shall be the one to take me.'

Malcolm gave a strange smile. 'We shall see.'

He spat on the ground before Duncan. 'I'm a Scot. It shames me to think this cur is of my blood and I'll not have it said the McCrieffs harbour a traitor. The clan will deal with him.'

'That isn't good enough,' Ewan said. 'He'll be taken to Stirling for the court to decide his fate. Hand him over.'

'Temper your tongue unless you want to fight all three of us,' Malcolm cautioned. 'I hated your father, but I respected him. I know nothing of you. Defy me and you'll make an enemy for life.'

Ewan smiled grimly.

'I'm a Lochmore. You're a McCrieff. I assumed that would be the case anyhow. I'll fight you if I have to, though I think Scotland has lost enough men already.'

'Ha! You've got balls after all,' Malcolm said, respect creeping into his eyes. 'In that case I offer you a choice, Lochmore. Duncan and Mademoiselle Vallon or the knowledge of why Rory Lochmore's body was taken.'

The choice was impossible. He burned to see Duncan brought to justice, a trial in the open and a sentence of death, if he was found guilty, but he desperately wanted to discover the secret of Rory Lochmore's grave. There was something he wanted more than either of them and there was only one way to ensure that.

'Give me Duncan and Marguerite.' He looked Malcolm in the eye. 'Take your son and his men and leave.'

Duncan swore. 'Uncle! No! The McNab land was meant for Donald. To give us more than the Lochmores have. Why should we have so little?'

Malcolm silenced him with a glare. Connor

and two Lochmores seized Duncan by the arms and dragged him towards the castle.

'He'll be kept safely until an escort can be arranged to return him to Stirling. I'll see he has a fair trial.'

Malcolm returned to his horse and whistled to Donald to follow. Ewan waited until all the able-bodied McCrieffs had left before turning to Marguerite. Aware that he was being watched by men from both clans, he intended to do nothing more than give her an arm to lean on, but by the time he was at her side he was trembling from head to toe with the need to touch her. He gathered her to him in an embrace he had thought never to have again.

'Oh, Maggie. Oh, lass. What did he do to you?'

Her fingers were ice against his neck. He pulled her beneath his *brat*, cleaving to her, and she melted against him. Desire rose within Ewan, but greater than the urge to have her was the need to comfort her, to keep her close. Ewan buried his head in the ruin of her hair, wetting it with tears.

'You're crying,' she sniffed.

He couldn't tell her about the beach. Not yet, when his heart was still raw from the devastating belief that his world had ended. He had to keep holding her to convince himself she was not a ghost after all.

'Your beautiful hair,' he murmured when he was capable once more of speaking.

'It doesn't matter.'

She tightened her arms around his waist. Ewan groaned as the sharp stab of pain in his ribs recalled the other injured men. 'I must attend to my people. Will you help me?'

She stroked the swelling beneath his eye with her fingertips. Her touch was fire on the aching skin. 'I can be useful here. Let me start by attending to you.'

Hand in hand they walked to the gatehouse, where Ewan issued instructions for the wounded to be taken to the Long Gallery. Marguerite tied a veil round her head and began ordering servants how best to treat the injured, throwing herself into staunching blood and wrapping wounds. Ewan watched with a smile. The small woman commanded his household better than he commanded soldiers. She glowed more than she ever had in court at Stirling. She needed a purpose to come alive.

Thanks to Marguerite's nursing, death did not claim many men. She worked tirelessly in the company of the castle women. Ewan buried the churlish jealousy that he could not claim her for himself, while relishing the excuse to delay what must prove to be a heartbreaking conversation.

* * *

Ewan threw a feast a week later, gathering the clan from villages all over. Bonfires burned again outside the castle walls, this time in celebration. He distributed the alms owed, adding more to compensate for the lives lost in the siege. There was dancing and feasting long into the night. Ewan walked among the men, thanking them for their service. His heart lifting as each man called him Laird. He had discovered the traitor as he had promised Morayshill. He had fought and won his first battle as Chief of the clan. He had faced down Malcolm McCrieff. Not as an equal yet, but the seeds had been planted.

And yet his heart was lead.

Marguerite was dancing, head thrown back in laughter. She wore a dress of orange and brown. Lochmore colours. She had few clothes to choose from, but Ewan wondered if she had picked the gown to match the *brat* he wore.

When he was sure their absence would not be noted Ewan beckoned her over and they walked to the chapel. Ewan stopped at the door. He could not face entering the crypt and seeing the empty space where Rory should belong. To be reminded of his great failure.

'You could have had the answer to your question, yet you chose Duncan,' Marguerite said.

Was his regret so obvious she could read it on

his face? It died instantly. With her at his side Ewan knew there could have been no other decision. He would brick up the tomb and leave Ailsa to rest in peace. The secrets of the past could sleep with her. There would be a new beginning for a new laird. He reached for Marguerite's hand.

'While Duncan was free you would never have been at ease. Now you have no need to hide and you can return to France without fear.'

Her fingers stiffened. She slipped her hand free. 'Yes. Of course. Thank you.'

Ewan bowed his head. What had he hoped? That she would stay here in a country she hated after everything she had endured.

A question burst from him. 'Did Duncan speak the truth about a child?'

Her hand strayed to her belly, but she shook her head uncertainly. 'It would be too soon to say. I thought he was going to strike me and it was the first thing I thought of to stop him.'

There was no child. He had no right to ask her to stay.

'I've sent word to Stirling requesting an escort for Duncan. I can appreciate you might not wish to travel with them, but when you are ready to leave, tell me and I will make arrangements,' he said. 'They could be here within a week and you can be in France before October is out.'

'I shall not go immediately, if you permit,' she replied. Her eyes searched his face and he realised she was looking for the same confirmation he wanted.

'I would like you to stay as long as you wish,' he said warmly.

'As long as I wish?' She raised her eyes to his. They were almost fully black in the darkness, but the distant light of the bonfires made them gleam. 'That might be a very long time, Ewan.'

He had not touched her since the day of the battle, but now he drew her to him. It was a cold night after all. She came to his arms willingly, lifting up on to her toes so that their lips were close. Ewan's scalp prickled and his stomach flipped over with unbearable desire. He drew a sharp breath.

'Maggie, what are you doing?'

'Ewan,' she breathed, putting her lips close to his ear. 'I am trying my hardest to seduce you.'

'Are you saying farewell?' he asked.

'No.' She raised her brows in surprise. 'Why are you making it so difficult?'

He took her face and gazed into her eyes. 'Because I experience such joy when I take you in my arms that I do not know if I can bear the pain when you leave me.'

Even as he spoke he was lowering her to the ground and sinking with her. She lay back on the grass, arms raised behind her head and looked at him with an expression that was a combination of trust and desire. He brushed his fingers over her lips, enjoying the way they parted as he touched them.

'I keep saying no more and I keep breaking that vow.'

'Then stop vowing something so foolish.' Marguerite sighed, tilting her head back and closing her eyes so that her long lashes lay on her alabaster cheeks.

Ewan moved his fingers slowly up to her cheekbones, then brushed them over the closed eyelids before replacing his fingers with his lips and following the same path. His hands moved to her hair. He ran his fingers through it as he loved to do, watching the strands catch the light of the bonfires, but stopped when the silken blackness ended far too soon. Marguerite opened her eyes.

'It will grow back,' she murmured.

'It reminds me how I felt when I saw your braid.' He looked at her bleakly. He withdrew his hand, bunching his fist as cold perspiration washed over his brow. 'Knowing it meant Duncan had you. It was the worst thing I've ever experienced.'

'Is that true?'

He closed his eyes, holding back tears. 'No.

When I couldn't find you on the beach was much worse.'

He gathered her into his arms, burying his face in what remained of her hair and clutching her tightly against him as the memories of the footprints on sand came flooding back, turning his stomach to acid. He wanted to hold her like this for ever, never letting her out of his sight until he stopped trembling at the thought of her being taken from him. He was not sure that day would ever come.

'I thought you had died, Maggie. I wanted to die myself.'

Marguerite wriggled and he feared she was trying to break away from him, but she only moved until she was able to slip her arms around his back.

'You care that much?' she asked.

'More than I can say in your language. More than I can express in mine. If I said you could stay as long as *I* wished, you would never see France again.'

'Then ask me.'

His pulse hammered, drowning out the distant pipes and drums. He asked not the question he wanted to, but the question that plagued him.

'Why do you want to stay? You've made it clear you hate Scotland.'

'Because there is nothing for me in France any

more and everything for me here.' She gave him the sweetest smile he had seen in many years.

He took her hand and pressed his lips over her knuckles.

'I'm not an expressive man, Maggie. I love you so deeply it hurts. It terrifies me that I might fail to show you or tell you. That you might think even for a day that you do not command my heart.'

'I know that. You chose me. You defended me. You kept me safe even though I made your life a trial. When I am in your arms I feel ecstasy I never imagined could exist. I don't want to give that up. I love you.'

She stroked a finger down Ewan's arm, igniting fires. To think he had suggested returning her to France. He did not want to contemplate what he would have done if she had agreed. He could suppress the question no longer.

'Will you marry me?'

The smile that filled her eyes was all the answer he needed. He seized her by the hand and pulled her to her feet. 'Come quick. While there are still witnesses.'

Hand in hand they ran through the castle gate, stopping before the largest fire.

'Clan Lochmore, listen to me. Before you all I make this vow.' He pulled the ribbon from the pouch at his belt, took Marguerite's hand in his and wrapped it around them both. He lifted their joined hands for all to see.

'I will take this woman as my wife. To have and hold and love as long as I live.'

Amid cheers he kissed her.

'If I am with child,' she whispered. 'If I do…'

He put a finger to her lips, determined not to let her dwell on dark possibilities in this gladdest of times. 'Whatever happens I will be with you. Whatever the future holds for us, we'll face together. Always.'

Epilogue

There was grey in Marguerite's hair. Not many strands yet, but Ewan had noticed them as she sat before the window in the morning sun and brushed it loose from her night-time plait. He didn't care. Ewan knew there was grey in his hair and beard, too.

Now, at sunset, it was more evident as they strolled arm in arm through the grounds of Lochmore Castle. Ewan wondered if she had noticed, but wisdom and long experience as a husband, and father to daughters, told him not to mention any faults. It was a balmy August evening with a sky of burnished bronze and copper stretching endlessly away over purple waves, warm enough that they needed no cloaks, and Ewan wanted nothing to disturb the peace of their evening walk.

'Janie is getting larger by the day,' Marguerite

said. 'But she's doing well and seems cheerful. I don't think she'll suffer when the baby comes.'

'Aye, Hamish picked well there,' Ewan said. 'Struan and Janet breed strong daughters.'

Their oldest son, Hamish, was recently married at twenty-six, almost the age now that Ewan had been when he had become Earl of Glenarris. A tall lad, Hamish had Ewan's figure, but his mother's eyes and temperament. Ewan felt a slight pang of sadness that old Hamish had never met the child named after him, but it passed. Ewan had no intention of dying yet, but knew that when his time came, Lochmore Castle, the lands and its tenants, would be in as capable hands under Hamish as it had proved to be under Ewan.

Marguerite put her hands on his shoulders. 'We'll have our first grandchild before Christmas. It scarcely seems possible!'

Her dark eyes gleamed with excitement. Their youngest child, Marie, was now eleven and considered herself too old to be babied. Marguerite would enjoy having young children to occupy her once more. Another generation of Lochmore children would sleep in the cradle Ewan had carved for Hamish. Childish voices and laughter would once again fill the courtyard and gardens where Hamish, Rory, Dominique, Margaret, Finlay and Marie had played in their younger days.

Ewan drew Marguerite close, kissing her deeply and thinking how lucky he was. She was still beautiful, with fine skin and a figure that was remarkably shapely after eight pregnancies. A little grey and lines at her eyes didn't diminish the way Ewan's heart leapt whenever she smiled at him. He'd sworn to love her every day and he had kept the vow with ease.

A loud expression of revulsion pulled them from the kiss. Margaret and Finlay, the twins, were walking through the new gateway from the beach path. They were fourteen years old and therefore acutely embarrassed to see their parents showing any sign of affection.

'Get away with you.' Ewan laughed. 'I'm kissing your mother.'

'Go tell Marie I shall be testing her on her scripture before bed,' Marguerite told them. She flicked her hand in the direction of the house to dismiss them and reached for Ewan's arm once more.

They continued their walk, intending to go through the new knot garden that Marguerite had designed and around the perimeter of the castle grounds on the route they always took, but thoughts of his father led Ewan to the old chapel. The heavy oak door had not been opened since Ewan had built a newer chapel ten years previously. Grass and weeds had grown high across the doorway. Ewan ground them down with the heel of his boot and tugged on the handle. It gave way with a creak and the door swung open with more ease than Ewan had expected.

Hand in hand, he and Marguerite made their way inside, coughing a little at the dust and musty smell they encountered. There was a puddle in one corner where a leak in the roof had sprung and birds nested in the eaves. Ewan ran his hand across the altar. It came away black with grime. Ewan hesitated at the top of the stairs before making his way down to the crypt. It was gloomy and the little daylight that followed him down the spiral struggled to gain ground in the shadows.

The wall Ewan had built to hide the desecrated tomb looked like it had always been there. Spiders had spun webs in the corners and dust had gathered along the edge of the stone floor. The plaster had faded and there were already a couple of large cracks in places. Anyone who didn't know what lay behind it would never be able to guess there was anything there at all.

Ewan rested his palms and forehead against the cold plaster, wishing he could make his presence known to the woman lying alone for ever on the other side of the bricks. He heard footsteps on the stairs. Marguerite draw near. He was always acutely aware of her presence.

'Did I fail him, Maggie?' he asked. 'Should I have searched harder or insisted Donald McCrieff told me where they'd taken him?'

Marguerite slipped her arms about Ewan's waist. She leaned against his back, kissing him lightly behind the ear, and sent a shiver of lust through him.

'Short of ransacking every building on McCrieff land and tearing them down brick by brick you did everything you could. Would Rory have wanted you to spend your life searching for him? Would either of them?'

He shook his head slightly. Marguerite was right. Who would he have asked anyway? Malcolm McCrieff had been dead and buried seventeen years now. Donald had become Earl, but spent most of his time drunk, gambling and whoring by all accounts. Duncan had been tried as a spy and executed. Ewan doubted any McCrieff descendent would care about a missing Lochmore.

'Were we wrong not to tell Hamish about this?'

'So our son could spend his life wondering?' Marguerite slipped around him, beneath his arm until she stood between him and the wall. She put her hands to his cheeks, pulling his head round so he was looking deep into her eyes. 'No. You made the decision that you were going to live for the future, not dwell on the past. Don't regret that now.'

Ewan looked into her eyes. In the shadows they were blacker than ever, her face white against the plaster. Ewan was struck by the memory of when he had first seen her and thought her to be a spirit, but as always she was alluring and loving and available. He had chosen saving her over finding Rory and he did not regret that for a moment. He wondered if Rory had loved his Ailsa as deeply as he loved Marguerite.

'You're right. Perhaps one day someone will find him and he'll be at peace, but it won't be us.'

He wrapped his arms around her and held her tightly. Marguerite pressed herself against him, bodies touching from hip to chest. She wrapped her arms around his neck. Ewan ran a finger lightly up her back, enjoying the way she wriggled beneath his touch. Even after almost thirty years of marriage he still found her irresistible.

Her deft fingers began teasing the points that attached his doublet to the top of his hose, running her fingers over the tips of the laces. Ewan felt mounting excitement beginning to grow within him. If her fingers worked their way beneath his clothing any further he would lose all control and he found himself longing for the past when he could roam around in *brat* and *leine* that could be pushed aside in a heartbeat.

'Let's go,' he murmured, dipping his head closer to her ear to whisper in it. 'It's getting cold down here and I'm far too respectable to think of swiving my wife up against a wall under the gaze of my ancestors when we have a warm mattress inside.'

Marguerite's eyes gleamed and she gave him a wide smile full of promise. She tugged one more point loose, then withdrew her hand from Ewan's waist, brushing it over his chest.

'Very well, my love. But I shall warn you, I've grown *very* cold down here and I will need a *lot* of warming up.'

Giggling like a pair of new lovers, they ran up the staircase, hands roving over each other. It was unseemly behaviour for a man past fifty, and their children would be mortified if they witnessed it, but Ewan didn't care. They paused briefly to ensure the door to the chapel was firmly closed, then hurried back home.

They did not look back even once.

* * * * *

MILLS & BOON

Coming next month

THE DETERMINED LORD HADLEIGH
Virginia Heath

'Thank you for your kind assistance this evening, my lord.' Continued avoidance of basic good manners was petulant. Penny's eyes finally lifted to meet his and she immediately regretted it. It was as if he could see right through her, past the determined and proud façade, to the uncertain and lost woman beneath. 'It is much appreciated.'

'No, it isn't.' Hadleigh grinned, his intuitive eyes dancing, and the sight did funny things to her insides. Why couldn't he be wearing his bland and inscrutable expression tonight? She knew where she stood with that. 'You would have rather walked over hot coals than have me help you and I cannot say I blame you. I behaved poorly on both our last encounters. Boorish, high-handed and arrogant with a healthy dose of sanctimonious mixed in. I had no right to attempt to force my will upon you or to assume I knew what was best. I've mulled it over long and hard since and chastised myself repeatedly for my crassness.'

Another pretty apology. Why did he have to be so good at apologies when she wanted to remain annoyed at him? Being righteously annoyed justified overt formality.

'You have flour on your face.'

'I do?' Her free hand swiped at her chin.

'Here…allow me.' His fingers brushed her cheek and Penny swore she felt it all the way down to her toes. She found her breath hitching as he dusted it from her skin, not daring to breathe out in case it came out sounding scandalously erratic. Which it suddenly was. As if sensing the new, potent atmosphere between them, his unusual, insightful amber eyes locked with hers and held. They both blinked at each other before he severed the contact and took several steps back.

Did he realise that the dormant female part of her body had suddenly just sprung to life? That her pulse had quickened or her lips tingled?

Continue reading
THE DETERMINED LORD HADLEIGH
Virginia Heath

Available next month
www.millsandboon.co.uk

LET'S TALK
Romance

For exclusive extracts, competitions
and special offers, find us online:

f facebook.com/millsandboon

🐦 @MillsandBoon

📷 @MillsandBoonUK

Get in touch on 01413 063232

For all the latest titles coming soon, visit
millsandboon.co.uk/nextmonth